KNIGHTS CORRUPTION MC SERIES

TRIPP

S. NELSON

Tripp
Copyright © 2017 S. Nelson

Editor
Hot Tree Editing

Cover Design
CT Cover Creations

Interior Design & Formatting
Christine Borgford, Type A Formatting

Tripp/ S.Nelson.—1st edition
ISBN-13: 978–1541002340
ISBN-10: 1541002342

All rights reserved. No part of this publication may be reproduced, distributed or transmitted in any form or by any means, including photocopying, recording, or other electronic or mechanical methods, without the prior written permission of the author, except in the case of brief quotations embodied in critical reviews and certain other noncommercial uses permitted by copyright law.

This is a work of fiction. Names, characters, places, and incidents are a product of the publisher's imagination. Locales and public names are sometimes used for atmospheric purposes. Any resemblance to actual people, living or dead, or to businesses, companies, events, institutions, or locales is completely coincidental.

If there is ever a time you feel like you just want to give up, dig deep to find your strength and continue to forge ahead. The results will be that much more rewarding.

PROLOGUE

"*STOP!* IT'S NOT WHAT YOU think," she cried, clutching the back of my cut and trying to pull me off the man I found in our bedroom. In *our* fucking bed. "Tripp, please...."

I wrenched my body to the side. It took only seconds before she got the hint and her hands fell to her sides.

"If you don't back the fuck up, Rachel, you're gonna regret it," I warned. The blood pumping in my veins was thick, my heart threatening to explode the more enraged I became. I'd never put my hands on a woman in anger before, but this bitch was pushing my limits for sure. Bad things happened when I lost control, and although I'd be justified to flip the fuck out right then, I still tried to keep it together. As best I could.

My thoughts pored over the past couple months, trying like hell to shove the haze of red from my vision. The mysterious incoming texts late at night. The sudden trips out with friends she hadn't spoken to in months, if not years. The out-of-town trips she suddenly had to take to visit a sick relative, someone I'd never heard her mention before. All of her excuses should have screamed she was fuckin' around, but I'd been so busy with all the shit goin' on at the club I simply took her at her word.

What a big fuckin' mistake.

"You think you can fuck my woman and get away with it!" I roared, slamming the stranger against the wall, the thud of his head hitting the plaster echoing around the room. "I hope she was worth it 'cause now I'm gonna kill ya."

The guy sucked in a strangled breath, his eyes popping wide as I tightened my grip around his throat. He clawed at my hands, but it was useless. I knew I wasn't gonna snatch his life, but I sure as hell wasn't gonna tell either one of them that.

What the fuck did she see in this guy, anyway? His long hair was unkempt, his beard scraggly at best. I towered over the guy, and while I realized I was larger than most, my size didn't detract from the puniness of the man she'd chosen to fuck around with behind my back.

In retrospect, I'd stupidly decided to be faithful to Rachel. I'd had plenty of opportunities to fuck around, but I'd made a commitment. I thought we both had. I was a one-woman type of man, which was quite the conundrum in the lifestyle I'd chosen. Pussy flowed easily for everyone involved in the Knights Corruption. Shit, for all the clubs I'd known. And while most chose to partake, there were a select few who chose one woman and one woman only.

Foolishly, I'd been one of them.

As I glanced at Rachel, my heart splintered a little more with each passing second. She was still trying to convince me to let go of the guy, fear in her eyes at what she thought I was gonna do. She had feelings for this fucker, which meant whatever she'd felt toward me had waned. We had our issues but I thought we were good . . . all things considered.

"Please," she continued to beg. "Let him go, Tripp. I promise it won't happen again." She grabbed my arm and tried to yank me back, but her feeble attempts only served to irritate me further. I needed to get outta there, but not until I'd finished teaching them both a lesson. Squeezing tighter still, I only released my grip when the guy's eyes closed, his lungs ceasing to struggle for air. I hadn't killed him, although I wanted to; I'd merely choked him out. As soon as I backed away, releasing my hand from around his throat, his limp body slumped to the floor. I waited to see if Rachel would rush toward him but she didn't, although her eyes kept flicking from mine to his and then back again.

Turning fully toward her, I shook my head when I saw the look of fright on her face. She had no idea what I had planned for her, probably thinking I'd killed her lover and that she was next. Apparently, she didn't know me at all. Or did she? I'd killed before, sure. Numerous times, in fact, but always in retaliation or defense. Never because of infidelity. Although, I'd never been put in this type of situation before.

Stalking toward her, I assessed her body language.

Fear.

Regret?

Didn't matter. I was done with her, but that didn't stop me from retaliating. Her back slammed against the wall, her hands coming up in front of her to protect our bodies from colliding. I came to a halt inches from where she stood pinned, my jaw clenched and nostrils flaring. I was so enraged I had no idea what to say. I wanted to wrap my hands around her throat just like I'd done with that fucker, but instead I kept them at my sides. My nails dug into my palms, drawing some of my attention away from thoughts of hurting her.

When moments passed and still I hadn't moved, she reached out and cupped my face. "I'm so sorry, baby. It'll never happen again. I swear." She flicked her eyes to the unconscious man and then back to me. It was then I noticed her pupils were dilated. She was on something, but since her choice of drug varied, I had no idea what it was. "I've just . . . been so lonely. You're always gone, and when you're here, you're not really with me."

I gasped as if she'd sucker punched me in the gut. "Are you fuckin' kiddin' me? You're trying to blame me for you bein' a whore?" Fury boiled my blood. I jerked my head away from her hand, her fingers falling from my face. I stepped closer, my chest brushing against hers. She stood before me completely naked. Having caught them in bed together, she'd never had the chance to throw on clothes. And while the thought of fucking her senseless normally arrested me whenever I saw her big tits and round ass, her standing before me with not a stitch of clothing on right then only served to disgust me.

Another man had been inside her. Tasted her. Promised her God only knew what, and from the looks she kept sneaking at him, she professed her own hopes and dreams to that bastard as well.

She reached for my hands, but I shrugged her off. "I'm not blaming you. But you can't blame me either. I know you've fucked around on me, and although I didn't cheat to get back at you, I'm not gonna stand here and let you intimidate me anymore."

"What the fuck are you talkin' about?" I yelled. "I haven't fucked anyone else for the past two years. Ever since we agreed to be together." As for the other bullshit she spewed, I couldn't help it. At six four and two hundred thirty pounds, I couldn't help but intimidate most people, even her. I admitted that I used my size to get what I wanted most of the time, and if I were being honest, I loved that she felt inferior right then.

Her eyes darkened, her posture becoming rigid all in the blink of an eye. Rachel could be a bitch when she wanted and right then was a prime example, trying to turn the tables on me to excuse her abhorrent behavior.

"You can say whatever you want, Tripp. I know you've fucked around, but I'm not gonna stand here and try to convince you to come clean." Pointing toward the man on the floor, she said, "I fucked him. Plenty of times. And now it's over, so the sooner you forgive me the sooner we can get back to us." Rachel had done a complete one-eighty in the span of minutes. At first, she played off her actions with remorse, apologizing with a look of guilt plastered on her face and riddled in her voice. And then she tried to blame me for fuckin' around, acting as if her cheating was merely a bump in the road of our relationship. As if that shit was normal and should be forgiven with no questions asked.

I wasn't gonna lie. She hurt me. But I wasn't gonna sit there and cry about it either. I refused to embarrass myself by givin' her the time of day any longer. No, she fucked up . . . and good.

I need alcohol.

Slamming my hands on the wall, one on each side of her head, I shouted, "Fuck you!" A quick thought of head-butting her flitted through my brain, and while the image satisfied me, I would never do such a thing. Retreating a step, I said, "We're fuckin' done. Get your shit and get out." Turning my back on her, I strode toward the hallway, shouting over my shoulder. "When I get back, you better not be here."

I heard her yelling but ignored her as I slammed the front door behind me. Two minutes later I was on the open road, embracing the wind and the feel of my bike between my legs. The rumble and vibrations calmed me. My grip on the handlebars loosened the farther I rode, putting as much distance as I could between me and the woman who fucked me over.

Had I known how my night would turn out, I might have stayed at home and watched her leave instead.

CHAPTER ONE

Tripp

LYING IN BED I TOOK a deep breath, willing the ache from my body, but it was useless. The evidence of the life I'd lived riddled my skin. I'd been shot more times than I'd like to recount, though thankfully nothing had happened to me in the past year. It was a nice change of events.

Absently tracing the scar near my heart, I thought about what I had to take care of later that day. Sighing, all I wanted to do was close my eyes and go back to sleep, but Marek wanted me to check out how shit was goin' at the new titty bar, Indulge. I had a hand in hiring the last round of talent, and four out of the five were still employed. We'd fired one of them for doing drugs; that shit just wasn't tolerated.

I believed someone had been hired to replace the chick we got rid of, but I wasn't sure. I'd been out of the mix for the past couple weeks, helping my prez deal with the final obstacle we faced.

Psych Brooks.

Leader of our most hated enemy, the Savage fuckin' Reapers.

All the brothers had taken turns standing guard to make sure that bastard got exactly what he deserved. Strung up like an animal in the basement of our club's safe house, he'd been deprived of adequate food and water, only being provided with the minimal amount to keep the breath in his lungs.

Daily beatings occurred, mostly at the hands of Marek, then Stone and Jagger. And that was because Psych had fucked with all three of their women. Sully had received the brunt of his abuse her entire life, seeing as how she was the daughter of the evil bastard. Her father never protected her, not once in all the years she lived with him. Shit, I hated even calling him her *father*, because he certainly was not.

When I broached the subject of Psych's demise, asking Marek when he was gonna end the fucker's existence, a sadistic grin lifted the corners of his mouth. Normally the image would have been out of character for the leader of the Knights, but whenever the subject of his wife's father was mentioned, the look was expected. "I'm not done with him yet," Marek would always respond. I understood, and while I agreed that he should drag out the man's torture as long as possible, I also wanted to be done with him. We needed to move on, and put the last link to our old life to rest once and for all.

But all in due time, I supposed.

Swinging my legs over the edge of the bed, I quickly stood and stretched my arms above my head, chasing away the last traces of sleep. Padding toward the bathroom, my mind was a flurry of thoughts, none of them bringing me an ounce of comfort. I was up next in the rotation at the safe house, and while I didn't mind gettin' a little bloody in the name of payback, I'd much rather chill out at home.

After a hasty shower, I grabbed some clothes from my closet, dressed, and snatched my keys. An hour later I pulled up to the safe house, shutting off my bike's engine and glancing around the garage to see who else would be joining me, if anyone. Looked like I was the first to arrive. Never paying much attention to who was scheduled to show up when, I strolled inside the house with thoughts of gettin' this shit over with so I could hit up The Underground on the way back. My home away from the clubhouse. The club's bar didn't bring in much of a profit, but it was my go-to when I didn't want to be surrounded by everyone.

We were on strict orders to keep shit as quiet as possible, so no more than three men were allowed at the house at any given time. Marek feared if people came and went at all hours, we'd draw too much attention and the neighbors would get suspicious. My thought, however, was that anyone who lived close would keep to themselves, fearing what would happen if they butted their noses into our business. The few times we did see our neighbors they averted their eyes and hustled inside their homes, slamming their doors before we even had the chance to nod hello. Not that we were out to make friends, but a welcoming acknowledgment here and there couldn't hurt. At least, that was my take on it.

Strolling through the kitchen, I snagged a beer from the fridge before venturing into the basement. The creak of the wooden steps echoed through the enclosed space, the ominous sound perking my ears with each thump of my foot. The scene I walked into was straight out of some horror movie.

A man shackled to a wall, head hung low and beaten so badly he was barely recognizable. But it wasn't some low-budget film; it was fuckin' real life, and the strung-up man was evil personified. Psych Brooks deserved every bit of pain he'd endured, plus whatever was left in our arsenal to deliver. So far, most of his teeth had been knocked out and his jaw was broken, which made eating impossible. The leader of the Reapers was on borrowed time since he could no longer take in food, so we made good with the time he had left. All the fingers on his right hand had been broken, along with his left femur. He'd howled when Stone had taken a sledgehammer to his leg, his wails the sweetest sound to our club's VP.

I was more of a subtle torture kind of guy—rubbing salt into tiny slits in the skin, shoving sharp objects under the fingernails, that sort of shit.

Once I'd hit the last step, I covered my nose with my hand. "Holy fuck, it reeks down here!" For a split second I thought I saw Psych lift his head and grin, but it could have been my eyes playing tricks on me. The man was more than beaten down, holding on to the last remaining threads of his life.

Marek had told us all that with each of our visits we were to inflict some sort of pain on Psych, making sure to save the big shit for him. Broken bones, stretching his limbs by tugging on the chains—all that sort of shit was permissible, but no one was to slice him open or cut off anything. That was to be left for our prez.

Ever since Sully had come into Marek's life, I'd witnessed the changes in him. Before her, he was a serious guy, but pretty laid-back. Not too much rattled him. He took things as they came, reacting when necessary and taking appropriate action.

These days, Marek barely cracked a smile, except when his wife was around. He'd aged a few years in the short span of time since her arrival. His expression was a constant grimace, and his eyes had taken on a darkness only a few of us could relate to. But it was all understandable. Knowing what Psych had done to his daughter her entire life, what he allowed others to do to her, gutted Marek. He didn't have to voice it in order for it to be known to all of us. I only prayed that after he finally had the chance to purge, after he was able to rid the world of Psych, he'd go back to the man I once knew.

Revenge had a funny way of flipping you on your ass, however. For so long, thoughts of getting even fueled the desire for justification. But when it was all said and done, sometimes all you had left was a shell of your former self.

As I reached for the chains, knowing my form of torture that day was gonna be to stretch Psych's arms so far above his head he'd have to step on his tippy-toes or else risk popping out his shoulders, I heard footsteps above me.

"Grab me another beer," I shouted toward the stairs, not givin' a damn who was there as long as they brought me a replacement. I was gonna be there for a while and wanted extra suds to help deal with what was to come. I'd never say I was a fan of inflicting pain, but the shit didn't faze me either.

"A please would be nice, brother," Hawke responded, pounding down the steps so hard I swore I heard one of them crack. He tossed me the bottle before plopping down on a metal stool in the corner, rubbing his hand over his head. His hair was finally growing back after having been balded when his woman had found out he'd cheated on her. Their relationship had taken a turn after the incident which still gutted my little brother.

"You actually left Edana's side?" I asked in surprise. Ever since his woman had been beaten and raped by some of Psych's men, Hawke never left her alone, bringing her to the club every single time his presence was required. Marek had given him a short reprieve from dealing with some of the club's business, the trips to the titty bars on hiatus until he knew Hawke could handle it without being distracted. I'd talked at length with him over what happened with Edana, but in the end he was the one who needed to come to grips with it and decide what needed to be done.

"Yeah," he answered, taking a slow pull on his bottle. "I figured it was time for me to step up and start doin' my part again."

I'd always been protective over my younger brother, going to bat for him and sometimes helping him clean up his messes. An incident happened a few years back, a scuffle with some random guy who went after him after finding out Hawke had fucked his wife. And because I was tired of jumping to his defense because he couldn't keep his dick in his pants, I'd stepped back and let the guy get in a few good punches, my arms crossed over my chest, just watching the two of them battle it out. I knew Hawke could handle his own, even with traces of alcohol flowing through his blood, so it was merely seconds before my sibling had the man on his back, turning the tables and beatin' the shit out of him. I'd finally intervened when I saw that Hawke was doing some damage, dragging him off the half-conscious man. I'd also warned him that the next time he messed with a married chick and the husband found out, I'd jump in with the stranger and help teach Hawke a lesson.

One glance at the Reapers' leader and Hawke's eyes darkened with anger. "So what are we doin' to him today?"

"I think he's in need of a bit of a stretch, don'tcha think?" I grinned, glancing at Psych to see if he was even aware he had company. The slight shuffle of his feet indicated he was, and I had no doubt he knew he was in for one helluva day.

Nothing but pain.

CHAPTER TWO

Reece

"TWO MINUTES," CARLA ANNOUNCED AS she walked up behind me, looking at me through the mirror in front of my station. "Then you're up, hon." Even after a month of working at Indulge, nerves still managed to rattle me before each performance, something I feared would never go away. Then again, the moment I became comfortable with this job should be the exact moment I quit.

Carla disappeared to attend to the other girls, mending some of the outfits for the night's performances. The club's manager used to be a stripper, but all that ended the day she met her husband, Brian. She'd stopped taking off her clothes for money but stayed in the business to help the younger girls starting out, offering advice and keeping them out of trouble.

In the short time since I'd known Carla, she'd helped me tremendously, teaching me how to deescalate any situation, learning to read the men's body language and how to protect myself if they ever got a bit rough. I'd never had anyone look out for me before, and Carla would forever have my gratitude for seeing me as a person and not just an object. A commodity to own and possess.

Adjusting my auburn wig, I finished my makeup with another coat of mascara before standing and assessing the costume I'd chosen for my routine—a naughty schoolgirl outfit. Cliché but it worked, arousing the customers to ensure tips would be plentiful. With one final glance in the mirror I headed for the door, my heart thrumming fast.

"Good luck, sweetheart," Carla shouted behind me. I turned halfway around, enough to flash her an appreciative smile before focusing on what came next.

The whole stripping scene was new to me, but it provided me with an income, something I was never allowed to have before. Refusing to even think about my past, I focused on the remaining beats of the current song, blew out a long breath, and strode toward the back of the stage. I was up next.

I lost myself to the rhythm of my routine, allowing the spotlight to block the prying eyes watching my every move. The club was almost at capacity, which was both good and bad. I would surely go home with enough money to cover my room and put some food in the mini fridge that was supplied at the motel, but because of the number of patrons, I would surely be putting Carla's advice to good use. Most of the men were well on their way to Drunkville, their eyes surely not the only thing trying to get their fill of me that evening.

With each piece of clothing I removed my mind hid, drifting off to the only time I'd felt safe, loved—my childhood. Memories of vacations with my parents filtered in. Playing Army with my older brother because where we lived there were no other children. Escaping to my room after I'd been punished for misbehaving, only to have my mom come and comfort me. She'd explain why I'd been in trouble but always made sure to tell me she loved me to the moon and back, kissing my forehead before giving me her stern look telling me that I was still grounded. My dad calling me his little princess as he twirled me around in his arms, blowing raspberries on my cheeks until I laughed so hard I could barely breathe.

As the song increased in tempo, unwanted scenes barreled forth. Tears pricked behind my eyes but I refused to allow them to fall. My whole world imploded the night two police officers knocked on our door.

An accident.

Icy roads.

One driver, two passengers.

No survivors.

Thrusting myself back into the present, I focused on the numerous strangers watching me while I danced to the music, counting the seconds until I could disappear backstage once more.

CHAPTER THREE

Tripp

"I NEED YOU TO TAKE my place at Jagger's fight tonight," Stone said, straddling the barstool next to me. "Addy's goin' to her dad's for dinner." He tapped the bar and signaled for Trigger to grab him a beer. The resident bartender scowled and disappeared in the back, completely ignoring Stone's request altogether. Those two didn't have the best history, not since Stone went against club rule and got involved with Trigger's niece, Adelaide. Now the mother of his kid.

Hell, he and I didn't have the best relationship either. He forever gave me shit about hittin' on his woman, but he'd got it all wrong. Adelaide cared for me after I'd been dropped off at the gates of the club, shot four fuckin' times, bleeding out and left for dead. It was Adelaide who had nursed me back to health, and because of the bond we shared, our friendship had blossomed. Which was quite odd for me, seeing as how she was the only true female friend I had. I innocently flirted with her, sure, but who wouldn't—the woman was gorgeous. But she was more like a sister to me, and as time passed Stone had come around to the fact that I would never fuck someone I viewed as family.

Don't get me wrong, Stone and I battled. Quite a few times. Shit, he even punched me in the face for puttin' my hands on her belly when she was pregnant with Riley. But I let it slide because, as a man, I understood his possessiveness. Didn't stop me from fuckin' with him, though.

Every once in a while I could still rile him enough to throw me daggers.

"If she's goin' to her dad's, then why do I have to take your place at the fight?" I lifted my beer and drained the remaining liquid.

"'Cause Riley is sick and I need to stay home with her. Addy hasn't seen her dad in quite a while and doesn't want to cancel." Leaning over the bar, he grabbed a mug and poured himself a drink before sitting back down. "That good enough of an excuse for you?"

"What's your problem?" Certainly used to Stone's aggravated tone, I knew when something was amiss.

"Nothin', man. Just . . . I don't know. Shit, I don't wanna talk about it right now." Tipping his head back, he swallowed half his drink in two gulps. "Besides, I sure as hell ain't talking about Addy with you." Gone was his usual tone of contempt, replaced with a slight wave of familiarity, as if he didn't completely hate me.

Slapping his back, I gave him something to contemplate. "Well, if you ever wanna talk. . . ." I left it at that, not about to get all sentimental with Stone's ornery ass. He knew where to find me if he needed to get somethin' off his chest. Although I imagined he'd seek out Marek before anyone else, seeing how close the two of them were.

The club's VP opened his mouth but quickly snapped it shut when his phone rang. Pulling it from the inside of his cut, he glanced at the screen before answering. "Hey," he said before vacating his stool and walking toward the room he used when at the clubhouse. I had no doubt his wife was on the other end of that call.

The rest of the day passed quickly. Nothin' much goin' on at the club besides making sure everyone took their turns visiting Psych.

———◆———

I ACCOMPANIED RYDER TO JAGGER'S fight, standing guard outside the dismal office inside the ratty old warehouse until the prize money was secure. Ever since Jagger had killed a guy in the ring, the younger brother of a Reaper, he'd become the hot ticket of the underground fighting world. The prize money quadrupled and because Jagger was still undefeated, the pot grew with each bout.

"All good?" I asked, moving to the side as soon as the office door opened.

"Yup," Jagger answered, his black duffel bag swung over his shoulder as he walked past me. He instantly sought out his woman, having no patience for anyone else. Kena was huddled in the corner with her sister, Braylen, and of course Ryder was close by. The guy wouldn't admit it but he had it bad for her. He tried to play it off as nothing more than sex, but I noticed the way he watched Braylen when he thought no one was paying attention.

Kena's hands were going a million miles a minute and after Jagger responded, she grabbed his hands and smiled. When Kena was an infant, she'd contracted a virus, which had damaged the nerves in her larynx, prohibiting her from ever uttering a single word. Jagger had learned sign language in order to communicate with her, but there were times when he messed up, like right then.

"What did you tell her this time?"

"Shut up, man. You try and learn this shit and not mess up." Jagger's frustrations quickly disappeared when his woman signed something before kissing him.

I grinned as I turned my attention to Ryder. "You almost ready?"

"Fuck yeah I am." He looked pissed, which wasn't out of the ordinary where he was concerned, especially when Braylen was around. I swore those two were always arguing about something. "Remind me I can't strangle her," he mumbled as he brushed past me, completely ignoring the blonde-haired woman walking briskly behind him.

"I heard that," she shouted, smacking his arm when she'd finally caught up to him.

Shaking my head, I turned back to Jagger. "You're set to go there now, right?" He was up next in the rotation at the safe house.

"Yeah, Kena and Braylen drove so I'm right behind you. Just let me say good-bye first." Taking her hand, he led Kena past me and out of the dank building where he'd won yet another fight.

The newly patched-in member took joy in dishing out pain on the bastard shackled in the basement. Psych dared to orchestrate the kidnapping of Kena and Adelaide. And to make matters even more serious, he'd been brazen enough to put his hands on Jagger's woman.

I'd only been paired with Jagger a few times since we'd taken Psych, and every time I inwardly cringed, witnessing the former prospect's rage toward the leader of the Savage Reapers. Or I should say ex-leader, seeing as how his life was gonna be snatched soon enough. Although, if it were up to Marek, Psych would live the next ten years rotting away in that basement.

Once outside, Jagger and Ryder walked the women to their car. Kena was all smiles while Braylen's scowl was enough to make *me* flinch. A couple of minutes later, the two men strolled back to where we'd parked and straddled their rides. We all kicked over the engines at the same time, the rumble of the three bikes sounding like fifty, echoing around us in the empty streets.

A sense of calm descended over me as I gripped the throttle, picked my legs off the pavement and drove off down the street. Jagger and I hooked a right toward the safe house while Ryder turned left, no doubt headed back toward the clubhouse. Something had been bothering Ryder lately, and I knew it was more than the arguments with Braylen, but damn if he clammed up every time I asked why he had a stick up his ass. Instead of answering, he would grunt and reach for a beer. If and when he got his hands on hard alcohol, then and only then would I be truly concerned.

The hard shit and Ryder just didn't mix. I'd witnessed it a couple times and never wished to again. That man had some demons lurking inside him, and for some reason his whole personality completely changed with the consumption of whiskey.

Pushing thoughts of Ryder aside, I focused back on what I had to take care of in the upcoming week. After that night, I had a few days to myself, my only obligation making sure everything was running smoothly at Indulge.

Little did I know a simple check-in at our newest titty bar would change everything.

CHAPTER FOUR

Reece

TAKING A DEEP BREATH, I shoved all nervousness aside as I stepped on stage. The music I'd selected began to play, the beat of the tune vibrating from the speakers and wrapping around me like some sort of blanket—which was an odd sentiment, seeing as how I was about to take off my clothes in front of a bunch of horny men. Losing myself to the music was the only way I managed to continue stripping. I closed my eyes and allowed the thrum of the song to live within me, swaying to the idea that my life was exactly where I wanted it to be.

Which was false, of course.

No little girl dreamed of dancing naked, straddling a pole while lusty men looked on. I certainly hadn't. But I didn't have a choice. When I mustered up enough courage to leave my life in the shadows, I had fifty dollars to my name. Taking my clothes off was the quickest way to make the money I needed to survive.

Shield myself from my past as best I could and hope for a better life.

A calm life.

A safe life.

Swinging my legs around the pole, I hoisted myself until I neared the top, slowly positioning my body until I was turned upside down. My strong thighs stabilized me while my hands gripped the pole so I didn't fall if I accidentally slipped. Which had happened before, but thankfully only when I'd been practicing my routine, not live on stage.

I unlocked my legs and spread them into a wide V, strategically placing my arms so I had a better hold. I slowly lowered my body until I reached the floor, going into a split before bouncing my ass up and down on the stage to the climax of the song. I soon let go of the pole, seductively crawling toward the edge of the stage and the men who were waving their money in the air.

The outfit I'd chosen that evening was a men's white dress shirt, buttons opened to my navel. The sleeves were rolled up twice and a dark gray tie hung loosely from my neck, dipping between my abundant cleavage. A hint of teasing without showing everything. Not until I decided to. Of course, what was underneath the shirt left very little to the imagination, the white lace thong barely covering me. I always wore wigs while working, a helpful tip from Carla. That night I wore a short blonde hairstyle, quite the contrast to my long chestnut-colored hair.

I only had a few minutes left on stage, choosing a longer rendition of "Gone" by The Weekend. His voice was sultry and seductive, perfect for dancing and enticing men out of their hard-earned money. At my core, I was innocent and naïve, but whenever I stepped on stage I took on a different persona. A woman out to get as much from a man as I could. Ensnare them. Make them think they're the only guy in the room. Make them *want* to keep watching me long enough to get paid.

Pushing myself on my knees I slowly unbuttoned the rest of my shirt, pulling the material apart once the last button slipped through its hole. Running my hands over my breasts, I shielded them from view until I'd received a few more bills tucked securely in the garter around my left thigh.

"Let's see those tits, sweetheart," an older, balding man yelled, swaying from side to side from obvious intoxication.

"Yeah," his buddy agreed from behind him.

Giving them both a sexy grin, I pointed to my garter. For as drunk as the bald guy was, he stuffed his money under the lace wrapped around my leg with ease.

Gripping both sides of my shirt, I slowly pulled the material away from my body. This was the part I hated, losing what little clothing covered me. But it was part of the job, so I mentally flitted away from the scene in front of me. I never allowed myself to see the men once my shield had been stripped away.

Their images all blurred together.

Faceless people in the crowd.

I knew it was my choice to strip, but it didn't make it any easier. And since there was a strict no-drugs policy at the club I couldn't even contemplate taking something to help numb me. I had to endure until I came up with a better way to support myself.

If that ever happened.

Shrugging the shirt off my shoulders, I tossed the material to the side of the stage. I knew what they expected and I gave it to them. Kneading my breasts, I pinched my erect nipples a few times before running my hands down my body. Knowing my song was coming to a close soon, I rose to my feet and sauntered toward the pole. Twirling a few times, I came to rest in front of it, sliding down slowly until my ass was a few inches from the ground. I played with the flimsy strands of my thong, teasing the men surrounding the stage with small glimpses of my bare pussy.

Indulge was a fully nude club, and even though I was required to rid myself of all clothing, I chose to always do so when I didn't have much time left on stage. Other dancers spread their legs wide when they bared themselves, but I never did.

I couldn't.

Standing and swiveling around so my back was to the crowd, I bent over and hooked my thumbs under the lace of my thong, slowly dragging my panties down my toned thighs. As soon as the scrap of material pooled around my ankles, I stepped free of them and kicked them toward the back of the stage.

The last few chords of the song drew near. I turned back around to face the crowd and caressed the pole as if it were a lover, running my hands up and down the metal, the coolness of it distracting me from the countless pairs of eyes staring at me. I trailed my hands down my body, shielding my pussy quickly before baring everything.

Thankfully the last note of the music sounded, signaling that my time was up. Bills were thrown toward me once they knew my show had ended. Gathering the money tightly in my hands, I continued to plaster a smile on my face, winking at a few of the men before finally disappearing off stage.

Each of us had a secure locker in the back of the club. Stuffing the wad of cash in mine, I pulled out my next outfit for the evening, complete with my favorite red wig. I sipped on my watered-down vodka on the rocks to help take the edge off.

If I'd known how my evening would turn out, I would've ordered a few more drinks.

CHAPTER FIVE

Tripp

IT'D BEEN THREE DAYS SINCE I last visited the safe house. My next rotation was in a day or so, depending on when Marek decided to pull the trigger—either literally or figuratively—and fuckin' snatch Psych's life once and for all.

Striding through the back door of Indulge, I passed by a few of the staff, nodding in acknowledgment as I headed toward the front. I spotted Hawke near the bar, throwing back shots as I approached.

"Bout fuckin' time, brother," Hawke shouted over the music, slapping me on the back. "What took you so long?" His brows rose but his attention wavered once one of the strippers walked by, throwing him a smile before heading toward a table of men.

"Thought you were all done with that." I signaled the bartender for a drink, turning back toward Hawke after ordering.

"I am," he said, "but I can still look. As long as I don't touch." His smile faltered, and I knew he still struggled with what happened to Edana. She'd gone looking for Hawke and had been viciously attacked by a few Reapers right outside this place, only allowing her to live so she could deliver a message that they were comin' for everyone we loved. Retribution for Marek stealing Sully away from her father.

I knew Hawke still harbored guilt for putting his woman in that situation, even though it hadn't been his fault. Yes, he'd had a hard time keeping his dick in his pants, but all that changed after Edana's attack. He confessed he hadn't touched another chick since, and I believed him. I saw the look of pure terror and pain in his eyes when he held Edana, doing his best to comfort her and assure her that he would rain all hell down on the Reapers for daring to touch her. As volatile as Hawke and Edana's relationship was, they loved each other, although at times it seemed only logical to question.

"How is she?" I didn't have to say her name for him to know who I was talking about.

"She's healing physically, more each day, but she's still fucked-up in the head." Hawke finished the rest of his beer, slamming down the bottle in frustration. "She's been having fuckin' nightmares, and when I try to hold her she lashes out and hits me. She doesn't even know it's me until she's fully awake." Running his hands through his hair, he dropped his head and groaned. I'd heard his anguish because I stood so close, but to everyone else, it just appeared as if he was drunk. "I don't know what to do for her. I feel so goddamn helpless, man," he confessed.

I had no idea what he was going through, but my heart bled for him just the same. Shit like this was one of the main reasons I chose not to get attached to a woman. Bad things happened all the time in our world, and the less people I brought into it, the better. Besides, the last chick I'd shacked up with betrayed me, and who the hell wants to deal with that fucked-up situation again?

"It'll get better in time. Just be patient."

"Easier said than done," Hawke grumbled. As he was about to say something else, Arianna, one of the dancers, shimmied next to me and wrapped her arms around my neck, pushing her fake tits against my chest. Rising up on her toes, still significantly shorter than me even in heels, she pressed her mouth to mine.

"Hey, baby," she cooed, licking her glossy lips before trying to kiss me again. But I was prepared that time. Unlocking her hands, I gently pushed her away. Yeah, I'd fucked her a few times when I was drunk and horny, but settling between Arianna's legs again wasn't something I was interested in any longer. To be honest, it shocked me that she'd been able to convince me to fuck her more than once. But like I said, I was drunk for all three occasions.

"Not tonight," I warned, keeping my voice as casual as possible. She reeked of cheap cologne, no doubt from giving a few guys some up close and personal time. Disappointment shrouded her face, but the emotion quickly disappeared when Hawke leaned over me and gave her his winning smile.

"I can take you both on if that's what you want. It doesn't have to be just the two of us." She batted her heavily coated eyelashes at me before turning her attention to my younger brother.

I'd been around the block and was no stranger to threesomes, but never with another guy. And sharing this chick with my brother was the last thing that was goin' down tonight. No fucking way was I crossing swords with him.

"No," I said more firmly, pushing her back another step to clear her from my personal space. "Not gonna happen, so stop tryin'."

She gave me a fake pout before winking at Hawke. Fortunately, a few guys seated close to the stage caught her attention and she strutted toward them without glancing back at us.

Well, that was easy enough.

"You hittin' that?"

"Not anymore. I should've never started shit with her to begin with," I confessed, taking a healthy swig from my beer.

"Why? She cray?" Hawke asked, grinning because he knew I hated when he talked like some teeny-bopper.

"Cray? Really?" He laughed before hitting my shoulder with his. "To answer your question, Arianna's probably in the vicinity of crazy, yes, but I never paid much attention to say for a hundred percent." Finishing off my drink, I gestured for another.

"Same thing, sweetheart?" Carla asked, wiping down the bar in front of us.

Before answering her question, I asked, "Why are you serving drinks tonight? I thought we just hired someone to do that." Swiping the bottle she'd passed me, I gulped half of it down before she responded.

"She called off. Said her kid was sick or something." Waving to someone at the far end of the bar, she smiled before leaving to tend to a customer.

I liked Carla. She was an ex-stripper turned manager. Anyone who spent five minutes with her knew she had a good head on her shoulders. Smart. Savvy. Compassionate. She kept the patrons in check with her stern, no-nonsense tone, all while helping the dancers, whether it be with costumes, dance routines, or talking them through a bout of stage fright.

Carla was a powerhouse of a woman. Not in stature, standing at just five foot five, but in personality. She was attractive, although not my type. If I had to guess her age, which I would never do out loud, I'd put her in her early to mid-forties. Her shoulder-length, honey blonde hair was styled into a flattering bob-type hairdo. Thin yet curvy, she definitely caught the attention of many of the men who frequented the club, a fact her husband, Brian, didn't appreciate. He'd almost knocked out one of the men ogling Carla when the drunken patron decided to get a bit handsy. Luckily, our security stepped in and threw the guy out on his ass before Brian attacked him.

Flinging the bar rag over her shoulder, she slid a shot glass toward Hawke and gave him a wink. He responded with an appreciative nod before throwing back the amber liquid, slamming the glass on the bar when he finished. Carla had a nurturing way about her, and when she'd found out what had happened to Edana, she tried to comfort Hawke in the only way she knew how—by giving him a drink right before he knew he even needed one.

"Hey, I meant to ask you this earlier. How's the new dancer working out? Any issues?" Finally sitting on the barstool, I rested my right foot on the rung, my left on the ground. Strumming my fingers on the bar top, I patiently waited for her to respond, my eyes taking in the action around the club.

"She's quite somethin'." Carla chuckled, the teasing tone to her voice enough to draw my attention back to her. Smiling big, she jerked her chin toward the stage. "In fact, you can see for yourself. She's up next."

CHAPTER SIX

Tripp

THE TONE OF CARLA'S STATEMENT had me on edge for a reason I couldn't explain, except that I knew something was about to change for me very soon.

Apprehension stole the air from my lungs.

Swiveling around, my eyes darted toward the area of the stage I knew the girls emerged from, my posture becoming more rigid with every breath I took. Before I could berate myself for being ridiculous, Craig's voice, our announcer, crooned through the speakers.

"Call your wives and tell 'em you'll be late tonight, fellas, because our next dancer is gonna grace us with one more performance. She's sexy. She's alluring. She's temptation incarnate."

A thunderous roar erupted before he'd even finished speaking, the spotlight hitting the stage and the music pumping from the sound system in time to the appearance of the next dancer.

It was a sensual song, one I never expected to hear in a place like this, but I guess that's what made her performance unlike any other.

A thin blanket of smoke rolled across the stage, quickly dissipating when the mystery woman appeared. Seduction drifted off her in waves as she walked toward the pole. Every step she took was predatory, the sway of her hips and the confidence in her body language instantly grabbing my attention. Hell, she entranced every fucker in the club. I saw the evidence as I quickly scanned the room.

Hopping off my barstool, my heart pounded faster as I approached the stage. Hawke shouted something behind me, but I couldn't hear him. My only focus was on her. I had to find out what the invisible pull was drawing me toward her. My breathing accelerated as I moved closer, and I realized right then that I was powerless to stop whatever was happening to me.

When I stopped a few feet from the stage, I finally saw what all the fuss was about. Everyone around me faded into nothingness, the once-deafening shouts from the men muffled. The thrum of the music lessened as my eyes latched onto the woman rocking my world.

She was the most beautiful creature I'd ever laid eyes on, and I'd seen plenty of gorgeous women in my thirty-two years. I had no idea what her name was, however, because Craig's announcement had been shrouded by the shouts of excited men.

She wore a tiny, white sheer top tied just underneath her full breasts, accompanied by a skirt so short it barely covered her ass. But I guess that was the sole purpose.

Her long red hair fell to the middle of her back, the curls bouncing and moving with every step she took. Her stomach was flat and toned, her legs long and lean. When she turned away from me and bent over I thought I was gonna come in my pants. Her heart-shaped ass was a work of art, and the only thoughts I had were of me sinking my teeth into her soft, pliable flesh.

Before I knew it, I'd advanced closer, surely blocking the view for some of the other patrons. But ask me if I cared. Besides, even if they had a problem with me obstructing their view, they weren't stupid. If they didn't know me personally, they could easily see from the cut I wore that I belonged to the club who owned this place. And if that weren't enough of a deterrent, my sheer size would have them thinking twice about opening their drunken mouths.

Our newest dancer slowly moved around the middle of the stage. Her delicate fingers popped the buttons of her shirt, purposely taking her time for the much-needed buildup, working up every man in the place. Her actions fueled something inside me, an unfamiliar rage simmering deep within. I wanted her performance to be for me and me alone. But the thought was stupid.

She's a fucking stripper.

Of course her little dance was directed at whoever would throw her money. Another fact which stirred my fury from a simmer to a slight boil.

What the hell is wrong with me?

The song picked up tempo and her lithe body contorted around that damn pole with expertise. Her shirt was wide open, exposing her full, natural breasts for everyone to see. She took a spin around the pole, jumping and hooking her legs above her head before slowly sinking down toward the floor.

She was magnificent.

I was knocked back from my fantasies when I saw her approach, her eyes locking with mine as she came closer.

I found it difficult to breathe, as if all the air had been sucked out of the room. I was stuck in place, entranced by the woman in front of me, and the gleam in her eyes proved she was aware of my new predicament.

A small smile tilted up her full, luscious lips as she watched my reaction. Reaching up, she grabbed her shirt and slowly let it slip off her shoulders, then off completely. Keeping her gaze pinned on me, she grabbed her breasts and pinched her nipples, twisting her hips to the beat of the music.

I couldn't look away.

What I really wanted to do was jump onto the stage and whisk her away, but not before covering her up. I couldn't stand that there were at least a hundred pairs of eyes raking all over her exposed flesh. It was driving me insane, but there wasn't anything I could do about it.

Was there?

Before I could entertain my odd thought, she sank to her knees and crawled toward me, engulfing me further in her web. It wasn't until she was a few feet away from me that I noticed something different about her. From afar, she appeared every bit the stereotypical stripper, playing her part to make her money, but up close, her bluish-gray eyes told a different story. They held an innocence, an inexperience which just didn't seem plausible. It was the oddest contradiction.

They say the eyes are the windows to the soul. If that were true, then I could see that all of her hopes and dreams had been dashed, yet she forged ahead, seeking a light that might be just within her reach.

Hope and desperation battled for dominance behind her beautiful pupils, the dueling emotions rather intriguing. I tried, but I couldn't look away. I thought I heard Hawke's voice yell for her to take it off, but I ignored him, even though I wanted nothing more than to punch him in the face for watching my woman get naked.

My woman?

So entranced with my new feelings, I hadn't realized she was so close. Her soft palm caressed the side of my face, her touch pushing all of my other thoughts to the side, and causing my lungs to seize up. I knew right then that if she continued her silent assault on my senses, I was gonna cause quite the scene. Picking up on my body language, the tick of my jaw and clench of my fists quite obvious and telling, she removed her hand and moved back, eventually lying on her back and spreading her legs wide in front of me. In front of everyone.

I'd never wanted to fuck a woman more than in that moment. I kept picturing burying my cock inside her, feeling her clench around me as I made her come over and over again. Absently, I reached down and palmed my dick, trying to calm my arousal so I didn't embarrass myself in front of her and every other fucker present. Even though I tried to will my dick to soften, it only became harder, painfully straining against the fabric of my jeans.

I almost lost it when her fingers hitched inside the waistband of her tiny skirt, shimmying the material down her long, shapely legs until she was wearing nothing but a thong. After thirty seconds of pure torture, she rose to her feet and stepped back toward the center of the stage, her fingers dancing over her skin, continuing to tease and torment me.

She continuously honed in on me as if I were the only man in the room, something I quite liked, although I knew it wasn't true. The final beats of the song faded before she'd had the chance to remove her last piece of clothing. Indulge was a fully nude club, but right then I'd never been so happy to see one of our dancers break the rules.

She disappeared from the stage, taking with her our brief yet binding connection.

CHAPTER SEVEN

Reece

CATCHING MY BREATH BACKSTAGE HAD nothing to do with the exertion I'd endured during my performance. Instead, it had everything to do with the man who'd thrown me into another world. Dammit! I'd been so distracted with him that I'd never removed my thong. Rules of the club were to get completely naked, and I broke that rule. I sure as hell hoped I didn't get fired because of it.

Pushing aside my building paranoia at the thought of losing my job, I reverted back to thinking about the man who'd distracted me. It was weird to acknowledge, even to myself, but the painfully handsome stranger made me feel things I hadn't felt in years . . . if ever. He seemed different than every other man present, locking eyes with me like he wanted to expose his innermost secrets. A strange thread of connection quickly formed between us, still lingering in the air even without being in his presence.

Shaking my head, knowing my thoughts were utterly ridiculous, I tried like hell to forget about Mr. Tough and Sexy as I prepared for the rest of my evening, which thankfully was close to being over.

After quickly freshening up, I ventured back into the lounge area to search for someone who was receptive to a private dance. I'd become rather popular during my short employ at Indulge, so I never encountered any problems earning my keep. The entire time I searched for my next customer, my eyes flitted around the spacious room in search of the gorgeous stranger who'd made my heart leap in my chest just moments earlier. But I didn't see him. Maybe he'd done both of us a favor and left.

Berating myself for acting like some kind of lovesick puppy, I squared my shoulders, raised my head high and plastered on the most seductive smile I could muster. Striding across the room and looking for my next customer, I eyed a table full of businessmen. They seemed harmless enough, as harmless as men could be with naked women surrounding them and alcohol flowing freely.

Circling the table, I stopped next to a good-looking, dark-haired, younger guy, touching him on the shoulder to garner his attention—not that his eyes weren't already on me the entire time. "Hey, handsome. Do you want a private dance?" There was no way he would turn me down, not with the lust-induced haze he battled while leering at me. I shut down my inner voice, deciding I needed to right the wrong of not shedding all my clothes earlier. Besides, there had been many times when I'd had to grind up on a fat, ugly man, so when I encountered the chance to entertain someone pleasing to the eye, I jumped all over it. Figuratively as well as literally.

Grabbing my hand tightly, he said, "You don't have to ask me twice, sweetheart." He rose from his chair, practically knocking it over in his haste. "Let's go." His friends egged him on as I led him across the club, the smell of alcohol around him evident but not quite at an alarming level.

As we headed toward the private rooms located in the back of the club, my eye caught sight of someone off to the right, sitting in one of the more secluded sections of the establishment.

Him.

The one who drew me in with nothing but his mesmerizing green eyes.

The one who spoke to my soul.

I guess he didn't leave after all.

Desperate to distract myself from wishing I were with the mystery stranger instead, I practically ran toward the room I needed.

Closing the door to the private space, I guided him toward the single chair in the center. Once he sat, I stepped back, being sure to give him my sexiest smile before turning around to hit the button for the music. All of the selections in the private rooms were seductive beats, nothing fast-paced. The idea was to drag out the dance as long as possible, hoping the customers would engage in another. Most times, it worked.

After my stage performance, I'd changed into a simple, short black dress which buttoned up all the way. It fell just below my plump ass cheeks and dipped very low in the front, practically exposing my very erect nipples. The cold blast of the air conditioning was always kept on high, ensuring our *arousal*.

Shutting my eyes, I allowed the steady strum of the song to guide the flow of my body, swaying my hips while my hands danced over my skin. In my head, I was somewhere else. Alone. Not about to take off my clothes for some man I'd never met before. Just when I'd found my happy place, *he* popped into my head. The way his eyes bore into mine while I was on stage. The way his breaths increased and the slight thumping of his pulse intensified the closer I stalked toward him. The way his jaw muscles clenched when I saw him glance at the other men surrounding the stage. He didn't like that their eyes were glued to me, much like his were. It was slight, and quick, but I didn't miss his possessive demeanor toward me. And I should have been frightened, but I wasn't. I wanted his attention. Hell, I think I even wanted his hands on me while I danced, although that was definitely against the rules.

I circled the guy's body, all while lightly touching him. First it was on the shoulder, letting my fingers trail over the fabric of his jacket. Then I ran my hand down the front of his chest, slowly unbuttoning his shirt halfway. Pleased when I felt defined muscles underneath, the guy was a nice change of pace from some of the men I had to deal with. So why couldn't I stop picturing *my* gorgeous stranger?

Straddling my customer's lap, my thighs pinning him to the chair, I ran my hands through his thick hair. Gripping his curly tresses, I yanked his head back so he was looking straight up at the ceiling. I heard a rumble erupt from his throat, knowing he was completely turned on—as if the evidence of his arousal straining against his pants wasn't already a sign.

But then he tried to touch me, and that was a big no-no. A violation of the rules. Well, *my* rules. I knew for a fact there were girls here who had sex with some of the men who came in, but I wasn't into that. The show I gave them was just that, a show. Dancing. That was all I'd ever do with these customers.

Apparently, this guy had other intentions.

"Nuh-uh-uh, big boy. No touching allowed," I gently advised as I pried his hands off my ass and put them back on the arms of the chair.

"Ah, come on. All I want is to touch you. I won't bite, I swear. Well, not unless you want me to." He winked as if the gesture would make me change my mind. The lights were dimmed low but I could still make out his every feature, as I'm sure he could mine. I knew he noticed the warning look on my face, and when he made a move to grab me once more, I quickly removed myself from his lap and backed up.

I needed the money, so instead of calling security in to remove him, I tried my best to dispel the intensified moment. And fast. Needing him to focus on me and not my unwillingness to let him grope me, I grabbed the top of my dress and slowly pried it apart, the buttons making a delicious sound as each one popped open.

And we have success.

He licked his lips while his eyes devoured the very sight of me, his anticipation heavy for my next move. The skin of his hands turned pale, his grip on the chair certainly intense. Until it all became too much for him. Slipping his hand down his pants, he started to stroke himself, and I knew my situation had gone from tricky to unnerving. The way his eyes darkened frightened me, but I tried like hell not to show it.

My hands stilled on the last two buttons of my dress and I stopped dancing. Taking one step back, I told him, "There's no touching allowed in here, honey." A fake smile plastered on my face, my tone left no room for argument. I prayed he'd see I was serious and simply comply so I could finish, but something told me that scenario wasn't going to play out for me.

"But I'm not touching you," he responded, looking confused.

I pointed at his crotch. "No touching at all, not even yourself."

Instant irritation contorted his expression, his eyes suddenly becoming darker than before. I knew he'd been drinking, but as the situation unfolded I realized there was something else wrong, something more dangerous. If I had to guess, I'd say he was high. On what, I had no idea, and I didn't want to stick around to find out.

"That's a fucking stupid rule if you ask me," he shouted, rising from the chair and taking a single step in my direction. "I'm paying good money, and if I can't touch you then I sure as hell should be able to stroke my cock if I want." There was fire in his eyes, and I knew I'd lost control of the situation. I frantically tried to figure out how I was going to move past the irate man and escape.

While I contemplated my next move, I put as much distance between us as possible. "Well, those are the rules and you have to abide by them if you want me to finish my dance." I didn't want to finish, not at all, but I'd say anything I needed to. "Can you please sit down so I can finish for you?" I asked as I popped another button, plastering on another fake smile to trick him into thinking he wasn't frightening the hell out of me. The plan I'd come up with was to make him sit back down before I ran toward the door. Toward safety.

But he had other ideas.

Still standing, he barked, "How about you get fuckin' naked and do what I'm paying you to do." He crushed the space between us in two long strides, grabbing my arms before I could retreat. Standing at five foot eight, decently tall for a woman, I appeared much smaller with him towering over me. I'd been in these circumstances before, unfortunately—a hazard of the job—but usually the men were weak and drunk, easily persuaded to comply with my rules. This guy, however, was different. He scared me, and if I didn't escape soon I feared he was going to attack me, uncaring if he hurt me or not. For all I knew, he *wanted* to hurt me.

"Please let go," I pleaded, trying to shrug out of his bruising hold. When his grip intensified, I started to tremble. "You're hurting me." Still nothing. "Let go of me," I screamed. "Now." I tried to appear strong and fearless, but my tone betrayed me.

"You're not going anywhere until I get what I paid for, you little slut." With his final word, he shoved me so hard I fell on my ass, instant pain shooting up my back and breaking out at my shoulders. Shock knocked me dizzy, allowing him to start to disrobe. He loosened his tie and ripped his shirt open in a flash, the muscles I thought were so appealing minutes before terrifying me now. His fingers popped the button of his pants before quickly working on his zipper as he approached my crumpled form.

Thankfully, the daze I'd been in dissipated and I shot to my feet, making a run for it. He caught my wrist as I rushed past, however, whipping me around and slamming me against the nearest wall. I tried to fight him off but I was simply no match. "Get off me, you bastard!" I cried, fear setting in that no one was going to hear me. Not over that damn music, both inside our room and out. My only saving grace would be if someone happened to be walking by at that exact moment.

"Now," he said, as he gripped the sides of my dress, "we're gonna have some fun." Popping the remaining button of my dress, he ripped the material from my body and tossed it to the floor beside me. I tried to cover myself, but he grabbed my hands with one of his and held them above my head. Trying to kick him did nothing but earn me a punishing grip to my slender waist. "Keep on fighting me, sweetheart. I love a good struggle."

There was nothing I could do. I was utterly helpless. My arms were restrained and his hips were pinning my own to the wall, adhering my fears to his excitement. His lips roamed over my neck, biting and licking me as if he wasn't forcing me into this position.

I continued to struggle, but the only thing I accomplished was wearing myself out. When my attempt at escape became futile, I started to cry. Honestly, I'd been surprised it'd taken me that long for the tears to start flowing. While I was lost to my breakdown, his free hand moved from my waist and down my body, traveling over the skimpy material covering my sex.

He rubbed his fingers over my core, trying to gain entrance by sliding the lace to the side. "You'll like this. I promise," he mumbled, his ministrations becoming more persistent. I wriggled in his hold, finding a spurt of energy, and as he took a small step back I finally found my opportunity to attack.

His face was mere inches from my own when I struck his nose with my head. A chilling sound erupted from his mouth before he released me and stumbled back, his hands instantly flying up to cover his face. Blood coated his fingers, but I didn't hear bone crunching so I doubted I broke his nose. *Pity.*

Before I could skate around his enraged form, he leapt at me and tackled me to the ground. "You fucking bitch!" His knees made good work of pinning down my arms, so the only thing I could do was shake my head from side to side. As if that was going to help me. I closed my eyes, willing my mind to float off to a safer place, but I was stuck inside that darkened room with a man who was hell-bent on taking what he thought he was owed.

Drops of his blood hit my cheek, forcing me to open my eyes and face the reality of what was going to happen. I decided to plead with him once more. "Please don't do this. Please just let me go." I begged him over and over, but it was no use. And my silly attempts to buck him off barely registered. He was simply too strong.

His hands wrapped around my throat before another word left my lips. Dots flashed behind my eyes. I started to fall under an all-too-familiar darkness, and although I did everything in my power to stop it, I feared all of my efforts were in vain. If I fell unconscious, he'd surely have his way with me. Not that I could do much while I was awake, but at least if I were lucid, I'd still have a shot.

The darkness would still my struggle.

The light would give me a fighting chance.

CHAPTER EIGHT

Tripp

I RESTED MY HEAD AGAINST the top of the booth, taking in all the activity of the club, but nothing I saw distracted me from *her*. The mysterious woman who not ten minutes prior had burrowed into the deepest parts of my brain.

"I thought you were leaving," Hawke yelled, slapping my shoulder before taking a healthy swig of his drink.

After *her* performance I knew there was no way in hell I was leaving any time soon. My inner voice had convinced me to stay, so I slinked into the nearest booth and attempted to cool my overactive thoughts with some hard alcohol.

"Nah," I responded nonchalantly. "I'm gonna hang out a bit longer." I never made eye contact with my brother for fear he'd pick up on something I wasn't completely sure of myself. Hawke may play a dumbass most times but the guy was super observant.

"Uh-huh," he mumbled, throwing back a shot before his head twisted to the side. Slapping the table, well on his way to becoming drunk, he shouted, "'Bout time you fuckers got here." Turning my head, I saw Ryder and Breck approach, both of them looking like someone killed their dog, if they'd had one.

Neither one of them said a word as they nestled into the booth next to Hawke and me, spreading out enough so we weren't crammed together, which would just be weird. Ryder reached for my scotch but I slapped his hand away before he'd grabbed the glass.

"What the fuck, nomad?" he yelled, quickly retracting his hand.

"You know damn well you ain't gettin' any of this shit."

"Who died and made you my keeper?" His scowl would have scared most people, but not me. Besides, I knew Ryder enough to know that he wouldn't make good on any threats while he was sober. And by sober I meant no hard alcohol flowing through his veins. Otherwise, all bets were off.

"Beer," I said, taking a healthy swallow of my drink.

"What?"

"Beer, you bastard. That's all you're gettin'."

"We'll see about that," he growled, shoving Breck from the booth so he could get out. Luckily, I caught Carla's attention and shook my head while pointing at Ryder who was fast approaching the bar. But my warning was unnecessary; everyone who worked the bar knew not to serve Ryder anything but beer.

Turning my attention back on Breck, I asked, "Why the face?"

No hesitation before he spilled. "Marek's ridin' our asses about the rotation with Psych. He's coming unhinged and it's scaring the shit out of me."

"*Coming* unhinged?"

"Well . . . more than usual." He shook his head as if he disagreed with some sort of inner dialogue, locking eyes with me before he frowned.

Ryder striding back to our table pulled all of our attention.

"You fucker. That chick wouldn't serve me what I wanted," he griped before pushing Breck farther into the booth so he could sit back down.

"Why you want that shit anyway?" Hawke shouted over the music, tapping the top of the table in beat with the song.

"I could just use a shot of something to help take the edge off."

"Why?" Hawke repeated. "Braylen getting on your nerves?" My brother laughed, and seeing the look on Ryder's face only made him laugh harder. "Shit!" he exclaimed. "Never thought I'd see the day when the big bad Ryder was all twisted up from some fuckin' broad."

"Fuck you. I don't even know what Edana sees in your dumb ass," Ryder goaded, knowing damn well Hawke was gonna retaliate. Which he did, seconds after Ryder shut his mouth. Hawke jumped up from his seat and lunged over the table, reaching out to grab Ryder's cut, the volatile look on his face warning everyone around him he was set to explode.

Pulling him back, I shoved Hawke back in his seat, throwing my arm across his chest to try and keep him contained. Which was quite challenging because he kept trying to go after Ryder, who sat across from us with a fuckin' smirk on his face.

"Calm the hell down!" I shouted to my brother, putting more pressure on him to stay still. Finally he did, reaching for his drink and draining the rest of it before tossing the empty beer bottle at Ryder. Thankfully our Sergeant-at-Arms ducked at the last minute.

"Isn't it your duty to make sure there's no chaos in the club?" I asked, glaring at Ryder. He knew damn well any mention of Edana was a sore subject, the guilt that consumed my brother on a daily basis over everything that had happened to her borderline debilitating.

"What? Like keeping the peace and shit?" He laughed, shaking his head in disbelief at the idea.

"Yeah, you ass."

"Like that'll ever happen." Ryder slumped back in the booth, baiting Hawke with the narrowing of his eyes. It was as if he wanted to fight with him.

Deciding to change the topic, I coaxed Breck into telling me more about his outburst. "So, is someone not doing their part babysitting our prisoner?"

"No. Everyone is doin' their part."

"So what the hell is the problem?"

Tapping the table as a distraction, Breck glanced to Ryder before speaking. "Marek feels we're not inflicting enough pain on Psych." From the tone of his voice I knew the subject bothered him. Breck had no problem inflicting pain on someone when necessary, especially to the likes of that fucker, but I knew he didn't get off on that shit either. None of us did. Well, apparently Marek did, but could I blame him? The man had every right to inflict as much agony on Psych Brooks as possible, but at some point he had to let go and move on.

"He's draggin' this shit out. It's not good. Not for him or any of us."

Bingo.

Leaning forward, I gave Breck my best advice. "Look, this whole situation with Psych will be done whenever Marek deems it so. He's working through some shit, not only for himself, but for Sully." Resting back against my seat, I finished with, "We're just gonna have to be patient. He can't prolong it forever. Have you seen Psych's condition? If I were a betting man, I'd give him a few more days at best."

Swallowing the rest of my drink, I shoved it toward Ryder. "You can suck on my ice cubes if you want. I'm sure there's some scotch left on them." The corner of my lip twitched in amusement watching his reaction.

"Fuck you," he grated, grabbing two of the cubes from the glass and throwing them at me. I dodged them, but Hawke hadn't been so lucky.

"What the fuck?" he yelled, tossing them right back at Ryder. A hint of a grin appeared on my brother's face, but it was gone before anyone else saw it. At least they weren't tackling each other to the ground.

The thing with men that many women didn't understand was that we could argue, and even go to blows, but a few minutes later it was done with. We were all brothers and, as such, we had each other's backs. Sure, we got on each other's nerves, and sometimes a battle ensued, but we didn't hold grudges. When it was done, it was done.

With the exception of Trigger and Stone. Trigger still harbored some ill feelings toward Stone for going against code and gettin' with his niece. Their relationship wasn't as bad as it once was, especially after Riley was born, but anger still reared up every now and again when Trigger spoke to the club's VP.

The antics at our table took my mind off *her*. Slightly. Peering around the club, I still didn't catch a glimpse of her. I wondered if she left for the evening. All of a sudden, thoughts of where she lived, how she got there, and if she was being careful bombarded me. Why I cared about the safety of a woman I'd never met baffled me, but the questions and concerns were present nonetheless. After ten minutes, I decided to put my crazy thoughts to rest.

Straddling a stool at the bar, I waved Carla over. "Did the new girl leave already?" I tried to appear as disinterested as possible, but her smile told me she knew I was anything but. I averted my eyes but her silence pulled my attention back to her. "What?"

"I told you she was quite somethin', didn't I?" She smiled bigger at my intrigue. I didn't answer. Instead, I raised a brow in irritation. Carla laughed. "No, she didn't leave yet. I believe she's in the back room giving a private dance."

My hands instantly clenched the edge of the bar, the look on my face surely telling Carla that I was less than pleased with the news. Although I couldn't explain why, not to her and certainly not to myself.

Rising from my seat, I walked across the open area and headed toward the private rooms. Only one was in use at the moment, the green sign above the door reading 'Occupied.' Every step closer had me on edge, my heart racing so fast I swore it was gonna beat right out of my goddamn chest if I didn't get a fuckin' grip.

I was ten feet away when I heard a man shouting. Then I heard a woman's screams, pleading with him to get off her. And I knew I only had seconds before something horrific happened to her, if it hadn't already. Not stopping to check if the door was unlocked, my shoulder hit the thick wood and splintered the frame.

Berating myself for ever taking my eyes off her in the first place, a mistake I would never make again, I rushed into the room and threw myself at the man pinning her to the ground. My sheer size, mixed with my surprise attack, was enough to knock the guy to the ground in no time, wailing on him with my fists while he did his best to defend himself. He tried to throw a punch, but all that got him was a broken wrist. My rage poured from me in droves, the adrenaline coursing through my veins hyping my need to end the fucker. My fists were still flying at him when hands grabbed at me from behind, tugging me backward to get me to stop.

"Tripp!" Ryder shouted. "Come on." I tried to shrug him off, but he wasn't the only one pulling at me; my brother was helping to diffuse the situation as well.

"Bro, he's right. Come on. You did what you needed to. It's over." Hawke had no idea what was going on, but he knew I would never attack someone without a damn good reason. It took me a few extra seconds to calm down enough to hop to my feet, leaving the other guy on the floor still breathing. Unfortunately.

Gripping my hair, I turned around and found the woman I'd rescued cowering in the corner, her knees pulled tightly to her chest as she buried her head from view. I could see her body trembling from clear across the room and I wanted nothing more than to protect her, to soothe her worries and comfort her. A stranger. A woman I'd seen for the first time on stage, dancing for a crowd of men. A woman who willingly came into this room with a stranger because she wanted to make extra money. A woman who would put herself into this very same situation again in the future.

Not if I have anything to say about it.

Disregarding my crazy thought, I moved toward her with my hands held in front of me to show her I meant no harm. The commotion caught the attention of not only my men but Carla and the guy we had working security that evening.

"Oh my God!" Carla cried. "What happened?" She took a step toward the woman, but I stopped her.

"Don't. I got her," I said, crouching and resting my hands on her shoulders. "Look at me." She ignored me and kept her head down. "Look at me," I said more forcefully, while still keeping a hint of compassion in my voice. Finally, she complied, lifting her head slowly until her eyes connected with mine. "What's your name?"

"Reece," she whispered. Tortured blue-grays shredded me, the hurt and fear lingering in her gaze pumping my anger to new heights all over again. It was then I noticed she'd been choked, the bastard's fingerprints bruising her delicate neck, the reddened area already starting to darken.

Barely controlling myself, I reached for her hands and guided her to her feet, pulling her into me to shield her nakedness from everyone present. Without turning around, I shouted to Hawke, "Get him the fuck out of here and make sure he understands that if he ever comes near this place, or her, again that we'll snatch his life from him."

As Hawke and Ryder dragged the bastard past us and from the room, she began to tremble more, wrapping her arms around my waist and trying like hell to disappear. If she could've climbed inside my body, I swore she would have. After what felt like forever, I dislodged her hands from around me and took a small step back. I shrugged off my cut and wrapped it around her. The sight of how it swallowed her up was almost comical, but at least she was covered.

"Thank you," she said, her voice small and frail. I nodded before turning my attention to Carla, who was still standing close by. "Can you stay with her for a second?"

"Absolutely." Carla drew Reece into her embrace, whispering something in her ear in an effort to comfort her.

Stalking toward the security guy, I grabbed his collar and shoved him against the wall. "Where the fuck were you? Why weren't you watching the cameras?" I roared, slamming him against the wall once more. "You could have prevented what happened to her." Stunned, the guy went mute on me, eyes widening in fear for his life. "Where were you?" I repeated.

"I'm sorry. I . . . I was . . . busy," he stumbled over his words.

"Busy doin' what? Gettin' your dick sucked?" The surprised look on his face told me I'd hit the nail on the head, and it took everything in me not to snatch him by his throat and squeeze the life out of him. "Well, I hope it was worth it because you're fired. Get your shit and get the fuck out of this club before I make it so you can't walk outta here," I threatened.

Spinning around, I headed back toward the two women. "Carla," I said, pulling Reece from her arms and back into mine, "I need you to tell all the girls they aren't to mess with the men when they're on duty. Ever. And give the guys the same message. Because if this shit happens again, I'll rain holy hell down on whoever fucks up."

"I'll take care of it," she assured, glancing quickly at the younger woman and then back to me before giving me what looked like a thankful smile.

Once it was just the two of us standing in the middle of the room, I stepped back to put some distance between us. With my fingers under her chin, I slowly lifted her head. "How's your neck? Because it looks pretty fuckin' bad."

"Nothing I can't handle," she confessed.

"Fuck!" I shouted, calming my tone once I saw her flinch. "Sorry. You don't have to be afraid of me. I won't hurt you. I promise."

"I know."

Looking into her beautiful, soul-captivating eyes, I knew she meant what she'd said. Those two simple words of acknowledgement were all I needed to forge ahead with my plan.

CHAPTER NINE

Reece

WHAT I FELT WHEN IN this man's presence was unlike any other emotion I'd ever experienced. His concern wrapped around me like the warmest of blankets, his desire to protect me settling my wayward nerves. My nakedness shielded by his large leather vest, I clutched it tighter and walked next to him as we headed toward the exit. I had no idea where he was taking me, and for the briefest of moments I didn't care. All I wished to do was live in the existence that a stranger rescued me. A stranger who captivated my attention and never let go. I didn't understand the pull I felt toward him, but after the night I'd had, all I wanted to do was forget about what happened and try and salvage an ounce of dignity before I broke down in front of the large man walking beside me.

"You're not working here anymore," he blurted, making me stop dead in my tracks while he continued on ahead. He hadn't realized I stopped following him until he happened to turn his head to the side, expecting to see me beside him. The look of anger mixed with fear on my face propelled him to walk back toward me. "What's the matter?" he asked, as if he hadn't just stolen my livelihood right out from under me.

Cinching his vest tighter around me, I narrowed my eyes before speaking, trying to choose my words wisely. But as soon as my lips parted, I rambled like some sort of fool. "How . . . how is it my fault? I didn't provoke him. I swear. I was only trying to give him a lap dance, and then he stroked himself and when I told him to stop he got angry, and when I tried to escape he got angrier and came after me and . . . and . . . I'm sorry." After all that, I ended up apologizing for being the cause of the eruption at the club that evening.

The stranger's head cocked to the side and studied me for a moment before asking, "Why are you . . . ? What's the matter?" Truly looking confused, he rested his hands on my trembling shoulders.

"I need this job," I pleaded, lowering my head in nervousness. "Please don't fire me. I swear it won't happen again." How I could promise such a thing was beyond me, but I did. I'd say anything I needed to, no matter how ridiculous, to ensure I kept my job. I wasn't above begging and groveling, having been doing it for years. Raising my chin I stared at his broad chest, covered by a thin white T-shirt. Imagining what his naked torso looked like distracted my overactive brain, if only for a few seconds. Lifting my chin higher, I had no choice but to finally look at him, the frown marring his handsome face quite puzzling.

"I'm not firing you for what happened. But I won't lie and tell you that you're gonna continue to work here. It's not happenin'." His fingers trailed over the tops of my arms, and even through the thick leather covering me, the contact heated my skin to scorching levels.

I needed space.

"I said I was sorry. It'll never happen again." *There I go again with my half-assed promises.*

"You're goddamn right it won't happen again. I'll make sure of it." The muscles in his jaw jumped, his fingers digging into my arms in what appeared to be anger.

I couldn't figure out why he blamed me entirely for that bastard attacking me.

Shrugging out of his grasp, my own anger took hold, but experience told me to watch my tone. Although, all reasoning aside, there was something about the man brooding in front of me that told me he wouldn't physically lash out at me.

"What makes you think you have the authority to fire me?" I grasped at straws, but hopefully throwing a legit question at him would make him take his attitude down a notch.

Apparently, I was about to be schooled.

"First off, I told you I'm not firing you. Well, not exactly. And second, who *I* am is your boss. See the patch on that vest coverin' ya? It says 'Knights Corruption.' The very same club that owns this place." Cocking an arrogant brow, he leaned down and said, "So I hold all the authority, sweetheart."

Captured in a good old-fashioned stare-off, it wasn't until Carla placed her hand on my shoulder that I turned my attention away from the man in front of me and on to her.

"You okay, hon?" she asked, concern for my well-being written all over her pretty face.

"Yeah, but . . . I just got fired." I tried to remain strong, but the hitch in my voice gave me away.

"What do you mean?" Stealing my space, she stood in front of me. "Tripp, what is she talkin' about?" Pinning her hands on her hips, she asked, "Did you really just fire her?"

Tripp?

"She's not workin' here anymore." The look on his face left no room for argument, but that didn't stop Carla.

"She didn't do anything wrong and you know it."

"I know that," he argued.

"Then why?" Carla pressed, reaching behind her and grasping my hand, funneling her support through her touch.

"I'm not justifying my choice to you or anyone. It's done. Let it go." He stood taller and crossed his arms over his broad chest, his muscles stretching the fabric of his shirt.

His size should have intimidated me, but it did the exact opposite—I felt safe next to him, protected, like nothing in the world could harm me. And even though he'd just fired me, I couldn't help but commit every facet of this incredible man to memory. Carla's next words shoved me out of my assessment and back into the increasingly tense situation.

"Stone left it up to me to find Heather's replacement, and I did. So you can't stroll in here and undermine me. That's not how any of this works." Tripp remained still, only the repeated arch of his brow a giveaway that he was even listening. Carla huffed and stepped closer, releasing my hand in the process. Shoving a finger into his thick chest, she said, "You don't scare me, Tripp, so stop trying."

His response was sudden. He reached around the club manager and snagged my wrist, gently pulling me behind him as he strode quickly toward the door. "It's done, Carla, so find another girl."

When I ventured a glance behind me, I saw Carla shaking her head, her lips moving so rapidly I was sure she was having quite the conversation with herself.

"Where are you taking me?"

"Home," he answered, never bothering to look at me.

"I don't need you to take me anywhere." I tried to pull free from his grip but he only tightened his hold. "I'm fine by myself. You've had your say. You've fired me, so stop confusing me with pretending you care what happens to me. I can make my own way home."

He continued on, walking so fast I tripped over my feet in my haste to try and keep up. When I smacked into his back on my lurch forward, he stopped and spun around, his hands instantly steadying me. "Sorry," he apologized. "I walk fast when I have a purpose." Then he did something which completely threw me off-kilter—he smiled . . . and I swore I thought I was gonna faint. In an instant, all the anger and frustration I'd felt toward him melted away.

The way his green eyes lit up captivated my soul. Odd sentiment, I know, but so very true. The breath in my lungs stung after endless seconds, but I wanted to remain frozen in the moment, relishing the odd peace catapulting me into a different place in time.

"Are you okay?" he asked, his fingers dancing over the tops of my arms once more. Closing in on my personal space, he stood so close I had to crane my neck just to see his face. His warmth enclosed me, his intoxicating scent flicking on a switch inside me that had been off for a very long time.

I wanted nothing more than to wrap my arms around his waist and nuzzle myself into him, to rest my head against his chest and feel the thrum of his heartbeat, but of course I held back. He'd think me some kind of fruitcake if I did such a thing. Instead I stood tall and allowed myself to escape inside those entrancing orbs of his.

"You okay?" he repeated, cocking his head to the side while waiting for an answer.

"Y-yeah. I'm fine," I finally responded, my hold on his vest unrelenting as I used it to keep myself covered. "But I'd like to get dressed before we leave." Knowing he wasn't going to make the first move and back up, I retreated a few steps, his hands falling to his sides.

Music vibrated from the speakers. Men shouted at the naked performer on stage, their hoots and hollers blending into one another's. A glass shattered in the distance, followed by a few choice words from Carla. A woman's laughter rang out into the sexually charged air, but none of it registered completely. It was as if I existed in a daze, everything around me a mirage. As if it weren't really happening. But dead center in the mix of the cloudy vision of the club stood two people, everyone else fading into obscurity with each second ticking by.

Tripp and me.

Our eyes devoured the other, the air between us shared.

Our worlds were colliding, exploding and threatening everything we thought and knew. I saw the shared experience in the twinkle of his eyes and in the way his full lips kicked up in the corners, smiling because he saw the same recognition in me.

Finally, after what felt like an eternity, Tripp nodded before pushing a strained puff of air through his lips. "Go. Put some clothes on and grab your things. I'll be waiting right here." His tone told me everything, and I knew I'd better hurry before he lost his patience and dragged me out of the club. Naked or not.

CHAPTER TEN

Reece

"ARE YOU FUCKIN' HIM?"

I knew exactly who'd asked the abrupt question, my locker door thankfully blocking the woman from sight. But I couldn't hide behind the metal barrier forever. Once the latch clicked closed, I turned my head and gave her a fake smile.

"Can I do something for you, Arianna?" I asked, wishing she'd just leave me alone. Ever since I started working at the club she'd given me a hard time, throwing me nasty glares, hiding my costumes and makeup, and making snide comments. I got it—she didn't like me, although I couldn't fathom why. I'd never done anything to her, but I gave up caring, especially when Carla told me she was only acting like that toward me because she was jealous of all the attention I was getting from the customers. The same customers who used to fawn all over her.

"You hard of hearin'? I asked if you're fuckin' him," she repeated, haughtily crossing her arms over her chest and pushing her fake tits up higher.

"Who are you talking about?"

"Tripp."

"You know him?"

"Oh, honey." She laughed. "I know him *real* well." She winked and licked her thin lips, dropping her arms to her sides before stepping closer. "I fucked him so many times I've ruined him for any other bitch."

If Arianna weren't such a nasty person she'd actually be attractive. Close to my five foot eight, she had a nice build, although she'd gone a little overboard with her implants. Only my opinion, of course. She also caked on the makeup, something I thought was a waste of time because the men weren't too concerned with our faces. She wore wigs like the rest of us, but the first time I saw her natural reddish hair, all thick and wavy, I'd been jealous. That was until she opened her mouth and snapped at me, asking why I was leering at her. Ever since then I'd tried my best to stay clear of her whenever we worked the same shift, but she always seemed to seek me out for her own amusement.

"Well?" she pressed when I remained silent.

"I just met him." I had no idea why I gave that answer, but I couldn't think of anything but the truth.

"Well, he won't want your simple ass anyway, so don't even bother."

I chose not to engage, pushing past her and grabbing my purse and bag from the bench, along with Tripp's vest.

As soon as Arianna's eyes latched onto his leather, she gave me the nastiest look. "You just met him? Then why do you have his cut?"

"His what?"

"His cut," she sneered, pointing at the vest in my hand.

"He gave it to me until I got changed." I hadn't wanted to continue the conversation, but I found myself babbling on nonetheless.

"Well, since I'm going home with him tonight, I'll give it back to him." She reached out and tried to snatch it from my hands but I moved back, clutching his property tightly. A possessiveness I'd never encountered before took over. I couldn't explain it and I didn't have time to, not before Arianna stepped closer and tried to grab the vest once more. Thankfully, Carla interrupted us; otherwise, I had no idea what would have happened. I'd already endured enough that evening, and another fight was the last thing I needed.

"Arianna, you're not done with your shift. Let's go," Carla demanded, pointing toward the door for her to leave.

"Fine," she scoffed, "but remember who he'll be fuckin' later, sweetheart." She narrowed her eyes, trying her best to intimidate me before knocking into me on her way out the door.

"What the hell was that all about?" Carla's compassion for me was comforting, but I was tired and the only thing I wanted to do was leave. End this night and lose myself to sleep until the dawn promised a new day.

"I have no idea," I lied, not wanting to explain because I didn't completely understand myself.

Following Carla, I walked across the main room until I stood behind Tripp. He didn't know I was there, as was apparent by his conversation with whoever was on the other end of the phone.

"That's fine. Yeah, I don't care. Whatever you need." He sighed. "I said I don't care." Those were his final words before he hung up. Tucking his cell away, he turned around and practically bowled me over since I'd been standing so close. He looked confused for a moment, grabbing a strand of my hair and twirling it around his fingers. I'd removed my wig, my long chestnut color clearly a surprise to him.

"I was beginning to think I'd have to come and collect you." No smile traced his lips that time, which led me to believe he was completely serious. Did he not trust that I'd leave the club on my own accord? That he'd have to personally escort me out? And why was he insistent on driving me home? Why not just put me out and be done with me? I'd just met this man, yet already he confused the hell out of me with not only the way he looked at me but the way he made me feel. I should've been infuriated with him for firing me, but I wasn't. Well . . . I was, but I also wanted to spend more time with him, defying all reason and logic.

Placing his hand on the small of my back, he guided me toward the exit. Before we made it, though, Arianna came out of nowhere and grabbed Tripp's arm. "I'll see you later, baby," she fussed, glaring at me quickly before looking back at Tripp. Before he could answer, she pressed her nasty lips to his and strolled away.

A twinge of jealousy roared through me as I put one foot in front of the other rather quickly and walked farther away from Tripp. I should have known he wasn't going to let me get too far ahead of him, the feel of his hand on my waist annoying yet comforting.

"I don't know what she's talking about," he said, pushing the door open for me.

Without looking back, I responded. "None of my business. Just like it's none of your business who I go home with." Being snarky wasn't a trait of mine, but I found it came in quite handy just then.

I half expected him to come back with a retort but he remained silent. I knew my comment bothered him, though; I could just feel it.

The darkness of the evening was a perfect shield, so I kept my eyes straight ahead while we walked side by side across the large parking lot. I had no idea where I was going, but I kept on anyway. Eventually, I'd figure it out. The motel I was staying at was only a mile down the road. Worst-case, I'd walk the entire way, although the heels I had on would kill my feet before I made it there.

"I'm parked over here," Tripp announced, grabbing my hand and hauling me toward a motorcycle. Once we neared his ride, I shook my head and retreated. "What's the matter?"

"I'm not gettin' on that," I refused, pointing toward the hunk of steel. "I'll find my own way back."

"I won't let anything happen to you. I promise." Reaching out his hand, he waited for me to come closer, but I never did.

"I don't want to." No way was I going to straddle that machine. There was absolutely no protection between me and the pavement if something went wrong. Helmets only helped to protect the head from being crushed. What about the rest of my body? I just couldn't trust my safety to a complete stranger, even though said stranger was most likely an excellent rider. Fate had lashed out at me enough during my life, I wasn't about to tempt the fickle bitch and simply hope for the best.

While I was caught up inside my own head, he pulled his phone out and dialed a number. "Get out here. In the parking lot. I need your keys. Because I said so." He hung up, not once taking his eyes from me. Moments later, the door swung open and a man walked straight for us. He was good-looking, his dark hair the same shade as Tripp's, and the closer he came the more I could see a resemblance between the two.

"How am I getting home?" the man asked, throwing me a smile

before tossing his keys at Tripp, staggering to the side before righting himself.

"I'll have someone come get you."

"Why don't you just let me take your bike?" His jumbled words gave away that he was a little more than tipsy.

"Because, brother or not, I'd have to kill ya if you put a scratch on my bike. Seeing as how your ass is drunk and all."

"I'm not drunk. Just feelin' nice," he blabbered, winking at me before turning his attention back to Tripp.

"Shut the fuck up and get back inside." Tripp stepped closer and whispered something in his brother's ear before ushering him back toward the club. Turning around, he strolled toward me, grasped my hand and led me toward a dark-colored truck. "I would've introduced you, but he's not in any shape not to be crass, or even remember he met you for that matter. It'd just be a waste of time."

Opening the passenger door, he waited until I'd slid inside and buckled up before rounding the vehicle to his side. Turning over the engine, he drove across the lot and came to a dead stop at the edge, glancing over at me for directions.

"Take a right. My motel is a mile down the road." I settled into my seat and waited for him to propel the truck forward, but we remained immobile. "What?" I asked, admiring his profile during the ensuing silence, losing myself to the image of his chiseled jaw and slight stubble.

"The Buckshot Motel? That's where you're staying?" he asked incredulously, turning on the interior light and shaking his head before peppering me with more questions. "How long have you been there? And why . . . why in God's name would you choose that place? Do you know what a cesspool it is? Of course you do, but what I can't figure out is why you're staying there." He rambled on until he wasn't even directing his words at me any longer. His demeanor was borderline snobby, which was quite comical coming from someone who looked like him. He was the furthest thing from uppity, yet he took it upon himself to condemn the only place I could afford, essentially making me feel worse about my predicament.

"Well?" he asked, raising his voice as if I hadn't been paying attention the entire time.

"Yes, I'm staying there, and it's because I can't afford anywhere else. I've just moved here and I had a whopping fifty bucks to my name. I was lucky to find a job right away, so at least I wasn't out on the streets." Turning my body toward him so he didn't miss the angry look on my face, I continued, "But now you've gone and fired me—for something that wasn't my fault, I might add—so now it's a great possibility that I'll be homeless in a few weeks if I don't find another place to work. So thanks for that." The more I spoke, the angrier I became, although I tried to rein in my temper because my feet were killing me and the thought of walking a mile in the dark in these damn heels was too much. If I watched my tone maybe he'd follow through and give me a ride back to the 'cesspool.'

We stared at each other, the slight tick of his jaw and squint of his eyes telling me something was going on inside that gorgeous head of his. He bit his lower lip, and I wanted nothing more than to dislodge it from his straight white teeth and suck on it. *Oh my God! What is wrong with me?*

Moving my body to face the front once again, I said, "Please just take me home."

"Home?" he scoffed, flicking off the light before pressing on the gas and turning left.

"Where are you going? I said to take a right."

"You're not going there."

"But my stuff is there."

"We'll get it tomorrow," he said matter-of-factly.

"Where are you taking me?"

"To my place. You can stay there until you find something better. No way am I dropping you off at that shithole, and since I don't trust that you'd be safe there, I'd be forced to stay with you . . . and no way that's happenin'."

There he goes rambling again.

CHAPTER ELEVEN

Tripp

I CAN'T BELIEVE SHE EXPECTED me to drop her off at the Buckshot Motel. The place was well known for druggies and whores. They even rented the rooms by the hour, for Christ's sake.

"How did you get back and forth to work? I know you don't have a car if the only thing you could afford was that fuckin' place." My hands tightened on the wheel, my impatience for the entire evening coming to a halting close.

She remained silent for a few moments before answering, most likely pissed at me for putting down her choice of living arrangements. But I didn't give a shit. Someone had to tell her, and that someone may as well be me. "I'd walk," she answered, angering me more than I already was, "or I'd hitch a ride with Carla or one of the other girls who live close by." The entire time she spoke she avoided lifting her head. Why did her refusal to look at me bother me so much?

I couldn't believe I hadn't thought about this before, but I wondered if she had someone waiting for her back at the motel. "You got a man?" I blurted, holding my breath until she uttered a response.

"No."

"Good."

"Why good?"

"'Cause if you told me you did, it wouldn't stop me from bringing you to my place." I had no idea why I was saying what I was, but the words tumbled out before my fuckin' brain could filter them. I only prayed I wasn't freaking her out.

Miles passed before she spoke again. "Tripp?"

"Yeah."

"Is that your real name?" she asked, resting her elbow on the frame of the door.

"Is that what you were really gonna ask me?"

"Yes." She answered so quickly I knew her response was forced.

"I don't know you well enough to tell you my real name, sweetheart," I countered, smirking at the sudden back and forth between us, the topic thankfully lighter than before.

"But you're willing to take me back to your place. Which, by the way, I don't think is a good idea."

"Oh yeah, and why's that?"

"Because you're a stranger. And I don't make it a habit of going back to strangers' homes." Her arm fell from the doorframe and both hands rested in her lap, picking at the edge of my cut.

"If that's bothering you"—I gestured toward my vest—"you can throw it in the back. I'll grab it when I get out."

"No, it's fine. The heaviness of it is actually keeping me warm. California nights sometimes get a bit chilly."

"The way you said that I'm assuming you're not from here."

"No, I'm not." She wasn't gonna give me anything more unless I pressed.

"Where are you from, then?"

"Maine."

"Why did you move here? You chasin' a modelin' career or somethin'?"

"Yeah, I was hoping to get my big break twirling around the pole." She chuckled. "It obviously didn't work." A lightness drifted off her and whatever tension had been strangling the air between us lessened.

"So why California, then?" I asked once more.

"I'd rather not talk about it." Short and to the point, the tenseness creeping back into her posture warning me to let it go. So I did, for the time being.

She didn't speak again until twenty minutes later when we turned down a narrow, darkened gravel road. I'd been renting a cabin ever since Marek had asked me to stay on and oversee the progress and daily running of Indulge.

Clearing her throat, she blurted, "You're not planning on killing me, are you?" A nervous laugh escaped, irritating me more than I let on.

"Do you think I'd save you from that asshole only to turn around and kill you?"

"I hope not." Another uneasy laugh. "Thank you for that, by the way. I really appreciate it, even though I got blamed for it."

"Why do you keep saying I blame you for him attacking you? Because it ain't true. The only one to blame is that fucker. Him and him alone, so please stop sayin' otherwise."

She twitched in her seat, her nerves getting the better of her. I could tell she wanted to confront me, yell at me, tell me right where to go, but for some reason she held back.

"What?" I asked, finally pulling to a stop in front of my place.

"If . . . if you don't blame me, then why did you fire me?" When I opened my door the interior light came on, illuminating her beautiful face and her confused expression.

"Because I don't want you to ever put yourself in that situation again. It isn't safe." I climbed out of the truck and shut the door before she could come back with a retort. When I arrived at her door, I opened it up and extended my hand. Hawke's truck was high and I didn't want her to lose her footing while climbing down.

As soon as her palm touched mine, I closed my eyes and reveled in the warmth of her touch. It was brief, yet calming. I took her belongings, including my cut, from her hands and led her toward the porch.

"You have a beautiful home," she said in awe, her voice like the softest silk, weaving its hold around every fiber of my being and entrancing me.

"Thank you, but it's not mine. I'm just rentin' it for now. But if I stay on, I have the option to purchase." A large front porch ran the entire length of the cabin. Sometimes I'd sit in the lone rocking chair with a beer in hand and watch the sun disappear behind the horizon, often wondering what the future held for me and my club. There were plenty of nights I'd wished to share the scenery with someone, but until I met Reece, I hadn't realized how lonely I'd been.

She walked quietly beside me, the only sound coming from the rocks of the pathway kicking up beneath our feet.

Once inside, I tossed everything I'd been carrying on the nearest chair and walked to the kitchen. "Do you want something to drink?"

"Water will be fine."

After I handed her a bottled water, I intently watched her twist off the cap, raise it to her mouth and take a healthy gulp before licking water droplets from her plump lips. When she finished, she placed it on the table closest to her and stood in front of me, playing with her hands in nervousness.

When the silent awkwardness became too stifling, I spoke up. "I have some clothes you can change into."

"Are you married?" she asked, stepping back and bracing herself on the chair behind her. Her bluish-gray eyes widened, and although I didn't understand her appall, all I wanted to do was put her out of her misery.

"No, I'm not married."

"Oh," she said, rushing out a breath of air. "I thought when you said you had some clothes for me that you had access to women's clothing."

"No, I meant I have some shorts and a T-shirt you could wear. Or not. If you prefer to sleep in the nude, please don't let me stop ya." I chuckled to help relieve some of the tension, but it did nothing to stop her body from reacting. Averting her eyes, her cheeks flamed the sexiest shade of pink. How someone could take their clothes off for a living yet look so embarrassed by the mention of sleeping nude was quite the conundrum. She certainly wasn't what I expected at all.

Dismissing her slight discomfort, she switched the subject, although what she chose to say irritated me. "I don't want to be in the way when Arianna gets here, so if you'll show me where I'll be sleeping, I'll get out of your hair."

"What the hell are you talkin' about? Why would Arianna be coming over?" My entire body tensed. I hated that Reece thought there was anything going on between me and that bitch. Yeah, Arianna was a bitch. I saw the way she talked to everyone at the club; I just chose to ignore it when I buried myself between her legs because I was obviously out of my mind.

"Because she told me she was."

"When?"

"When I was getting changed at the club. She cornered me and asked me...." She trailed off before finishing, becoming quite flustered again. Her blush intensified.

Oh this is gonna be good.

"What did she ask you?"

"I don't remember," she lied, lowering her head to avoid further eye contact.

"Reece...." She kept her head down. "Look. At. Me," I demanded, the gruffness to my tone leaving no room for argument. After several seconds, she finally raised her head. "What did she ask you?"

Her teeth played with her bottom lip in nervousness. All sorts of images of what I'd love to do with those lips ran through my head, but before I lost myself to them, she answered. "She asked me if I was fu-fucking you." Surprisingly, she kept her eyes on me after speaking, probably counting the seconds until I broke the suddenly charged connection.

"What did you say?"

Her mouth fell open. "What do you think I said? I just met you earlier tonight." Her mouth opened and closed a few more times, but no words escaped.

"So . . . you don't wanna sleep with me?"

"I didn't say that. I mean, that's not what she asked me." Her hands twisted errant strands of her hair. "Wait, what are you asking me?"

Rattling her was quickly becoming my new favorite thing.

Having too much fun to let it go, I pressed her further, crowding her personal space for the full effect. "It's simple. Do you want to sleep with me?"

"I don't know you."

"So what? It's a simple yes or no. Do you want me between those sexy thighs of yours or not?" She looked like a deer in headlights. "Okay, we'll table that question for another time." I should've been more sensitive to what she'd been through earlier, but I couldn't help but goad her. Besides, I took comfort knowing I'd never let anything bad happen to her again. From here on out she should consider herself safe. "And just so you know, Arianna won't be stopping over."

"Is she your girlfriend?"

"Hell no!" I shouted, lowering my voice back to a normal level after I saw her flinch. "Sorry. No, that chick is certainly not my girlfriend. Since you seem to want to pry into my business," I said, giving her a faux look of irritation, "I'm not involved with anyone."

"Oh," she simply responded, twirling a strand of hair around her finger again. A nervous tick?

"So you know what that means, don't ya?"

"No." Her voice was meek and unsure, a contradiction to the woman I believed her to truly be.

"That means you're free to hit on me as much as your little heart desires."

She blushed again, but at least that time her flush was accompanied by a smile.

Walking away was hard, but I turned my back to her and headed toward the kitchen once more. "You hungry?" I asked over my shoulder, rummaging through the fridge for something to make in case she said yes. I didn't have to face her to know her eyes were glued to me. As much as I wanted to turn around and catch her ogling me, I remained in position, acting as if I weren't completely distracted by her standing twenty feet away.

"No. I don't have much of an appetite," she admitted.

Closing the fridge, a rush of strangled breath passed my lips before I finally turned to face her and saw I was right. Her eyes were glued to me, but when her tongue peeked out and licked her lips I had to hold back from rushing toward her and crashing my mouth to hers.

Fuck! What was I thinking bringing her to my house?

Before I could delve into my confusion, my cell rang, 'Prez' flashing across the screen and pulling all of my focus.

"Yeah," I answered, my voice rushed, trying to tamp down my irritation.

"You're up."

"I thought that wasn't until tomorrow."

"Change of plans. Let's go," Marek demanded, hanging up on me before giving me the chance to ask if someone could take my place. Cursing under my breath, I glanced at Reece, hating that I had to leave her. But at least at my place she'd be safe. It was a small comfort.

If I'd had a choice, I would've stay holed up in the cabin for days—weeks, even. Who was I kidding? I'd stay locked away from everyone else for months if that's what it took to drive away my new obsession with this woman.

CHAPTER TWELVE

Reece

WHAT THE HELL WAS I *thinking coming here?*

My actions were completely out of character. Never mind that Tripp was a stranger; even though he'd rescued me, the way my body bristled when I was near him should've been a warning in and of itself. He was dangerous. The way his eyes devoured me. The way his body called to mine on the basest of levels.

All my thoughts became muddled whenever he crowded my personal space. Hell, even with the space currently between us I found it hard to think of anything other than being wrapped in his warm embrace.

Maybe it was nothing more than knight-in-shining-armor syndrome. Was that even a thing? I'd never had someone come to my rescue before, so maybe his saving me from that bastard earlier was the sole reason for my confusing feelings toward him. Even as my brain tried to convince me this was the real reason, my heart and soul knew differently.

"Come on," he instructed, striding from the room after speaking and leaving me no choice but to follow. Correction—I had a choice. I could have stayed glued to the spot, but my brain spurred me to follow him. Or was that curiosity? Or tangible attraction?

He disappeared around the corner and I had to jog to keep up, which resulted in crashing into the back of him, bouncing back and almost losing my balance. Luckily my hand shot out and I braced myself against the wall.

"You okay?" he asked, spinning around and grabbing my arms.

"Yeah, I'm fine," I said, quite embarrassed. "Your long-ass legs are to blame, you know." I tried to make light of my clumsiness, and from the smile on his face, it'd worked.

"My long-ass legs?"

"Yeah. I had to run just to keep up with you. What are ya, seven feet tall?" He stood taller and smiled bigger, his rugged beauty almost knocking me on my ass for real that time.

"Six four."

"You're the biggest man I've ever seen," I blabbered, continuing to crane my neck just to see his face. My confession rattled me even though it was an innocent statement.

"You ain't seen nothin' yet, sweetheart." He chuckled, licking his lips before turning away from me and strolling into what I assumed was his bedroom.

Standing in the doorway, I watched him dart about the room, disappearing into a closet before reentering the space. Grasped in his hands was a plain red T-shirt. "Will this do?"

"For what?"

"For bed. Or like I said, you could sleep in the nude. But if you go with that option, you better lock this door or I'll be payin' you a visit." He wriggled his brows and I found him even sexier than before. A playful Tripp, albeit inappropriate, tugged at something inside me, but I didn't want to dissect any of what I was feeling right then.

"What about the shorts?"

"What shorts?"

"You said you had a T-shirt and shorts I could change into. So, where are the shorts?" I shuffled my feet but beyond all reason kept my eyes pinned to his. I found our banter soothing, although the sexual attraction toward him ran rampant inside me, threatening to erupt at any moment if he didn't walk away.

With a few simple steps, he towered over me, holding his shirt in front of me. "I think this will be plenty. It'll hide . . . everything." Why did he look disappointed after he spoke? Standing so close tested my restraint. I feared if he didn't move back, and do it soon, I'd throw myself at him and beg him to have his way with me. Which, much like going home with a stranger, was completely out of character for me.

Pulling me back from my fantasies, he pointed toward the bathroom and said, "You can change in there."

"WHAT SMELLS SO HEAVENLY?" I rounded the corner as my stomach threatened to eat itself.

"I thought you said you didn't have much of an appetite," he responded, wiping his hands on a nearby dishtowel.

"Well, it's back in full force now." Walking up behind him, I moved to his right to try and peer around him but he shifted at the last second, blocking my view of whatever he was dishing out on the plate. Because I couldn't see the food he'd prepared, I did the next best thing. Taking a deep breath, I inhaled the delicious aroma, closing my eyes and allowing the savory smell of bacon, eggs, and pancakes to waft through my nose.

"Did you just smell me?"

I was still lost to the aroma of a home-cooked breakfast when Tripp surprised me with his question. My eyes popped open and my lips parted in surprise. I took a step back and fervently shook my head. Words escaped me, and in my silence I allowed myself to quickly take in the man in front of me. The smirk on his face was most definitely arrogant, but for some reason it worked for him. Made him sexier, if that were at all possible. His shirt stretched across his broad chest and the image of what lay just underneath was anything but hidden. He wore dark-washed jeans, the fabric fitted in all the right places. When I looked lower I saw he was barefoot. I'd never been so happy to see a man's feet before.

"Well . . . did you?" he asked again.

"Uh . . . what?" I shook my head and tried a different response, something that didn't have me sounding like a complete idiot. "No, of course I wasn't smelling you. I was smelling the food."

"Are you sure? Because I've been told I smell incredible."

"I'm sure you have, and by plenty of women at that."

"Not anyone who counted," he offered. A fleeting look passed over his features but was gone before I could read into it. Retreating a step, he glanced at me from head to toe, similar to what I'd just done to him. His quirked brow made me self-conscious all of a sudden, even though I was fully clothed. "I like you in my shirt."

Finally peeling my eyes from him, I looked down at the oversized shirt covering my body. With my gaze still averted, I responded. "Yeah, it does the trick."

Tripp cleared his throat, but it wasn't until he did it again that I raised my head. The way he stared at me was as if he wanted to eat me alive, and given the sexual tension between us I could only imagine exactly where he'd like to start on my body. Clenching my thighs together, I tried to squelch the sudden throbbing, but it was useless; the only thing that was gonna help me right then was a cold shower. I tried to think of something to say but the only thing my lust-induced brain could come up with was "You have a stain on your shirt."

"Where?" He pulled the material away from his body and I caught a peek of his lower abdomen. *Look away.* But I couldn't. "I don't see it," he huffed, pulling his shirt higher up his body so that I had a full view of his stomach. Can men have eight-packs? Because he sure as hell did.

"It's right there," I answered, tearing my eyes away from his naked skin and stepping closer until my hand covered his, moving the shirt until I touched the stain. "Here."

He smiled, looking at where our hands touched. "Hazard of cooking, I suppose." Swallowing my sudden brazenness, I stepped back and pulled my bottom lip between my teeth. I was nervous, sure, but it was more than that. Desire. Want. Lust—you name it.

"Looks like I better take this off before I stain it again."

Before I processed his words completely, he lifted his shirt, revealing first his defined abdominals and then his pecs. Furrowing my brow at the sight of the many scars littering his torso, I didn't ask what had happened, figuring it was too personal for him to reveal such a thing to a stranger, even though he'd insisted said stranger stay with him that evening.

When his shirt had finally cleared his head, he tossed it on the seat closest to him, his eyes pinned to mine. Watching, waiting for some kind of reaction.

"Better?" he asked, leaning against the counter so I could take him all in. My mouth suddenly went dry. My heart hammered inside my tightly coiled chest, and an ache I was becoming familiar with bloomed between my thighs. "Reece? Are you okay?"

"Huh?" I continued to visually devour him, committing every facet of his incredible body to memory. I was completely shameless.

Tripp pushed himself off the counter, his muscles flexing and taunting me. *Yeah, completely shameless.* "I asked if you were okay." The deep gravel of his voice ricocheted through me and made my lustful state even worse. *Get a grip, woman.*

"Oh yeah, I'm fine. Sorry, I didn't mean to stare. You just caught me off guard when you stripped in front of me." My nervous laughter told him everything.

"I hardly call that stripping. Now, if I took off my jeans. . . ." The corners of his full lips kicked up in amusement again.

I knew if I didn't change the subject I would completely embarrass myself in front of him. No doubt he was used to women throwing themselves at him, and the last thing I needed, or wanted, was to be included in that group. No, Tripp was a stranger, someone I'd just met earlier that night. Even though I essentially owed him my life for his protection, it didn't change the fact that I didn't know him. Sure, I was attracted to him, but that's all it was—physical attraction. Nothing more.

He must have realized I'd become uncomfortable, although I doubted he knew the extent of why, because he turned around and finished dishing out the food he'd cooked. "Sit down," he ordered, his tone demanding yet gentle.

As soon as I situated myself, he placed the plate in front of me. "It's the only food here. I hope you don't mind breakfast." He stood beside me stock-still until I made a move, so I dug in to keep from focusing on him any longer. Only then did he walk out of the kitchen, returning several minutes later fully clothed. And although I was thankful that he'd covered himself, I couldn't help but feel a pang of disappointment.

CHAPTER THIRTEEN

Tripp

I TOYED WITH FIRE. BRINGING her back to my place wasn't the smartest move I'd ever made, yet I couldn't seem to help myself. From the first time I laid eyes on her I knew I never wanted to look away.

I just about lost my shit when she entered the kitchen wearing nothing but my shirt. Yeah, it covered her completely, but her full tits pressed against the material, drawing my attention right away. I'd seen her naked earlier when she danced for me . . . and every other man at the club. And it was knowing what my shirt hid that tortured me.

Regretfully I had to leave her to take care of club business. I was already late, and I knew Marek would lay into me even worse if I didn't hurry my ass up and get to the safe house.

"I have to go." Eyeing her plate, I saw she'd eaten every last morsel.

"Where? Will you be gone long? You're going to leave me here all by myself?" She showered me with questions, her nervousness wafting off her in waves.

"I have to tend to some business at the club. I probably won't be back until tomorrow. Late morning. But feel free to make yourself at home. If you wanna take a shower, there're plenty of towels and anything else you'll probably need. Not so much chick stuff, but shit to get the job done." All at once, I felt heat rush through my body. Not only was I picturing her naked in my shower, with her hands running all over her toned and supple body, but I rambled on like some kind of idiot. Taking a much-needed breath, I finished with "You'll be fine until I get back."

Grabbing my keys off the table, I walked toward the door, telling myself not to turn around for fear I'd never leave. But her voice stopped me, the innocence of her tone undoing me.

"Tripp?"

With my back still facing her, I answered. "Yeah."

"I'm scared." The lilt of her voice tugged at my insides, urging me to swing around and pull her close. But I understood myself enough to know that if I drew her into my embrace I wasn't gonna let her go.

"Why?"

"Because of everything that happened earlier."

Shit! There was no way I couldn't face her, the fright she felt lacing each word. Letting go of the handle, I spun around and walked toward her. Her fingers toyed with the hem of her shirt. *My* shirt. Her breath quickened the closer I stepped, and the fear I heard in her voice was mirrored by her expression.

"He won't hurt you again. I promise."

"I know."

"Then why are you scared?"

"I don't know. When you told me you were leaving, I just got nervous. I can't explain it, other than to say that I feel safe when you're near. I know I don't know you, and you could very well still be a killer," she nervously joked, "but it's how I feel." Looking around the wide-open space, she added, "And now you're gonna leave me here all alone."

Reaching for her hand, I intertwined my fingers with hers. "You'll be fine. This place has a state-of-the-art security system and you're out in the middle of nowhere." Grimacing, I realized that probably wasn't the best thing to say. Nothing like making her feel even more secluded. "What I mean is that the chances of anyone approaching this place are nil to none. You'll be safe until I get back. But if it would make you feel better, I'll give you my number in case you need me. I mean, need to call me." *There I go again with the awkward fuckin' rambling.*

"Okay," she agreed, pulling her hand from mine to root through her purse. Finding her cell, she handed it to me and I input my name and number before giving it back. "I feel better knowing I can reach you."

She looked like she wanted to say something else, possibly apologize for being so scared, but she remained silent.

"Call me if you need to. Okay?"

"Yeah."

Uncertainty weighed me down as I walked out of the cabin, and while I had no idea why, I knew the woman standing on the other side of the door had just changed my life forever.

CHAPTER FOURTEEN

Tripp

THE SMELL OF BURNING FLESH assaulted me as soon as I stood at the top of the basement stairs. Pulling my shirt up to cover my nose, I tentatively walked down the steps, curious as to what the hell was goin' on down there.

"How does that feel, you motherfucker?" I heard Marek shout, the roughness of his voice quite unsettling. I knew Psych's demise was being carefully cultivated by our leader, but it wasn't healthy anymore. Not that any type of torture was *healthy*, but his revenge against Sully's father was taking a toll on him none of us could have predicted. He was coming apart piece by piece, so quickly I feared there'd be nothing left to the man I followed without question and admired immensely. He was transforming into someone else, and there wasn't a damn thing anyone could do about it. We just had to wait and see what hell he'd eventually succumb to when this shit was all over.

Stepping into the shrouded darkness of the basement, a single dull overhead light doing its best to illuminate the dank space, I saw Psych still shackled to the wall, hanging limply from the iron restraints above his head. The man was a shell of his former shelf, his dark, shoulder-length hair greasy and limp. He looked like death. Fuck, he even smelled like it.

Marek stood in front of him, a blowtorch in his right hand. The flames lit up the darkened corner of the room, and when the torch touched Psych's chest, his garbled groans filled the air. I hated the leader of the Savage Reapers as much as anyone else, but what Marek had been doing to him since he'd taken him had become too much. I wanted to slit the guy's throat and end it already, but I would never steal Psych's last breath. That was for Marek to do. His final 'fuck you' to the man who'd been his biggest enemy. The man whose club had killed his father during a routine run. And the man who'd abused Sully her entire life.

The Knights and the Reapers had been at war for as long as I could remember, going back decades; that alone was justification for killing Psych. But add in all the evildoings that he horrifically subjected his own daughter to, and it was a recipe for . . . exactly what had been going on ever since they'd stolen him from the warehouse where he held Adelaide and Kena hostage.

"Prez." I walked up behind Marek and placed my hand on his shoulder. He flinched but never turned around. Removing the torch from Psych, he lowered his arm, the flame still on and bright.

"'Bout fuckin' time you got here, Tripp. What the fuck took you so long?"

"Sorry," I said, continuing to talk to his back. "Had some stuff I had to take care of."

"Does that stuff include the new stripper from Indulge?"

What the hell? How does he know about Reece?

I didn't respond, instead trying to remove the torch from Marek's hand, a gesture he didn't appreciate. "I'm not done yet. Step back," he ordered, raising his arm and bringing the torch so close to Psych's leg the flame licked the hair before burning through the flesh of his thigh. Psych's head shot up and at first I thought he'd tried to plead with me, but the sounds coming out of his mouth were nothing more than hallowed moans. Sounds of torment so unnerving I had to turn my back and block out the image in front of me.

After several minutes, Marek finally laid the torch on the metal rolling cart, the clanking sound grabbing my attention. I thought maybe he was done for the evening, that he'd grab his cut he'd laid over the chair in the corner and walk from the room without another word.

How wrong I was.

What happened next flipped my leader's world upside down, ripping his guts from him, taunting and clouding everything he'd ever known.

Psych's lips parted and incoherent sounds poured forth. He was trying to say something, but we couldn't make out what exactly until he cleared his throat, wincing in obvious pain before attempting to speak again.

"What did you say?" Marek shouted, stepping close to the shackled man.

"Family." One word, mangled or not, we both understood.

"You don't know the first thing about that fuckin' word," Marek spit at him, his fists clenching uncontrollably. The vein in his neck throbbed and I feared for my leader's life if he didn't get ahold of himself.

"Maybe you should just ignore him, Prez," I encouraged. "Nothin' this piece of shit says is worth listening to."

"I know." Even though Marek acknowledged what I'd just said, it didn't stop him from probing Psych to continue.

"Fuc . . . kin' fam . . . ily," Psych spoke again, the two words not making much sense to us.

Gripping the strands of his hair, Marek balled his fist and punched Psych in the face, snapping his head to the side from the jolt. "What are you tryin' to say? Spit it out already."

Psych inhaled a shallow breath before opening his mouth once more. "I said—" He coughed, garnering whatever strength he had left before continuing, "Fuckin' family." Another short breath. "How does . . . does it feel . . . to fuck . . . your family?" Each word was strained, each syllable rattling the unbearable tension in the air. Psych didn't make any sense, but he pressed on nonetheless. The evil glint in his eyes proved he knew he'd gotten his captor's attention. Even in his current state, barely hanging on to life, he reveled in fucking with Marek's head.

"What the fuck are you talkin' about? You're not makin' any sense," Marek growled, his frustration rubbing off on me.

"Yeah, what the hell are you trying to say, Reaper." His club's name tasted like poison on my tongue, but I refused to say his name. Something tangible bristled in the air surrounding all of us, and had I known what it was I would have killed Psych before he parted his lips once more.

Shifting his feet, the clank of the chains binding him to the wall filling the air, Psych lifted his head the best he could and glared at Marek. "Why do you . . . think . . . this war started, boy? Huh?" He dropped his head for a brief moment, doing his best to gain momentum for what was coming next. With a broken jaw, it was hard for him to speak so when he did, he did so slowly, mumbling most of his words.

"Because your fuckin' club couldn't stick to your territory and got greedy. The Reapers intercepted a shipment meant for the Knights, and shit popped off. A few of our men, my father's men, paid the ultimate price. All because of you."

The lines on Marek's face deepened, the redness of his eyes intensifying with the stress barreling around inside him.

The prickling unease in the room heightened, drawing us all into its clutches. I moved closer to Marek. It was intentional. My gut told me he was gonna need my support in the next few minutes.

"That's not why," Psych said, coughing up blood before spitting it out, the string of saliva hanging from his lips while he spoke again. "It's because I fuc . . . ked your. . . ." His words trailed off while he succumbed to another coughing fit. Strangled breaths of air tempted his life, but he pressed on. "Mother," he finally finished.

Marek's eyes widened as he took a step back. I read his body language; all he wanted to do was decimate whatever was left of Psych's body, but he restrained himself. Barely. Marek glanced toward me, a silent plea in his gaze before he turned his attention back on the Reaper.

I was now certain that the Knights Corruption leader would be lost in a haze of rage . . . and perpetual agony.

"You're lyin'!" I shouted in Marek's defense.

Completely ignoring me, he continued to focus on the man unraveling in front of us. "I'd say ask your ol' man, but . . . he's rottin' in the ground." Psych could barely breathe, yet he somehow mustered up enough strength for a sinister laugh. The man was evil incarnate; I was convinced of it now more than ever before.

"You're just sayin' this shit to fuck with me because you know I'm gonna snatch your life from you soon, and there ain't a damn thing you can do about it." Marek began pacing, mumbling to himself the entire time.

"I'm not. It's . . . the truth." Psych's chest constricted, more blood spurting from his mouth and hitting the concrete under his feet. "Forcing that bitch wasn't what fucked with your ol' man," he spit out. "It was when she . . . she got kno. . . ." He took a breath. "Knocked up . . . that did it."

Marek halted all movement and whipped his head toward Psych. I tried to interfere but I was too late. He rushed toward the wall and pressed his forearm across his enemy's throat, screaming and shouting at him the entire time. I saw the look in Psych's eyes. He knew he'd gotten to him. He'd managed to pluck at the raveling thread holding Marek together and completely destroy it.

"You worthless piece of shit! You'll say anything just to goad me. Why? Do you want me to end your pathetic existence? To relieve you of this torture? Because that ain't gonna happen. So spew all the garbage you want because I know it's a lie." Marek took a quick breath. "My mother was only pregnant one time. With me."

Psych pushed back against Marek's arm, getting as close to his face as he could. "I know."

All of a sudden I found it difficult to breathe, my lungs seizing in astonishment. And if I'd felt that way, what the hell was Marek goin' through?

"You know . . . what . . . that means? Do ya . . . *son*?" I swore I heard the last piece of Marek's sanity splinter apart. "I'll ask ya . . . again." Psych's chest convulsed in a short coughing fit, blood dripping off his chin, making him look like a madman. "Do you like . . . fucking family?"

Vehemently shaking his head, Marek released his hold on Psych and backed up, knocking into the rolling cart. "You're fuckin' lyin'!" he roared. "You'll say anything at this point."

"'fraid it's true. Son."

"Stop saying that!" Marek cried out, unraveling further with every second. "No," he whisper-shouted. "No, it's not true. You would've said something before today. You would've tortured my ol' man with that shit." Marek's eyes darkened the longer he engaged Psych.

"You th . . . think I'd ever claim yo . . . you? You're the fuckin' enemy. The sh . . . shit under my shoe," he sputtered, more blood escaping his mouth.

"Shut the hell up, Reaper!" I shouted, stepping closer with a knife gripped tightly in my hand. His eyes flew to the weapon and when I took another step toward him, he grinned. He wanted me to stab him, probably prayed for it, but I wouldn't give him the satisfaction of killing him. For as much as I wanted Marek to end him right then, I knew he'd do it when he saw fit.

"Tell me . . . somethin' . . . son," Psych goaded, "how does it . . . feel knowin' you were . . . fuckin'—"

"Shut the fuck up!" I yelled, hoping my shouts would drown out his garbled words. But they didn't. Nothing would stop Psych from having the final word, pushing the president of the Knights into madness.

"Your sister?" Psych finished, grinning like the biggest fool before his head fell in utter exhaustion.

CHAPTER FIFTEEN

Tripp

EVERYTHING HAPPENED SO FAST I didn't have time to intervene, which was probably for the best, all things considered. I didn't want to be the one to step in and try to calm Marek down enough to reason with him. Otherwise, *I'd* probably be the one sucking in my last breath.

In the blink of an eye, Marek grabbed a knife from the cart and barreled toward Psych, the old man's eyes widening a fraction before the corners of his thin, cracked lips curved into an ominous grin.

"Marek!" I shouted, not quite sure what else I was gonna say after calling out his name. Whatever he did to Psych was justified, but I feared if he killed him now he would never get the answers he needed. But maybe he didn't care about that. Hell, he didn't appear as if he cared about anything but snatching Psych's life and sending him straight to hell. Exactly where he belonged.

His arms were a blur of movements, blood spurting forth from Psych's body so fast his life source coated the floor in mere seconds, expanding and covering ground so quickly I had to take a step back or the crimson river would have surrounded my boots.

Marek had finally lost it, his hand plunging the knife into the Reaper over and over again, ripping open the thinly veiled skin covering his organs. At one point, soon after he first attacked, Psych's bowels started to spill from his body. But that didn't stop Marek. It seemed to only fuel his rage, pushing him beyond the scope of sanity. Surprisingly, Psych was still alive, his short breaths few and far between, his lungs amazingly still functioning. That was until Marek plunged the knife through Psych's chest, directly into his heart. Twisting the blade ensured our enemy would leave this world in the next few seconds.

When he finally exhaled his last connection to this life, Psych's entire body went slack, pulling on the chains and testing their hold. Dropping the knife to the floor, Marek finally retreated until his back hit the wall, his eyes on Psych the entire time, as if he weren't completely convinced he'd died. My eyes followed my prez's steps. When he finally slid down the wall and hung his head in his hands, his mind, body and soul completely defeated, only then did I glance over at the state of our enemy.

The sight was something out of a fuckin' horror movie. It looked like Jason Voorhees had destroyed Psych with a machete. His stab wounds were so extensive I couldn't tell where one ended and the next started. Most of the skin was completely shredded, half of the damage coming from being burned off, the rest from Marek's uncontrollable rage. Some of Psych's organs were exposed and hanging from his still form, the image regrettably burned into my memory forever.

"It can't be true," Marek whispered. The room was eerily silent, allowing me to hear every disbelieving word he uttered. "He was lyin'," he continued, speaking to himself more than to me. But I needed to answer and try to bring him back to reality, whatever that might look like now.

"Fuck, Prez," I comforted, squatting down so we were closer to eye level. "He could have definitely been lying." What I failed to say was, *"And he could have been telling the truth. Sully could really be your sister."*

Dropping onto my ass, I braced myself against the wall and mirrored the leader of the Knights. And that's how we stayed for at least an hour, both of us trying to come to grips with what Psych had said. Whether or not Marek wanted to admit it or not, the Reaper could have very well been telling the truth, saving his final blow of retaliation for the end.

"IT AIN'T GOOD, BROTHER," I exhaled into the phone. I'd called Stone when I didn't know what else to do. "He's completely lost it. You need to grab a couple of the men and get over here." A few choice words from the VP of our club and he fell silent. "Oh, and make sure to bring the cage 'cause Prez is in no shape to ride back on his own." Finishing the conversation, I hung up and paced in the kitchen, looking inside the fridge a few times, hoping that some alcohol would magically appear each time the light went on.

I tried to persuade Marek to come upstairs, but he refused to budge from the spot he'd glued himself to on the floor. Every now and then he'd glance over at Psych, vehemently curse, and then drop his head again, mumbling incoherently and sounding like a certified crazy person. Maybe he was. Maybe he'd gone off the deep end and split from reality. Looking at him, anyone would agree. Parts of his hair stuck up, his hands gripping the strands in delirium. His eyes were bloodshot. His month-old beard was unkempt, and blood covered his hands and clothes.

He looked like a deranged killer.

Well . . . truth wrapped its ugly hands around that new reality.

I jumped to my feet two hours later when I saw headlights pull up the driveway, the squeak of the garage door solidifying that reinforcements were there. Rushing to meet them, I rounded the van to the driver's side. "Stone, thank God!" I wasn't normally one for such exclamations, but the situation I was in surely called for one.

"Where is he?" Ryder patted me on the shoulder as he passed, Trigger and Jagger hot on his heels. Their only priority was getting to their president, but I needed to fill them in on just what they would walk into once they breached the basement door.

"Hold up," I shouted, following them through the kitchen. Trigger grabbed the handle and just as he tried to yank the door open, I slammed my palm on the wood to make sure I had my say before they went down there. "I've seen some nasty shit in my life. I've *done* some nasty shit, but what's down there is somethin' else." The seriousness of my tone left no room for doubt. Only when I had all of their attention did I continue. "Marek lost his shit. For real, and Psych paid the price."

"Good," Jagger sneered, his jaw clenching while he waited for something more to come out of my mouth.

"I'm not sayin' he didn't deserve every bit of our leader's fury, but something was said down there that pushed Marek over the edge. And I'm not sure if he can come back from it, especially if it's fuckin' true." I mumbled the end of my statement but I knew damn well every man standing in front of me heard me.

"What the fuck are you talking about?" Stone rushed forward, grabbing the handle and trying to pull the door open. But I kept it closed, even when our VP gave me a stern, disapproving look.

"I think I should let Marek tell you." Yeah, I wasn't about to tell them that our president may have married his own half-sister.

"Then back the hell up and let us down there, nomad," Trigger gritted out, mirroring everyone else's look of anger.

"Just be warned that it's quite the sight," I cautioned before removing my hand from the door. Trigger pulled it open and one by one they hurried down the steps. I debated whether or not I should go back down into the basement, and after several minutes of contemplating, I finally gave in and joined my brothers.

CHAPTER SIXTEEN

Reece

AGAIN I ASKED MYSELF WHAT the hell I was thinking going home with a complete stranger. The same stranger who left me all alone in his house, who took off in the middle of the night, explaining that he'd be back sometime the next day. And to add to the already odd scenario, he never told me the code for the alarm system, essentially locking me inside until he returned.

Having no idea what else to do, I grabbed my phone and dialed the number for Indulge, hoping and praying that Carla was still working. I desperately needed someone to talk to, and I feared if she'd already gone home that I'd sit and stew all night. I cursed Tripp, angry with him for firing me, or whatever he called it, all while still remaining thankful he'd come to my aid earlier. The situation was complicated to say the very least.

The phone rang three times before someone finally answered. "Indulge" was the only greeting that came through the line.

"Hi. Is Carla still working?"

"Who's this?" I knew without asking it was Arianna, and if she knew it was me she'd probably hang up. I couldn't risk it so I lied.

"Her sister." I tried to change the tone of my voice when I answered, still fearful she'd end the call.

"Hang on," she responded, shouting over her shoulder and away from the phone. Breathing a sigh of relief, I counted the seconds until Carla came on the line.

"Heather? Is everything okay?" she asked in a small panic. "Why are you calling so late?"

"Carla, it's me. Reece. Sorry about that, but if I told Arianna it was me I think she probably would've hung up on me."

"Yeah, you're right." She chuckled. "That one is a bit touched in the head, if you know what I mean. Why couldn't it have been her who Tripp kicked out tonight?" A brief silence ensued. "Sorry, honey. I didn't mean it like that."

"Well, that's why I'm calling. Sort of." Slouching back against the couch, I tried to get as comfortable as I could.

"Hold on a sec. Let me take this in the office. Too noisy out here." I waited until I heard the background noise of the club diminish, taking that extra time to figure out why exactly I'd called Carla in the first place. "Okay, all good." I didn't have to be standing next to her to know she was smiling, that she was exuding her support through the phone. "What's up?"

"I don't know. I. . . ." My words drifted off, but it wasn't long before Carla picked up on exactly what my worry was.

"Where are you, Reece? Are you safe?"

"Yeah. I think so."

"What do you mean you think so? Where did Tripp take you?"

I hesitated for a moment, knowing my answer would certainly raise some flags with her. "Back to his place."

Carla gasped. "Why? Why wouldn't he take you to your motel room? Well, I guess I understand why he didn't take you there. I've told you that place is dangerous, that you'd be much better off staying someplace else, but what the hell do I know, right? I've only lived around here my entire life." She rambled on for another minute before finally taking a breather.

"Are you done?" I kept my tone non-defensive because I knew Carla had my best interests at heart, and she was only worried about me.

"I think so."

"Good. Now can I continue?"

"Go ahead." Her smile had returned. I just knew it.

I wavered before letting her in on what Tripp said on the drive home. "He felt the same way . . . about me staying there, and since it was late, and I had nowhere else to go, he just took me back to his place."

"Where is he now?"

"I don't know," I answered truthfully. "He said he had some stuff he had to do for his club, and that he'd be back sometime tomorrow. That's all I know. But until then, I can't leave because he set the alarm and never told me what the code was. So I'm essentially trapped here." Closing my eyes, I tried to picture Carla's reaction, but the only image I could muster was of Tripp. The concern in his eyes when he'd crouched down in the private room at the club to make sure I was okay. The annoyance on his face when I'd told him where I'd been staying. The way his full lips kicked up in a smirk when he told me I was free to hit on him anytime.

"Tell me where you are. I'll have someone close up for me and I'll come get you," she offered.

"I don't really know where I am exactly. He lives out in the middle of nowhere." Then I suddenly remembered that his brother was at the club. Or at least he was when we left. "Is his brother still there?" I asked, hoping she'd say yes.

"Hawke? No, he left already. One of his buddies came to get him about a half hour ago."

"Oh, okay," I dejectedly responded. "I guess it's just as well, seeing as there's still the small issue of his alarm."

"Oh, I don't give a shit about that. I'll bust you out of there and he can deal with whatever happens."

"You'll bust me out of here?" I laughed.

"You know I will." Carla's amusement faded, quickly replaced by a serious tone. One which kind of freaked me out.

"Do you think I'm in danger here? You can tell me the truth." My heart rammed against my chest in anticipation of her answer. She obviously knew Tripp more than I did because of the way she spoke to him when he was in the midst of dragging me out of the club earlier.

"With Tripp? No. Not from what I know of him. He can be quite intense sometimes. Other times . . . he's laid-back, joking around to stifle a tense situation. He's a good guy. I don't agree with him taking you to his place, however. Although. . . ."

"Although what?"

"I'm sure I read it wrong."

"Carla," I said as sternly as I could. "What the hell are you talking about?"

"It's just . . . the way he kept looking at you. I don't know. It was off." What she told me momentarily freaked me out, until she finally explained herself. "Sorry, what I mean is . . . I've known Tripp for some time now and I've never seen him look at anyone the way he was looking at you tonight. Yeah, I've seen him interested in women before, but not like he was with you. He seemed bothered by the fact that you were even there, all while being intrigued at the same time. Again, I could be reading too much into it, so. . . ."

Out of everything she'd just said, it bothered me when she mentioned him being interested in other women. A small pang of jealousy surfed through me, even though I realized it was ridiculous for me to even feel such an emotion.

"Reece? You still there?"

"Yeah, sorry." I expelled a deep sigh. "I'm just thinking about what I'm gonna do for a job now." Then a thought suddenly came to me. "Carla, do you think you can talk to Tripp? Make him reconsider and let me come back to work?"

"Do you think that's such a good idea? Especially after what happened?"

"I don't have another choice. Not until I'm able to find something else. I need this," I pleaded. "I need this job. Please."

"Of course. I'll talk to him."

"Thank you." After several minutes we finally ended the call, Carla promising she'd do her best to try and convince Tripp to let me stay on at Indulge until I found another job.

I should've been pissed. I should've been scared. But I was neither.

Carla's reassurance helped to ease some of the anger and panic I'd felt. I had no idea what I would have done without her. Even though I'd only known her a short time, I considered her a true friend.

Deciding not to delve too far inside my various thoughts, I deemed it best to try and distract myself by exploring Tripp's home. If he was gonna leave me all by myself, then he should expect I'd go snooping through his things. Curiosity won out as I opened the drawer of the end table in the living room, finding nothing inside except a few motorcycle magazines and a remote for the television. Everything stacked neatly. Looking around the small living space, it was then I noticed that not one single thing was out of place. A few pillows were strategically arranged on the couch, a comfy-looking blanket thrown over the back. Not a single item littered the coffee table, or floor for that matter. Everything seemed to have its place, and the thought that Tripp was some kind of neat freak made me smile.

Wait . . . aren't serial killers anally neat? I lost my smile for a brief moment before I laughed out loud. "Get a grip, Reece," I mumbled to myself before heading toward the kitchen to grab some water.

Walking through the cozy cabin, I took it all in, immersing myself in Tripp's world. A small glimpse inside the man who'd saved me. The place was small, the only rooms in the front the kitchen and living room. A large stone fireplace took up the majority of the wall, and with the way the evening had dipped into the lower digits, I imagined relaxing on the brown leather sofa while a fire warmed me.

Toward the back was a short hallway which led to two bedrooms and a bathroom. Peeking my head inside Tripp's sanctuary, I glanced around the room and smiled. Again. What was with my lips kicking up whenever I thought about the gorgeous man who'd forced his way into my life? Taking a tentative step inside, looking behind me as if he was gonna show up out of thin air and catch me snooping, I marveled at the state of his room—neat, just like every other inch of this place. An overly large bed took up a lot of space, but seeing how big Tripp was, it made absolute sense. An end table and a five-drawer dresser were the only other pieces of furniture, a small walk-in closet tucked into the corner housing the rest of his belongings.

Glancing at the alarm clock, I saw it was late, reminding me that I was most certainly beyond tired. Raising my arms above my head, I stretched as best I could and bellowed out the loudest yawn before turning and exiting the room. Walking only a few feet I came upon the bathroom. The thought of losing myself to a hot shower suddenly seemed like the best remedy to the horrible night I'd had.

As soon as the water beat down on my body, the steam enveloping and soothing me, I relaxed and pushed all thoughts of what had happened to the back of my mind. It was what I was best at—denial, oblivion. Over the years, I'd gotten very good at shoving life way deep down. It was the only way I could survive. Old habits were certainly hard to break, and because I didn't know any other way to cope I chose denial once more.

After my shower, I pulled Tripp's T-shirt back over my head, inhaling his lingering scent before pulling it down to cover my body. Images of the sexy biker rushed forward, and it was all I could do not to fantasize what he would look like completely naked. Normally such thoughts never entertained me, not even when I encountered a good-looking man while working. I always tried to keep that life separate from my real one, never mixing the two worlds for fear of the uncertainty. And even though I'd only been stripping for a short while, my promise to never mingle the two worlds had proved beneficial. *Until tonight.*

Tripp made me feel things without even trying. I'd never come across such a man before, someone who made me question my logic and instincts. I'd drive myself insane if I gave in to the need to try and understand why I'd suddenly become obsessed with him. Why he'd done what he had for me. Why I shoved aside my inner voice and got into his truck, allowing him to take me to his place. Why I'd thought about him almost every second since he'd left.

Deciding to forgo making myself crazy, I trudged back toward his room and crawled onto his bed, laying my head gently on the pillow. I would have curled up in the guest bedroom had there been a bed, but it appeared as if it was being utilized strictly for storage, the numerous boxes stacked perfectly. Not a shocker.

As I lay there, I took a deep breath and recapped everything that'd played out that evening. I refused to focus on anything that happened before Tripp had come to my rescue. No point in frightening myself over something I couldn't change. I strangely thought my body would refuse to succumb to sleep, that I'd unfortunately be awake for the rest of the night. But as soon as Tripp's face appeared in my mind, I smiled and slipped into the darkness of a comforting slumber.

CHAPTER SEVENTEEN

Tripp

"WHAT THE FUCK?" STONE ASKED, pacing back and forth in front of Psych before moving toward his best friend and leader. "Marek. What the hell happened, brother?" was all he could ask.

But Marek never answered. Instead, he remained on the floor where I'd left him, his head still in his hands as he mumbled the same thing over and over again.

"It can't be true. It can't be true."

He was slowly losing his mind, and so far I was the only one who knew why. The smell of the room had intensified over the past hour, and because no one had made a move to clean anything up, we were completely exposed to Psych's lifeless body and all the horrible smells his dead flesh emitted.

"Why does he keep saying that?" Jagger asked after pulling me to the corner of the room. My answer didn't come as easily as I thought it would've. There was a part of me that wanted to protect Marek as long as possible. Maybe if I told the others the reason he kept repeating "It can't be true," it would become all too real. So I stalled, trying to think of what to say. "I know you know something, Tripp. You were the only one here with him. Other than that fucker over there." Jagger pointed toward Psych, his eyes lingering on the dead Reaper for only a few seconds before his attention was back on me. "What can't be true?"

I waited, for what I had no idea. My lips remained sealed while my heart picked up its pace. Marek stepping back into reality and shouting for me to remain silent would have been extremely welcome at that point. But there was only silence. Even Ryder, Stone, and Trigger were quiet, whispering to each other every few minutes. All of us were contemplating the next move, but shock about the situation kept us locked into ambiguity.

Before Jagger could press me again for an answer, Stone closed in on us, his presence leaving no room for anything but the truth. "What the hell happened down here?" He looked back and forth between Jagger and me, but obviously I was the only one who could answer.

"What does it look like happened?" I whisper-shouted, doing my best to deflect from giving him—giving them all—the answers they truly wanted. "He fuckin' lost his mind and took it out on Psych."

Stepping closer, Stone gripped my shoulder. "Why did he all of a sudden lose his mind?" The VP of the Knights stood a couple inches shorter than me, but his domineering presence was larger than life. The stern look in his eyes told me he wasn't gonna let up until I told him something.

Quickly contemplating what I should say, my eyes veered over to glance at Marek, hoping he'd look at me and give me some kind of signal on how to proceed. But he did nothing, continuing to mumble to himself while he shook his head back and forth.

Tightening his grip, Stone demanded I let him in on what exactly happened. Why his president was on the fuckin' floor and actin' like some kind of mental patient. "Tripp, I swear to fuck if you don't tell me what happened. . . ." He didn't need to finish his sentence because it didn't matter what he threatened me with. I'd never let it get that far. We were dealing with enough shit as it was; there was no need to add to it.

Stepping back to give us as much privacy as possible, I blew out a breath and started talking. "When I came down here, Marek was torching him and shit. Fuck. I thought I was gonna lose my lunch from the smell. Anyway, out of the blue, Psych started talkin' about family and why the war really started between us and them in the first place."

"Greed and territory," Stone interrupted. "That's how it started."

"Not according to Psych."

Stone frowned, leaning against the wall while waiting for me to clear up the confusion. Jagger continued to listen, keeping his mouth shut so he could take it all in. Ryder and Trigger were across the room, crowded around Marek and trying to talk to him, to get him to snap out of whatever delirium held him captive.

"He lied. Whatever that fucker said . . . he lied." Stone's temper rose, but he kept it under control. "What did he say?" he pressed while clenching his fists.

"He said that the war started because he raped Marek's mother. That the Reapers and the Knights went to war because he raped her . . . and knocked her up."

"Fuck!" Jagger and Stone yelled at the same time, looking over at Marek to see if he heard what I'd just told them. But he didn't, still lost in his own world, which was probably for the best right then. At least until we got the hell out of there.

"That's not the worst part," I continued, running my hands through my hair as a stall tactic.

He hit my shoulder in frustration. "Out with it, nomad." Stone and I didn't have the best relationship, but it had been getting better over the past year. And if I didn't want to go back to him constantly giving me shit every time he saw me, and meaning it, then I better just spill the rest of what happened so we could all move on and deal with it. No matter the consequences.

"Psych indicated that he was Marek's father and asked Marek how he liked fucking his sister." I let the words linger in the air between us, allowing them the time to process what I'd just said. It didn't take long at all, their reactions mirroring what I'd gone through when it was being said for the first time.

"Is it true?" Jagger asked, staggering back a step before bracing himself.

"I don't think so," I answered.

"But it could be. Holy shit," Stone said, lowering his voice. "It could be."

"How do we find out if he was lyin'?" My question swirled around all three of us, waiting for someone to come up with a plan to either put Marek out of his misery or drive him further into it.

"Fuck if I know," Jagger muttered. His dark blond hair, which was normally strategically styled, was all over the place, looking more like Marek than I cared to admit. After telling them the reason for their leader's meltdown, Jagger tugged at his strands, practically ripping out chunks because he didn't know what else to do with his hands. He couldn't punch the wall; he needed them for his fights, his way of earning for the club.

Stone's eyes widened for a brief moment before he walked across the room and pulled open a drawer. Slamming it closed he looked inside another, then another before he found what he was looking for. With a baggie in hand, he grabbed a cloth from the rolling cart and closed in on Psych. Running the fabric down the dead man's chest, Stone tossed it in the baggie. Then he ripped out a chunk of hair from Psych's head, throwing that into the same baggie.

Heading back our way, he showed me the bag and said, "I'll have Addy contact someone and rush the DNA sample. Now all I have to do is convince Marek. He might fight me on it because of his fear that it could be true."

"Can you blame the guy?" I asked.

"Nope." That was all he said before we all dispersed.

Chapter Eighteen

Reece

GROGGILY WIPING THE SLEEP FROM my eyes, I swung my legs over the side of the bed. Tripp's bed. Resting my feet on the cool floor, I inhaled the moment and tried my best to take in my new predicament. Not only the room where I'd spent the night, but that I was now jobless. Jobless and essentially held captive. Okay, held captive might've been a bit strong of a sentiment, but it was kind of on point. Sort of.

While I sat on the edge of the bed, I recalled my phone call with Carla the night before, choosing to focus on certain parts of our conversation more than others. For instance, when she'd told me, "I've known Tripp for some time now and I've never seen him look at anyone the way he was looking at you tonight." Why did the recollection of her telling me that cause a flutter in my belly? Being careless in the past had led to some of the worst decisions I'd ever made, essentially endangering my life, and it was precisely why I needed to keep my head straight. No matter how attracted I was to Tripp.

Deciding I needed a shower to wake me up, I shuffled across the room with my head hung low and swung open the bedroom door, running right into a naked, muscular chest. Quick hands reached out and grabbed me as I stumbled backward, righting me before I ended up on the floor.

"Jesus Christ, woman!" Tripp exclaimed, his fingers still wrapped tightly around my upper arms. The heat from his touch instantly warmed me. No, scratch that—his touch enflamed me, torched me from the inside. So hot I thought for sure he'd snatch his hands back from the burn. My belly fluttered like it had once before while my heart beat furiously inside my chest. Licking my lips, I broke free from him and retreated, which was a mistake because I could see more of him. But distance was most definitely needed; otherwise, I feared I'd allow my hormones to take over and literally throw myself at him. Try and climb his massive, sculpted form.

"Sorry," I mumbled, trying like hell to avert my eyes from the practically naked man standing in front of me.

"No, I'm sorry if I scared you. I saw the door was closed and didn't wanna wake you. Although, come to think of it, it's almost noon." He smiled and crossed his arms over his chest. "Do you normally sleep in this late?"

I heard him speak but his words jumbled together. As if in some kind of trance, my eyes trailed over his body, devouring the sight of his rigid, cut muscles, the V of his abdomen disappearing behind the white towel wrapped around his waist.

When my gaze moved upward, trailing over his arms still crossed and muscles popping, I saw him lick his full lips. His smile intensified, and it wasn't until I finally looked him in the eye that I saw the glint of amusement. His short dark hair was wet, a few water droplets dripping off the tips and running down his neck.

"Like I said before, you can hit on me anytime." Dropping his arms to his sides, he brushed past me and walked toward his closet. I tried but I couldn't seem to peel my eyes away from him. The way he walked was mesmerizing, his gait confident and authoritative. Before I could even think to apologize for leering at him, his towel fell to the floor without warning. And there before me was the sight of his naked ass. His glorious, tight, round and muscular ass. I knew if I didn't turn around in the next second he was gonna ruin me for all other men going forward.

"You still there?" His voice rumbled through the air and startled me, but it was exactly what I needed to regain some of the composure

I'd lost when he'd dropped his towel.

I flipped around to give him some privacy. "Um . . . yeah. Sorry. I was . . . just shocked." I could hear the rustle of his jeans as he pulled them over his thighs, followed by the zipper and finally the clank of his belt buckle as he finished dressing.

"You can turn around now, sweetheart. I'm decent." He chuckled, the deep timber of his laugh making me clench my thighs together. It was obvious he loved getting a rise out of me. Was I that easy to rile up? Apparently so.

"Sorry," I repeated, sheepishly grinning to try and hide my embarrassment. I hated how he could fluster me so easily.

"Am I that awful to look at?" he teased, stepping closer until he was only a few feet from me. His eyes stayed pinned to mine, and the lazy way the corners of his mouth curved up was probably the sexiest thing I'd ever seen.

"You know you're not."

"You're quite the contradiction, you know that?" Intrigued by his odd statement, I took the bait.

"I don't understand. What does that mean exactly?"

"Well, for starters, you're a stripper. Or rather, you *were* a stripper." I couldn't help the slight irritation that flowed through me at the mention of my job loss. "You took your clothes off and danced for countless strangers, put yourself in a sexual environment all the time, yet you blushed when you saw me naked."

"How do you know I blushed? You were turned around."

"Because your cheeks are still red." He reached out and ghosted his fingers down the side of my face. I hadn't expected him to touch me, and when he did I couldn't stop my body from reacting. Again. My breath came out in short spurts as if my lungs had stolen my air, yet I welcomed the strange feeling. Before I did something stupid like lean in to him, I retreated.

"I have to go," I whispered, watching him closely for any sudden change in expression. Would he be angry that I wasn't fawning all over him? Especially when it was obvious he was attracted to me? Would he find me challenging and pursue me, try to convince me to stay to see if he could get what he wanted from me—even though I had no idea what that was? Well . . . I could take a guess, but would he be so brazen? Of course he would. I didn't see him as the type of guy to beat around the bush when it came to things he wanted.

But did he want me?

Oh my God! My brain was firing off in all different directions, most of my thoughts confusing the hell out of me.

"What's goin' on in that head of yours?"

"Just thinking that I overstayed my welcome," I lied, fiddling with the bottom of his shirt which still covered me. His eyes drifted to where my fingers gripped the material.

"I think that's my new favorite shirt," he confessed, veering the conversation—what little of it there was—in yet another direction. Holy shit, we were all over the place.

"Well, it's yours, so that would make sense." I had no idea what else to say, other than to make idle, meaningless chitchat. After several heartbeats, I chose to get back to the main point. *What was that again? Oh yeah. . . .* "I have to go."

"Where?"

"Back to the motel."

"I told you that you're not going back there," he snapped, reining in his sudden temper once he realized his outburst. He crossed his arms over his chest and stared at me, as if trying to will me into submission. I was sure most people followed Tripp's orders, but I wasn't gonna be one of them. Not when what he was saying was completely asinine.

"Where else am I gonna go?" Wanting to mirror his resoluteness, I put my hands on my hips and challenged him back. I was sure I was quite the sight, standing there in nothing but his T-shirt, hair tousled and looking a mess.

"You can stay here."

"With you?"

"What's wrong with that?"

Was he offended?

"Um . . . let's see. I don't know you, for starters. Besides, you fired me, remember? What makes you think I'm still not pissed off at you?"

My arms stayed glued to my waist.

It was then he decided to make a move, reaching me in only a few long strides. He stood so close I had to tilt my head back to see his face. "Are you?" His warm breath fanned my face and I couldn't help but wonder what his kiss would taste like.

"Am I what?" I asked dreamily, so lost to the image of his lips pressed against mine that I'd lost all rationale.

"Pissed at me?" He reached out and tucked an errant strand of hair behind my ear, the pads of his fingers trailing over the sensitive area just below my earlobe.

"Huh?" My eyes were half closed at that point, and my mouth had suddenly become quite dry.

Chuckling, he leaned down until his mouth was but a whisper away from mine. "Are you still pissed at me? For letting you go from the club? Or are you imagining yourself kissing me? Is that where that beautiful head of yours is at?"

I couldn't do anything other than stare at his mouth, the questions he'd just asked not even registering before I rose up on my tippy toes and pressed my lips to his, completely oblivious to how inappropriate my actions were.

"Aw . . . fuck it," he muttered before giving in and kissing me back.

CHAPTER NINETEEN

Tripp

WITH REECE'S LIPS PRESSED AGAINST mine, it didn't take long before I lost all control and demanded everything from her. I hadn't thought of anything else since the first time I saw her, which had been less than twenty-four hours before.

Our situation hadn't started off ideal, but that didn't seem to matter. Life threw me a surprise that flipped me on my goddamn ass, and I had no choice but to roll with it and see what happened. I wasn't a deep thinker. I wasn't a man who questioned "what does it all mean" or even considered something as unrealistic as fate, but I couldn't deny the attraction and pull I felt toward Reece. An odd feeling, one I'd never experienced before, not once during my thirty-two years. There was something different and special about her. About us together. I knew she was attracted to me, could see it every time she looked at me, but did she feel that same undeniable force?

Our mouths collided while our tongues dueled, both of us desperately trying to savor the taste of the other. When she nipped my bottom lip I swore my dick became so hard I thought I was gonna explode right then and there. With the way we were goin' at each other, it sure as hell wasn't gonna take much anyway.

"Let's get this off you," I growled, breaking away from her mouth and raising the hem of her shirt—my shirt, to be exact—until it cleared her belly. Several seconds passed. I waited, impatiently I might add, but she didn't protest, so I lifted the material over her head and tossed it somewhere behind me. My eyes traveled the full length of her, first stopping to take in the magnificent view of her round and perky tits, then moving lower to glance at the tiny pair of panties she wore which barely covered her. I stepped back to better take her in, and that's when I saw her skin blush the sexiest color of pink. When I remained silent, she became self-conscious.

"What?" she asked, swallowing nervously while I continued to devour the sight of her.

"You're perfect. Absolutely fuckin' perfect." I wanted my mouth to cover every single inch of her, starting with those full, kiss-bruised lips. Pulling her into me, I crashed my mouth to hers again, demanding she open up for me once more with the thrust of my tongue. I pulled back long enough to remove my own shirt, and then I was back to tasting her for what felt like forever.

She moaned, digging her fingernails into my shoulders as I walked her backward toward my bed. Reaching under her ass, I pulled her up my body and she instinctively wrapped her legs around my waist. The warmth of her chest pressed against mine felt like heaven. I could only imagine what it would feel like to slide inside her, the heat of her pussy surely enough to send me over the edge.

Once we reached the bed, I crawled on top and gently laid her beneath me, careful not to crush her delicate frame. The prickling awareness that she was gonna allow me to fuck her soon excited me all while making me nervous. To be more exact, I was nervous for her, not me.

I'd been with many women over the years and it never failed. Every time they discovered what I was packing down below, their eyes widened. Some of them had even looked a bit worried.

I was a large man. Everywhere.

My hands trailed along her sides, goose bumps covering the surface of her skin the more I explored. Gently biting the tip of her tongue, I pulled back and stared at her, loving the fact that she looked like she did because of me. Her skin was still tinged pink, her plump lips battered from my demanding kiss. Her eyes were half closed, desire pooling underneath so heady I could only imagine what I'd find if I ran my fingers between her legs. No doubt she was soaked.

"Tripp." She whisper-moaned my name when my fingers played with the top of her panties. Shifting positions, I sat back and tugged the material down her thighs until her bare pussy was no longer covered.

"I can't wait to taste you," I said hastily, ripping her panties the rest of the way off before spreading her legs and burying my head in between. But before I could savor her sweetness, she uttered three words which stopped me dead in my tracks.

"Make me forget."

She spoke the words quietly, but I'd heard them loud and clear. I clenched my jaw, knowing damn well I couldn't continue on without making sure she was ready to fuck me because she wanted to, and not to escape from what happened the previous night.

After the attack she appeared okay, only a slightly frightened reaction moments after I busted into that back room. I stupidly thought she was completely fine, even thinking she was over it. But I should have known better. Of course, she'd suppress her feelings. I didn't know of a single woman who wouldn't be shaken after something like that, which was all the more reason I'd never allow her to put herself in that kind of situation again.

You hardly know her. How can you protect her?

Choosing to ignore my inner voice of reason, I pushed off the bed and stood at the edge, contemplating my next move. Fuck, this was hard. There she lay, naked and ready for me, and my dumb ass refused to fuck her unless she was doin' it for the right reason. Goddamn, I hated having a conscience.

"What's the matter?" she asked, closing her legs and leaning up on her elbows. I wanted to wipe away her look of self-doubt and confusion, but I couldn't. Not until I made her tell me why she'd said, "Make me forget."

"Reece . . . ," I started, running my hands through my hair, tugging at the strands in sexual frustration. My cock pressed against the seam of my zipper, throbbing for a release I had a feeling wasn't gonna happen any time soon. My hesitation made her even more aware something was wrong, so she pulled the covers over her to hide her nakedness.

"Why did you stop?" she gasped, remaining silent for a moment before saying accusingly, "You really are married, aren't you?" She shuffled back on the bed.

"I'm not fuckin' married. I told you that before."

"Then why? Why did you stop?"

"Why do you want to fuck me?" I asked crassly, wincing at the harshness of not only my words but my tone.

"Because . . . I like you. And I thought you liked me too."

"Is that it?" I arched a brow and set my expression to skeptical. She remained silent, not quite sure how else to respond. "Do you want me to make you forget what happened, to take your mind off being attacked?"

It was she who winced that time. "Yes," she replied honestly.

Shaking my head, I reached for her hand and waited for her to give in. Once the heat of her palm connected with mine, I helped her from the bed, the blanket still wrapped loosely around her body.

"I can't do this." She opened her mouth to speak but I continued on, not allowing her to say anything. "I'm not fucking you until I'm the only thought in that head of yours."

"I don't understand," she responded. "I'm not thinking about anyone but you." She tried to tug her hand from mine but I only tightened my hold. In fact, I pulled her closer.

"You need me in order to help you forget. You said so yourself." Taking a breath, I continued, "You've been through a lot, and that's on me for thinking you were okay with it. I should have known better, but I got caught up in you. In the thought of us together." To relieve her of some of her mounting anxiety, I kissed her, my lips lingering over hers for several seconds. "I don't want our first time together to be tainted by your need to escape from something else."

My eyes widened in shock when she started to cry. At first it was a single tear, but then many more quickly followed. Her shoulders shook as she finally released what had been pent up since the attack. Without hesitation, I wrapped my arms around her as she expelled her anguish.

I normally didn't do well with a crying woman, but with Reece it was different. All I wanted to do was comfort her, to promise her that everything would be okay, even if I didn't truly believe every word myself.

A tightness gripped my chest, the anger I felt about what happened to her rising to new heights. Such vulnerability and confusion on her part had me wanting to erase the memory of the night before. But I couldn't. I didn't know how to help her, and that alone killed me.

CHAPTER TWENTY

Reece

I COULDN'T BELIEVE ALL THAT had happened in the course of twenty minutes. First, Tripp undressed in front of me, comfortable as could be with that unbelievable body of his. Then I fell under some sort of spell when he neared me, imagining all sorts of dirty things I'd love to do to him, and him to me. Then, as brazen as could be, I was the one who made the first move. With all of Tripp's flirtation, I was the one to kiss him. I was the one who encouraged what happened next without question. I allowed him to take over, to take off my clothes and lay me on the bed beneath him. I was the one who allowed him to put his head between my legs, and I was the one who essentially stopped it with my admission that I needed him to help me forget all that had happened in the past twenty-four hours.

As soon as Tripp rescued me I had something else to focus on entirely, whether it was the anger from being fired or my lusty attraction to the stranger who swooped in on one of my darker moments. What I wasn't doing was dealing with the near rape that had occurred. A part of me was used to violence, but I thought once I moved to California I'd be able to leave all of that behind me. The incident at the club proved otherwise, and instead of dealing with all of those raw emotions, I chose to deflect. To shove everything so deep down it was as if nothing happened.

But it had, and now I had to deal with it. Breaking down in Tripp's arms was apparently the first step.

After I'd dried all of my tears, I dressed in a pair of sweatpants and a fresh shirt he'd given me. Of course I looked ridiculous in the overly large clothing, but Tripp grinned when he saw me enter the kitchen, taking me in from head to toe. A flirty smile I was becoming all too familiar with played on his lips as I sat down to a bagel and glass of orange juice.

"Sorry, it's all I have right now."

"It's more than enough," I said before taking a bite.

I ate in silence, my breakdown before quite embarrassing. Looking up every now and again, I saw that Tripp was watching me. He would go from frowning, to biting his lower lip, which was extremely sexy, to cocking a brow. An internal debate no doubt wreaking havoc on his thoughts.

Eventually one of us had to speak. It just so happened that we decided that very same thing at the same time.

"So," both of us said, amusement in our tone at the coincidence.

"You go first," he insisted, taking a sip of his coffee. I watched the muscles of his throat swallow the hot liquid, then stared at his mouth as he licked his lips. "Reece?"

"Sorry. Um . . . well . . . I guess I should be going. Can you give me a ride back to the motel?" I'd hoped he wasn't going to give me a hard time about going back there. In reality, I had no place else to go.

"No." His answer was final. He placed his mug on the counter and crossed his arms, looking like he was preparing himself for an argument. Well, he was right. I hardly knew him; I wasn't going to let him dictate anything for me.

"No?" I asked incredulously, my tone raising an octave in disbelief, although his answer shouldn't have shocked me. I pushed my empty plate away and stood from the table, bracing myself behind my chair for support.

"No. I already told you you're not stayin' there. You can stay here.

With me."

"I can't do that."

"Why?"

"Because I don't know you. Plus, it's . . . inappropriate."

He laughed, uncrossing his arms and stepping forward, mirroring the way I rested my hands on the back of the chair. "Why is it inappropriate? Unusual. Quick. Those are the words I'd use before saying it would be inappropriate." Clearly he found me amusing, a sentiment which irritated me.

My brain couldn't function when he stood so close, so I couldn't come up with a defense as to why I'd chosen that word. Instead, I blurted out something else which came to mind. "I just can't stay. Please. If you won't take me back to the motel, then I'll find my own ride."

"You *can't* stay? Or you don't *want* to stay?"

He just wouldn't give up.

Looking away, I said, "I don't wanna stay." I lied, of course, but I figured he'd relent if he knew I didn't want to be there with him. Thankfully, it worked. But when I glanced back at him, I saw a look of disappointment and hurt cross his face. It was brief, but I caught it.

"Fine. But you're not goin' back to the motel. I'll find you a place you can crash at until you get back on your feet." I opened my mouth to object, but he cut me off. "No argument, Reece." His hardened expression softened. "Let me do this for you. At least I'll know you'll be safe."

I eventually nodded, giving him the go-ahead to make the arrangements.

CHAPTER TWENTY-ONE

Tripp

I LEFT REECE IN THE kitchen while I stepped out on the porch, closing the door behind me for added privacy. Since I couldn't force her to stay with me, I had an idea where she could stay. I just needed approval first.

"What?" Marek practically shouted into the phone, no doubt losing all his patience for . . . everything.

"Sorry to bother you, Prez, but I was wondering if I could set someone up at Zip's place. I need somewhere safe, and close to the clubhouse."

"For *her*?" His tone was curt, his question irritating me right away. But since I detected a slight slur to his words, I let it go.

"Yeah."

"Is this rash move on your part gonna come back on the club in any way?"

Confused, I answered as honestly as I could. "No."

"Then I don't give a fuck." He hung up before I could thank him.

Zip's place was the perfect solution, but as I smiled at the compromise, I couldn't help thinking about our fallen brother.

Zip was a good kid. Always trying to prove his loyalty to the club, even though there was never a need. Marek had entrusted him to follow

Rico Yanez, Rafael Carrillo's right-hand man. And when the leader of Los Zappas Cartel found out Yanez went behind his back and continued to deal with the Savage Reapers, our most hated enemy, it was enough to seal his fate. The proverbial nail in the coffin. When they'd finished with Yanez, they passed him on to us on Marek's request, where he was tortured and finally disposed of once and for all. Revenge for what he'd done to Sully.

When Psych found an opportunity to exact his own kind of revenge against our club, he'd managed to kidnap Adelaide and Kena, Stone and Jagger's women. Zip had been the one assigned to accompany them on their shopping trip, and devastatingly enough, he'd been killed when the Reapers ran him off the road. This club was everything to Zip, and we paid him homage by burying him on the compound. He spent most of his time at the clubhouse, so we found it only fitting.

Walking back inside, I saw Reece pacing in the kitchen. Her head was down, sections of her dark hair shielding her face from me. As soon as she heard the creak of the door behind me, however, she looked up and directly into my eyes. I swore a jolt of something indescribable ricocheted through me.

"So, I found a place for you to stay." Shaking off the odd sensation that'd just racked through me, I leaned my hip against the counter. Her fingers had been playing with an area on the bridge of her nose, and when she caught me looking, she dropped her hand. It was then I noticed a small scar, a dent in her skin indicating she'd broken her nose at some point.

Jerking my chin at her, I asked, "What happened?"

Her response was immediate and deflective. "What do you mean?"

"How did you break your nose?"

"How . . . ?" She gently touched the scar again. "An accident. I'd had too much to drink one night and tripped over the curb. Clumsy, really." Her nervous laughter screamed she was lyin', but I didn't know her well enough to demand the truth. So I let it go.

Deciding to focus on something else, I raked my eyes over her, her appearance making me smile. The woman was drowning in the clothes I'd given her, but she'd never looked more beautiful. No makeup, her long hair piled loosely on top of her head. Something innocent about Reece tugged at my soul, and I'd be damned if I wasn't gonna find out what it was exactly that made me feel the way I did whenever I was around her.

Staring into her eyes calmed me, all the while heightening my need to protect her. I could spend hours, days even, trying to dissect my newfound feelings, but I wanted to live in the moment with her.

"I can't let you do that." She broke into my thoughts by responding to my original comment about Zip's place.

"Well, it's done." I tried to come off as cool and casual, but my clipped words gave me away. More than anything I wanted her to allow me to do this without an argument, but with the small amount I knew about her, it shouldn't have come as a surprise when she pushed back.

"Tripp, I really appreciate everything you've done for me. Besides firing me, of course. But I can take care of myself."

The next words to leave my mouth were certainly a surprise. I didn't want her anywhere near Indulge, but I also knew I shouldn't stand in the way of her making a living either. Maybe if I relented then so would she, taking me up on my offer to put her up at Zip's place.

"If I agree to let you go back to work at the club, in a different position, will you stay where I want you to? Where I know you'll be safe?" Zip had installed top-of-the-line security, as we all had, and his place was close to the clubhouse, which turned out to be rather convenient.

After his parents had died years prior, Zip had assumed all responsibility for the place, even thinking ahead and leaving it to Marek in case anything happened to him. He was young, and whereas most guys his age weren't even thinking about wills and what would happen to their shit when they died, most didn't have danger creeping around every corner, threatening to snatch their lives in the blink of an eye.

"What position?" she asked skeptically.

"You can assist Carla with bartending. She's been on us to hire someone to help her out, so I doubt she'll have any complaints about the new arrangement."

There was but a minute of contemplation on her part before she answered.

"Okay," she said enthusiastically. "Yes, I'll stay where you want me to, but only until I save up enough money for my own place."

I could have offered her the money she needed, but I selfishly wanted her close by so I could check on her anytime I wanted. With her permission, of course.

"All right then, let's grab your things from the motel and I'll take you to your new place." I gestured for her to walk ahead of me, resting my hand on the small of her back. She flinched from my touch, but I saw from the flush of her cheeks that she liked it.

"I STILL CAN'T BELIEVE YOU stayed here," I growled, walking around the small room and tossing her stuff into a bag she had opened on the bed. The place was fuckin' filthy, the walls a dingy white and the seventies shag carpet a horrible shade of worn green. And the smell—holy fuck, it smelled like stale smoke, vomit, and piss. A white-hot surge of anger strangled me at the idea that she thought so low of herself she chose to stay in this dump. "What the hell were you thinkin', Reece?" I stopped in front of her and lifted her chin so she had no choice but to look at me.

Embarrassment stole over her skin and she tried to move her head, but I tightened my hold, all without hurting her.

"What were you thinkin' stayin' in this shithole?" I repeated.

"Stop it," she whispered, placing her hands on my chest and shoving me away from her. I stepped back only because I saw the sad look in her eyes and I didn't want to add to her already distressed state. "I told you I didn't have any money. This was the only place I could afford."

I couldn't help but press her for more information. More personal information. "Why didn't you ask your family for money, then? I'm sure they'd help you out."

With her back turned toward me, busying herself with gathering the rest of her things, she said, "I don't have any family. My parents and brother died in a car accident." She took a deep breath. "And I left my house so quickly I didn't have time to think about what I'd do once I got wherever it was I was going."

"What does that mean?" I tried to turn her around but she shrugged away from me, zipping her bag before quickly walking toward the door. Once outside, I decided to let the conversation die—for now.

I still had Hawke's truck from the night before, and thank God because it had started to rain on the way to the clubhouse.

"When can I start back to work?" Reece asked, tapping her fingers on the door rest.

"Tomorrow, if you want." My hands tightened on the wheel, a reaction she most definitely noticed.

"What's wrong?"

"What makes you think something is wrong?" My knuckles were turning white.

"Because of that," she said, pointing to my hands.

"I hate the thought of you around all those fuckin' men," I grunted.

"Are those men the same ones who keep making your club money?" She smirked, toying with a strand of her hair while giving me the coyest smile. While I didn't like the topic of conversation, I had to admit that I liked the relaxed mood she appeared to have switched into, especially since she seemed so upset moments earlier.

"Yeah. Doesn't mean I like you being in their line of sight, though." Blowing out a frustrated breath, I loosened my grip on the wheel. "Just stay behind the bar during open hours and we'll be fine."

"You mean *you'll* be fine," she teased.

"Yeah." I knew it was a lie as soon as the word left my mouth.

CHAPTER TWENTY-TWO

Tripp

TWENTY MINUTES LATER I PULLED into the clubhouse lot. "I'll be right back. Just have to grab the keys." I jumped out of the truck and was about to close my door when Reece's voice cut through the air.

"Can I use the restroom?" she asked, clenching her thighs together. "I really have to go and I don't think I can hold it." Her face scrunched up while she squirmed in her seat.

"Yeah, okay. Come on."

Leading her inside, I directed her to the bathroom while I headed toward the bar, having spotted Marek hunched over talking to Trigger. Slapping him on the back, I took the stool next to him. "How ya doin'?" I asked tentatively. His only response was a grunt, followed by a slew of drunken words.

Looking to Trigger, I frowned, to which he simply shook his head. He mouthed, "Not good," before serving Marek another shot. The only guys who knew about what was goin' on with our prez were the men who were at the safe house. We agreed not to tell anyone else until we found out whether or not Psych had been telling the truth. Once the DNA results came back, then we'd let Marek decide what to do next. Until then, we swore to keep our mouths shut.

Marek's cell vibrated on the top of the bar, Sully's face flashing across the screen before he reached over and rejected the call. "I can't," he mumbled before shouting to Trigger to pour him another drink.

"Are you sure, Prez?" Trigger asked, slinging his bar towel over his shoulder. "I think you've had more than enough. Don't you want to sleep it off? Or better yet, do ya want me to take you home? I'm sure Sully's worried about you. She keeps calling." Trigger looked to me for assistance, which I readily gave.

"Yeah." I tugged on his arm. "Come on. One of us will give you a lift home. I'm sure your wife is worried sick." I looked back to Trigger. "He hasn't been home yet, has he?"

"Nope. Been planted on that fuckin' stool the entire time. I'm surprised his drunk ass hasn't fallen off yet."

"I ca . . . can hear ya," he muttered, finally staggering to his feet and walking toward Chambers. "Bring me a bottle," he shouted before slamming the door to the club's meeting place.

He left his phone on the bar, and when it rang again, I answered. I probably shouldn't have, but I knew Sully would be worried. No doubt she'd already spoken to Adelaide and knew Stone had returned home.

"Hey, Sully."

"Oh. Hi." A brief silence ensued before she spoke again. "Who is this?"

"Sorry, it's Tripp." Trigger stared at me, disbelieving that I'd actually answer Marek's phone. He shook his head and walked into the kitchen, most likely not wanting to be part of me going behind our prez's back.

"Is Cole there? Why do you have his phone? Is he okay?" she asked, her words coming out faster and faster the more she spoke. "Did something happen to him?" Short pants of air hit my ear and I knew I had to calm her before she really freaked out.

"Marek is fine. He's just. . . ." I trailed off, not quite sure what to say to her.

"He's what?"

"Drunk." Short and to the point.

"Drunk? Why? What happened?" Before I could answer I heard someone in the background—Adelaide. Then I heard Stone's voice.

"Sully, give the phone to Stone. I need to speak to him." I thought for sure she'd give me a hard time, insisting I tell her about Marek, but she didn't.

"It's Tripp," I heard her say before Stone came on the line.

"Everything okay?" he asked.

"Not really. Marek's at the club, drunk and mumbling all sorts of craziness."

"Can you blame him?" he whispered. I heard the women's voices fading into the background and knew Stone had walked away from them for more privacy.

"Not at all. But you need to calm Sully down before she freaks out and makes things worse. Whatever you do, keep her away from here."

"Yeah, I got it."

"Good. Hey, did you give Adelaide that shit to get tested? Did you tell her whose it was?"

"I'm not an idiot, Tripp."

"Well, that's debatable."

"Fuck you. And no, I didn't tell her anything except that I needed her to put a rush on it. She knew enough not to question me about it."

"And by that you mean she asked and you had to promise her some kind of sexual favor to let it go." I laughed because I'd witnessed the dynamic between the two of them, Adelaide certainly giving our VP a run for his money.

"Fuck you," he repeated before hanging up on me.

I'd been distracted from the call and didn't notice Reece walk up behind me. She gently touched my arm to let me know she was finished and ready to go.

"Hey, babe," I greeted. *Babe? Where the hell did that come from?*

She looked as shocked as I felt, but smiled nonetheless while stepping back when I stood up. Guiding her toward Chambers, I asked her to wait for me while I disappeared inside. Once I'd retrieved the keys from Marek, who was slumped over the table while simultaneously yelling at me because I didn't have a bottle of booze with me, I took hold of Reece's hand and led her back outside.

"What the hell, Tripp?" someone yelled across the courtyard. When

I turned, I saw Hawke jogging toward me. "You still got my truck," he accused.

"I know. You were too damn drunk last night to drive so I did you a favor."

Glancing behind me, he jerked his chin at Reece before looking back at me.

"Who ya got here?"

Now that my brother was sober, I guessed it was time for official introductions. *So help me if he tries any slick shit, I'll put him on his ass.* Although he'd told me he was done with steppin' out on Edana, he still had a long way to go before I actually believed it.

"Hawke, this is Reece. Reece, meet my younger, uglier brother, Hawke."

"Don't you wish?" Hawke glared at me before nodding toward Reece, who was still standing behind me. "Nice to meet you," he finally said. "But I think you might have something wrong with you, you know . . . up here," he said, pointing to his temple. "Anyone willing to hang out with my brother just can't be right in the head." He laughed but soon grimaced when I punched him in the chest.

"Shut the hell up," I grated, a half smirk on my face when I finally turned away from him and walked back toward the truck, Reece quickly following. "I'm takin' your truck again. Be back later."

———◆———

ZIP'S HOUSE WAS A FIVE-MINUTE ride from the clubhouse, which put me at ease knowing I could easily check in on her. In case she needed me, not for my own selfish need to see her.

Yeah, keep tellin' yourself that.

We entered the modest home and I gave her the condensed tour, although there wasn't that much to see. The living room was first, followed by a dining room and finally the kitchen toward the back of the house. Upstairs, there were two bedrooms and a small bathroom. The entire place was void of any fancy décor, but it was clean and was a million times better than that fuckin' shithole of a motel.

Watching Reece take it all in, I knew I'd made the right decision bringing her here. Going over the security system left Reece in a panic, so I wrote down the instructions on how to arm and disarm it, explaining everything in more detail as I jotted it down.

Rooting through Zip's hallway closet, I came across a fresh set of sheets and a new blanket. After making up the bed in his room, knowing that's where she'd be sleeping, I said good night and instructed her to set the alarm as soon as I left.

As I walked back toward the truck I was struck by an odd sense of anxiety about leaving her all alone.

CHAPTER TWENTY-THREE

Tripp

BAG OF GROCERIES IN HAND, I unlocked the front door. As I approached the keypad to disarm the alarm, I noticed Reece had never set it. Annoyance and a hint of fear coursed through me that she was left unprotected all evening. Looked like we'd be having quite the conversation as soon as I saw her.

Placing the bag on the kitchen counter, I filled the coffee pot before checking out the contents of the fridge—empty except for some condiments. Like I said, Zip spent the majority of his time at the clubhouse, so it didn't shock me that he didn't have any food.

While I waited for the coffee to brew, I went in search of Reece, taking the steps two at a time and quickly reaching the top. I tried to tell myself not to appear too eager, or enthusiastic, or whatever would make me seem as if I'd been counting the minutes until I laid eyes on her again. Dispelling my impatience, I told myself the reason I was quickly walking toward her bedroom was because I needed to have a talk with her about safety. The sooner that issue was resolved the better.

Looking down at my watch before entering her room, I saw that it was just after eight. By most standards, including mine, it was still kind of early, so I assumed she was still in bed.

As soon as my eyes landed on her sleeping form, I relaxed, breathing a sigh of relief that she was safe. To be this worried about a woman I barely knew was uncharacteristic of me, but there was just something different about Reece. I felt it the first time I saw her dancing on stage, and again when I rescued her from that asshole. Every time we interacted, or touched, or laughed, I knew my world was changing.

Reece had thrown the covers off her at some point, the nightshirt she wore riding up enough that if she moved even an inch I'd be able to see her panties, if she was even wearing any.

I can dream.

Her hair fanned out on the pillow. Her arms were raised high above her head, and the first image that popped into my brain was her splayed out underneath me, instantly making me as hard as stone. My imagination took hold and I envisioned her in every position possible, all in the span of a minute. Before I even realized what I was doing, I'd reached out to touch her, but she moved before I could do so.

Then she moved again, mumbling something in her sleep as her chest began to quickly rise and fall. Tossing her head to the side, she opened her mouth as if to say something but no sound came out. Lowering her arms, she clenched the bedsheet and groaned. At first I thought she was having some sort of erotic dream, but that notion quickly flew out the fuckin' window when the word "no" left her lips. Over and over again. Then she began pleading with someone not to hurt her, that she wouldn't do it again. Was the guy who attacked her coming back to torment her in her dreams?

I knew I had to wake her from her nightmare. I tried to be as gentle as possible, knowing that I could frighten her even more if I tried to shake her awake, but the more she writhed around, I knew I had to pull her out of her dreams quickly.

"Reece," I called out, gripping her by the shoulders. "Reece, wake up. It's only a dream." I grew frustrated the longer she remained asleep, and it wasn't until I practically shouted at her that her eyes popped open. It took her a few seconds to realize where she was, and that whatever she'd been dreaming about was no longer a threat. Before that realization took hold, however, she scooted back on the bed and threw her hands up in front of her, as if to protect herself from me.

I knew it was instinctual on her part, but it didn't hurt me any less. I would never do anything to harm her, and I kept telling her that with the look of concern in my eyes. Eventually, the fright she felt faded, and it was only when the relief set in that she lunged at me. At first I thought she was gonna try and attack me, which I would've let her do to help her purge whatever haunted her, but I quickly understood that she needed me to comfort her.

"Tripp," she cried, flinging herself into my arms and snuggling into my chest. While I hated that her reaction stemmed from her nightmare, I couldn't help but love the feel of her against me.

"Was it that bastard who attacked you?" I asked tentatively, not really wanting her to answer but knowing she needed to in order to start moving past what happened to her. She remained quiet, hanging on to me for dear life. After several intense moments, I unlocked her fingers from around me and pulled back enough for me to look into her eyes. "Was that who you were dreamin' about?" She started to shake her head but then quickly nodded, looking down when she saw the frown on my face. "Reece. . . ."

"I don't remember." I knew she wasn't telling me the truth simply from the way she kept avoiding my eyes.

"Well, you're safe now," I soothed, running my hands up and down her arms in a show of comfort. I decided not to grill her about her dream. She relaxed, and so did I. "Come on. I brought you some food."

"Did you make coffee?" she asked, swinging her long legs over the side of the bed.

"Sure did." Those were my last words before I walked from the room, leaving her behind me to do whatever she needed to before she came downstairs.

———•———

"I HAVE SOMETHING TO TALK to you about," I said, waiting until she'd taken a seat at the table, a forkful of scrambled eggs poised at her lips, ready to be devoured.

"Okay," she responded, looking rather worried.

"The alarm," I started. "You have to make sure you arm it. Every time. I don't care if the door is locked. You can't mess up on this." She remained quiet. "It's very important. Do you understand?"

She nodded.

"No, I need you to tell me you get it. That you hear what I'm telling you," I pressed.

"Yes, I understand. Sorry."

"Okay. If I come here again and find out you didn't set it, I'll be forced to spank you." I meant to lighten the mood with a joke, but as soon as the words left my mouth, I knew I shouldn't have said them. That was until I saw her skin turn pink, the blush rising from her neck up to her cheeks. Her teeth captured her bottom lip and she briefly closed her eyes before looking at me again.

Because of her reaction, I never apologized, instead letting my sexual threat linger in that beautiful head of hers. Her eyes widened when I stepped closer, her breath hitching when I reached toward her to snatch her mug for a refill. A rush of air left her lungs when I turned around, and I couldn't help but adjust myself. I was so fuckin' hard that if she made a move on me I'd carry her back upstairs and fuck her so many times she wouldn't walk right for a week.

Needing another topic of conversation to focus on, even one I didn't particularly care for, I chose work. Reece now stood in front of the sink, washing out her cup and rinsing off her plate. My eyes were glued to her backside the entire time, until she turned around and caught me leering at her like some kind of creep. Or horny man. Yeah, I was goin' with sexually frustrated, horny man.

"Listen," I said, clearing my throat, trying like hell to get back on track and force all of the sordid images from my brain, "I have to head to the clubhouse to take care of some business, but I'll be back to pick you up at five for work."

"Why?"

"Why am I gonna pick you up?"

"Yeah. I can find my own way there. I don't want to put you out. You've done enough for me already." She shuffled her feet in nervousness.

"I don't mind," I insisted, my body language giving everything away, I was sure. My go-to intimidating stance was crossing my arms over my chest and spreading my feet, and while the last thing I wanted to do was bully her, I played on the only tool I had right then. I needed her to give in and do as I demanded; otherwise, I feared I'd go out of my mind with worry. And if I was constantly focused on Reece's safety, I'd be hampered from doing whatever I needed to for the Knights. Then I'd have bigger issues.

"I really don't—"

I cut her off, my aggravation increasing by the second.

"This conversation is over, Reece. I'll pick you up at five. Be ready to go." I gave her a fleeting smile before walking out of the house, a preemptive strike to any argument she may have come up with.

Chapter Twenty-Four

Reece

MY FIRST TIME BEHIND THE bar didn't go exactly as I'd hoped, but with each passing hour I'd mastered some of the skills needed not to break every damn bottle stacked on the shelves.

Tripp stayed true to his word and picked me up at five on the dot, hanging out at the club until Carla insisted his presence was only adding to my nervousness. He left reluctantly, but only after telling me what he thought of the outfit I'd chosen to wear—a short black skirt paired with a low-cut Indulge tank top. Carla had passed out the shirts to every woman who worked there, telling us to wear them to promote the club. Good for business and all that. They were designed to leave little to the imagination, but that was the point, to draw in men who would spend their hard-earned money on the girls.

"I hate the thought of all these men leering at you," he'd whispered in my ear while I poured one of the customers a beer.

"At least I have clothes on," was the only thing I could think of to say. He left soon afterward, peering around the club one last time before he disappeared outside. I had no doubt he'd have eyes on me in his absence, and I was proved right when his brother strolled through the front door not an hour later.

"I'M GONNA CHANGE REAL QUICK. I spilled beer all down the front of me," I yelled over the music. Carla smiled and nodded, tending to the multiple men waiting to be served.

"There should be extra shirts in the back. If you can't find any, check my locker. It should be open." She turned back toward one of the customers who wasn't taking waiting too well. Luckily, Carla knew exactly how to handle those types of guys. Besides, new security had been hired on to assist, just in case.

Once I'd reached the back room, I spotted a pile of the club's tank tops neatly stacked on top of one of the dressing tables. My bra had been soaked as well but there wasn't anything I could do about that, so I tossed my beer-soaked shirt on the floor and quickly pulled a fresh one over my head. I'd been too distracted with trying to hurry that I never heard her come into the room.

"Well, who do we have here?" Arianna sneered, the disgust she held for me certainly not hidden. I kept my back to her and didn't respond, engaging with her the last thing I wanted to do. My plan was to ignore her and head back out to the bar, but that never happened.

As I moved toward the door, Arianna stepped in front to block me.

"I thought they fired you," she cackled. Yes, *cackled*. It was the only word to properly describe the sound she made, the noise like nails on a chalkboard.

"Just from taking my clothes off. Apparently Tripp doesn't want any other man to look at or touch what's his." The words left my lips before my brain could filter them. I hadn't meant to goad her, but I had to admit that it certainly felt good. Really good. Arianna was nothing if not a bully, and if what I said was enough to leave her speechless, if only for a brief moment, then I considered that a success. No matter how short-lived.

When the shock finally wore off, she attacked. "You're lying. There's no way Tripp would ever hook up with the likes of you. You're . . . beneath me." She blew a strand of her over-processed hair out of her face. "He'd never bother with you after he had a taste of me."

The image of Tripp and Arianna together bothered me, although it shouldn't have. I had no claim on the man. I barely knew him. And even though it was apparent we were attracted to each other, that's all it was. But I didn't need to let this bitch know that.

As I was about to say something else to rile her up, my cell rang. And as luck would have it, Tripp's name flashed across the screen. What were the odds?

Turning my phone toward her so she could see who was calling, I smiled big and said, "Well, would ya look at that. Right on time." Arianna gave me the nastiest look as I swiped to answer the call. "Hi, sweetheart," I cooed enthusiastically, probably a little overboard but I couldn't help myself.

Arianna stood there in utter disbelief before she finally stomped out of the room, shouting at whomever was in her way before slamming the door behind her, leaving me extremely satisfied.

"Sweetheart? Well, that's unexpected, although I can't say I don't like it." The sound of Tripp's laughter soothed me, while the roughness of his tone anchored me into calmness.

"Sorry. Arianna was givin' me shit about you, so I decided to mess with her a bit."

"Don't pay her any mind, Reece. Seriously, she's not worth it." His words were clipped, which only spurred my next question.

"Do you still hook up with her?"

"What? Who told you that?" Tripp sounded flustered, which was odd coming from him. He seemed as if nothing would faze him.

"She did." Silence. "So, do you?"

"No, I don't."

"It's true, then? You did sleep with her?" I had no idea why I pried into his business, other than curiosity. And jealousy. Let's not forget about jealousy.

Letting out a ragged sigh, he answered, "Yeah, in the past. A few times. But no more. It was a mistake. One that'll never happen again."

"Which one was a mistake?" I pried further.

"What?"

"Which time you slept with her was a mistake?"

"Every time." A frustrated pant of air hit my ear. "Look, I don't wanna talk about her, so can we please drop it?"

Since Arianna was the last person I wished to discuss, I did as Tripp asked and let it go. He proceeded to change the subject, asking when my shift ended. I told him around three, and that he didn't have to worry because Carla would give me a ride home, to which he insisted on coming to pick me up. He was so adamant that I relented.

Besides, I really wanted to see him.

As soon as I ended the call, my phone instantly rang. I never bothered looking at the screen, simply figuring it was Tripp calling me right back.

"I know. I won't go anywhere until you get here." My tone was light with laughter, but when there was only silence, I pulled the phone from my ear and looked at the screen. Unknown. It wasn't Tripp who'd called me back.

"Hello?" Still no answer. "Hello?" I asked again. That time I heard someone breathing and my stomach flipped over in nervousness. "Hello?" I asked more timidly, praying the person on the other end would hang up without saying a word.

I got my wish when the call disconnected.

CHAPTER TWENTY-FIVE

Tripp

EVERY SINGLE DAY FOR THE past week, I'd seen Reece. I'd picked her up for work, hung out for an hour or so, and then returned later on to drive her home. She'd become more comfortable with her new role at the club, and although there were a few times when some of the drunk customers got a bit handsy with her, she seemed to handle them with no problem. That didn't mean I trusted anyone around her. Quite the opposite, in fact. If I wasn't there, I had one of the guys posted until I could return. We'd also hired additional security, not only for Reece but for all of the women at the club. Had to protect the club's investment, right?

On Reece's day off, we went grocery shopping. Something so mundane yet I enjoyed every second. Watching her flit from aisle to aisle brought a smile to my face. Even though the way we met wasn't ideal, it didn't deter me from delving into who she really was underneath.

During our many late-night talks, I'd convinced her to open up more about her family. She'd tell me stories from her childhood but then would quickly shut down as soon as she broached the subject of their accident. It was obviously still too painful for her to talk about. I'd switch the topic to that of past boyfriends, for my own torture, and she'd give me vague answers, her finger subconsciously rubbing the scar on the bridge of her nose. The desperate look in her eyes told me let it go, and I did. For the time being.

Something about Reece brought out my overprotective side, which I knew drove her crazy sometimes. She'd roll her eyes when I'd become a little more than animated trying to stress the importance of being aware of her surroundings. So in order to try and teach her a lesson, I went as far as to hide around the corner of Indulge, grabbing her when she'd come outside for some fresh air. She didn't particularly care so much for that little stunt of mine, shrieking out in fright before pummeling me with her tiny fists.

———◆———

"I DON'T UNDERSTAND WHY THE hell you won't tell me," I yelled, trying like hell to control my temper. But I failed. Big time. Only when Reece shrank back farther into the couch did I release a heavy breath and silently counted to ten. Tentatively approaching her, I stopped by the side of the sofa so as not to crowd her. "Sorry. I just want to get to know you, that's all. The good and the bad." I attempted to lighten the mood with a smile but couldn't. My body wouldn't allow the simple expression to form while my blood ran hot inside my veins.

"There's nothing to tell," she lied, pulling her knees to her chest in a protective stance. "Besides, I don't know anything about *you*," she threw back at me. "You won't even tell me your real name. Or anything about your family. Or how you came to be part of your club. I hear the other men call you 'nomad' every now and again. I've done some research. Nomad means you don't belong to any one place."

"Charter?"

"What?" She looked confused by my correction.

"They're called charters." The sofa dipped with my weight. I needed to sit for this, knowing damn well she was gonna take advantage and ask me all sorts of questions.

Rolling her eyes, something she'd been doing quite often, she asked, "Why did you decide to stay here?"

I knew what she was doing, deflecting to take the focus off her. I'd asked her about her previous relationship, again for my own torment, but she refused to give me any details.

The anger I'd felt just moments before slowly started to fade, although traces of it continued to pump through my veins. "Okay, fine. You wanna know some shit about me, I'll tell ya." I took a deep breath, giving off the impression I was annoyed. It wasn't totally off base. "You already know that Hawke is my younger brother, and although he can be quite the pain in the ass most times, we're close. I'd do anything to protect him, even if it's from himself. What else . . . ," I said, tapping my finger against my chin. "I've been with the Knights since my early twenties. Although he was never part of the club, my father had been friends with Marek's ol' man, as well as Stone's. I knew the guys growing up, so it just made sense to join. My father often worried about the goings-on within the Knights and didn't want me or Hawke involved, but he also knew enough about us that we wouldn't be deterred so easily."

"What does he think about it now?"

"He passed away last year. Cancer." I couldn't help the sadness that crept over me. Both Hawke and I were close with the old man, and it was a dark day when he died.

"I'm sorry," she said, reaching over to stroke my hand, her touch most definitely welcome.

"Thanks. Anyway, we were young and thrived on danger." I smirked but quickly stopped when I saw her reaction.

"Wait, what do you mean danger?" A worried look drifted over her face.

"Not anymore. Nothing for you to worry about where the club is concerned." I refused to elaborate. "Anyhow, I've always been sort of a loner, hence being a nomad." Judging by her expectant look, I continued on, revealing something I hadn't told anyone—the real reason I'd been in town the night some of the Reapers had attacked me, leaving me for dead in front of the Knights' clubhouse, four bullet wound scars a constant reminder of my carelessness.

"One night, I came home to find the woman I'd been living with fucking some guy. In our bed. Needless to say, I wasn't too happy. I almost killed him. I wanted to, trust me, but I didn't. After telling her it was over, I left and hopped on my bike. Before I knew it I'd arrived at The Underground, our club's bar. Because of what'd happened, I got drunk. Really drunk. And when I stumbled outside, there were a few Reapers waitin' for me. Still to this day I have no idea how no one saw them creepin' around outside." I took a deep breath. "They shot me, then dropped me off outside the clubhouse."

I paused to allow her to digest it all, her eyes wide with fright and concern. "I almost died. If it weren't for Adelaide, Stone's woman, I probably would've. She patched me up and looked after me while I recovered." I smiled at the recollection of how pissed Stone had been when Adelaide watched over me. I liked to think I was the reason he got his head out of his ass and finally pursued making them a legit couple.

"Who are the Reapers? Are they still after you?"

Hmm . . . how to answer that question.

"The Savage Reapers are a rival club. Real scum of the earth. And no, they're not still after me." Deciding to be as truthful as I could, I added, "Well, because of the hatred our clubs have toward each other, there's always the chance we could run into them. You know, not on accident." The worried look never left her face. "But now that their president is dead, I don't see them being a problem."

"He's dead? Did you . . . kill him?" she asked meekly, her bottom lip disappearing between her teeth in anxiousness.

"No, I didn't kill him." It was mostly the truth. While I'd assisted in his demise, Marek was the one who ended his wretched life.

Wanting to change the subject from something so grim, I allowed her to ask me a few more questions, hoping that by me opening up she would do the same.

"What else do you wanna know?" I prompted.

"Do you have any other siblings?"

"No."

"Is your mother still alive?"

"Don't know."

"Why wouldn't you know that?"

I tried not to appear as angry as I felt. "Because she took off with another guy and left us when Hawke and me were still young."

"And you never saw her again?"

"No. Next question," I barked. Reining it back in again, I said, "Sorry, I just don't wanna talk about her."

There she goes again biting that damn lip. All I wanted to do was reach over, pluck it from between her teeth and suck on it.

"That's okay. I know how that feels. Some things are better left in the past."

And there it was. She'd essentially just let me know that she wasn't open to discussing anything from her past. Eventually she'd have no choice, but we weren't there yet.

"Okay, I have one more question for you." She smiled so I relaxed.

"Shoot."

"What's your real name?"

"Cavanaugh."

"That's your first name?"

"Last name." While she was still processing my answer, albeit not the one she wanted, I asked for hers in return. "What's your last name?"

I thought for sure she would've refused, but surprisingly she answered. "Kendrick. Now tell me your first name," she insisted.

Shaking my head, I moved closer and ghosted my fingers down her arm, doing my best to distract her. I refused to give her the answer she wanted, but it wasn't because it was anything horrible. I simply loved playin' with her, knowing my refusal annoyed her.

"Nope.

"Are you running from the law or somethin'?"

"I told you my last name. Besides, if I were hiding from the police, do you honestly think I'd be involved with a well-known biker club?"

"Maybe. If you think about it, it's the perfect cover. Hiding in plain sight." She laughed, the sexual tension between us increasing. She continued to look at me expectantly.

"Not gonna happen, sweetheart. I don't know ya well enough yet to tell ya."

"Still?" she huffed, moving to tuck her legs underneath her. Turning toward me, she rested her arm on the back of the couch. "You've found a place for me to live, have picked me up and taken me home every night I had to work, seen me naked, and kissed me so passionately you made my toes curl."

"I made your toes curl, huh?" I winked, the corners of my mouth curving up in a wicked grin.

"You're so arrogant," she teased, slapping my arm in jest and allowing her fingers to grip my bicep a few seconds too long. Before she could pull away, however, I grabbed her hand and pulled her close, positioning her until she straddled my lap.

"What are you doing?" she asked breathlessly, short pants of warm air hitting my face her mouth was so close to mine. She moved on top of me to better adjust herself, and the second she rubbed herself over my cock I almost lost all gentleness and tore her clothes off right then and there.

Reece was still fragile. She tried to pretend otherwise, but I saw the pain hidden behind her beautiful eyes. An incident that would merely startle someone else sent her into a panic, if only for a few seconds. Glass shattering from one of the mugs behind the bar. Shouts from the customers when they got excited, which was quite often given the club they were in. No matter what it was, though, she always collected herself quickly, and if I hadn't been paying so much attention to her, I probably never would've noticed.

"What do you want me to do?" I asked. Placing my hands on her hips, I ground myself against her, licking my lips and drawing her attention from my eyes to my mouth.

"I don't know what you mean." She still tried to play coy, and admittedly I kinda liked it. Lifting the bottom of her tank top, my fingers grazed over her skin, her breath hitching from the heat of my touch. "That feels nice," she whispered.

"You know what else would feel nice? Great, in fact?" I continued to raise her shirt until I'd finally removed it altogether. She never protested. Never answered my question. She didn't do anything except wait for me to make my next move.

CHAPTER TWENTY-SIX

Reece

I'D BE LYING IF I didn't say that most of my thoughts were consumed by Tripp. The way he'd looked when he dropped his towel in front of me, baring his naked self and acting like it was no big deal. The way he'd watch me when he thought I wasn't paying attention. The way his kiss tasted when I'd been the one to shamelessly throw myself at him the day after I'd met him.

The way he made me feel safe.

The way he made inappropriate sexual jokes, like telling me he'd spank me if I forgot to arm the alarm system.

The way my body reacted to that statement.

The way he noticed.

So to be sitting on his lap, straddling him, our most intimate areas touching even though we were still clothed, left no room for imagination any longer. I knew exactly what he wanted to do.

And I wanted to do it too.

I wanted Tripp to strip me naked and have his way with me. As many times as he wanted. I needed to feel his lips against mine, to feel the warmth of his breath covering my skin as he positioned himself between my legs. I wanted to taste him on my tongue, to drive him so crazy with lust that he was barely able to control himself.

As soon as he unhooked my bra and tossed it aside, I finally gave in, knowing what was to come would be climactic, every pun intended. The chemistry that existed between us was palpable.

Undeniable.

Electric.

"Yes," I moaned, writhing on top of him and pushing my breasts closer to his face. Needing him to take me in his mouth, I brazenly taunted him until whatever resolve he had left shattered into pieces.

"Fuck," he groaned, latching on to my breast while toying with the other. The sensation was too much. Every flick of his tongue over my sensitive nipple. Every gentle tug of his teeth, his tongue soothing the bite so the line between pleasure and pain blurred together. "These are mine, baby. Do you hear me?" he asked, switching from one breast to the other, pinching the erect buds until I could barely stand it.

Tripp rose from the couch while holding me exactly in the same position. I wrapped my legs around his waist to ensure I wouldn't fall. Hell, I never wanted to separate from the man ever again. Our mouths found one another's as he climbed the steps and hurried toward my bedroom, our tongues dueling for dominance. But it was no contest; he took control like he always did, and I'd never been so happy to submit.

Once inside my room, he wasted no time before laying me on my back and ripping my skirt from me, quickly followed by my panties.

"I can't wait to fuck you," he groaned, kicking off his boots before removing the rest of his clothing, standing before me in all his glory. As my eyes trailed down the length of him, starting with his gorgeous face, to his sculpted chest and abs, then down to his . . . *oh my God!*

With furrowed brows, I leaned up on my elbows and stared right at his package. His overly large, extremely rigid, previously well-hidden surprise. I knew he was gifted down below when I'd felt it against my thigh earlier, but I never would have imagined just how big he was.

"What's the matter?" he asked, glancing down at himself before finally nodding. "Uh . . . never mind. I know what that look's for."

CHAPTER TWENTY-SEVEN

Tripp

SCRAMBLING UNTIL SHE WAS ON her knees, a position I'd envisioned her in too many times to count, she shook her head and looked at me with a twinge of fear in her eyes. "You don't honestly think that'll fit inside me, do you?"

If I weren't so fuckin' hard right then, the situation probably would have made me laugh. Reece pointed at my dick in disbelief, and while I found the whole scene flattering, I knew there was a chance I'd hurt her. And that was the last thing I ever wanted to do.

Before I could respond with some sort of reassurance, Reece crawled toward me, her tits heavy and begging for my mouth again. I wanted nothing more than to flip her on her back and plunge inside her, but I knew I could never do that. Not the way I wanted. Not until she became comfortable with my size.

Inching closer still, she glanced up at me before wrapping her hand around me, my cock twitching in her tight hold. "Fuck me," I growled. "Don't tease me too much or I'll be done before I even start."

"It's just so big," she whispered, stroking me from base to tip. Slowly. Tentatively. In awe at the sheer size of it. When a drop of pre-cum coated the tip, she swirled it around with her thumb, stroking me quicker than before.

"Reece . . . ," I warned, the look of failing restraint plastered all over my face. "You can't keep doin' that. Not unless you want me to come." My eyes were pinned to hers the entire time, and when I saw a small smile tilt her lips, I knew she was up to no good.

"I just wanted to touch it."

"Well, don't stop there, sweetheart." A wolfish grin spread across my face. "You can taste it if you want." On reflex, my cock jerked in her hand, emphasizing my offer for her to wrap her lips around me.

"I might just take you up on that," she said, licking her lips as if already preparing to swallow me whole. Well, not whole because I'd never fit.

The heated look in her eyes, mixed with the heaviness of my balls, told me that if she took me in her mouth I'd never last.

"Never mind. I don't want you to do it."

"No?" She drew closer until her lips hovered over me, the sight of her about to suck me into her mouth pushing me toward the edge.

"Reece," I warned again. "I'm serious. Don't. Not yet. I don't wanna come down your throat." No matter what I said, it didn't deter her from doing what she wanted. Sure, I could have stopped her, but there was a part of me that wanted to see what she'd do. She was clearly fascinated with me. Who was I to stop her from exploring my dick?

"I'll just do it for a second," she promised, opening her perfect mouth and wrapping her lips around me. Her tongue swirled around the tip, her cheeks hollowing as she sucked me in as far as she could, which wasn't much. But it was enough, all the same.

It took every ounce of control I had not to thrust inside her wet, hot mouth. So, to steady myself, I grabbed her hair and positioned her where I wanted her. She tried to take more of me but I pulled back, only allowing the tip to remain inside. I felt the ache in my balls building, threatening to explode soon if I didn't pull out all the way. But it felt too good—amazing, even.

"Goddammit!" I roared, restricting her movements every time she pushed to take more of me. Knowing it would all be over too soon, I pushed her back and I finally fell from her mouth. I swore it felt as if I'd run a fuckin' marathon. The air pushed from my lungs in heavy spurts, my chest rising and falling simply from lust alone. "You're gonna be the death of me," I told her, watching her smile widen. Her saliva made it easier for me to stroke myself while she watched, the desire in her eyes taking over in the form of sheer fascination. "Do you like watching me do this?"

She nodded, biting the corner of her bottom lip in excitement.

"Lie back," I demanded, kneeling once her back hit the bed. "Spread your legs."

"Tripp, I'm nervous," she admitted, worry etching faint lines around her eyes.

I'd better put her mind at ease, or she's gonna chew the hell out of that poor, abused lip.

"I'm not gonna fuck you yet. Not with my cock, anyway." Widening her legs, I lowered my head until my breath spread over her glistening pussy. "I can see you're ready for me, but just to make sure. . . ." I slid my tongue between her folds, the taste of her driving me insane.

There was no slow buildup before her back arched off the bed, her fingers pulling at my hair and thrusting her pussy against me. My tongue slid inside her, followed by two fingers, stroking that sweet spot until her toes literally curled.

"Oh . . . oh my God . . . yes," she panted, over and over again. With my free hand, I played with her tits, pinching her nipples and adding to the sensation racking her body. "Tripp. . . ." My name was like a prayer on her lips. A promise. An ode to something bigger.

I knew as soon as I wrapped my lips around her clit that she'd fall. While I wanted nothing more than for her to come on my tongue, I was also being quite selfish. The wetter she became, the easier it would be for me to push inside her.

"Does that feel good? Do you wanna come?" I asked, continuing to tease her until she answered.

"Please," she panted, her fingers gripping my hair to the point of pain. But I didn't mind. Not at all. It meant she was close to the edge. All I had to do was finish her off.

With one final stroke of my tongue, I sucked on her clit and pumped two fingers inside her simultaneously. Reece cried out, her moans the best sound I'd ever heard. The sight of her undid me, my own need to claim her intensifying the longer she rode out her orgasm.

When she'd finally come back down, she started to laugh. "Oh my God!" she exclaimed. "That was amazing."

"Then why are you laughing?" A smile toyed with my lips until I was full-on grinning. Her expression was infectious.

"Because I can't believe I've missed out on that all these years." While what she'd said was a compliment, I didn't ask her to elaborate because the thought of her with another man would torture me.

"Glad I could be of service." I moved up the bed and covered her still-quaking body with mine. "Do you know how many times I've pictured you like this, legs spread and ready for me?"

"Probably not as many as I have," she answered, a sly smirk staring back at me.

"Oh really?" I laughed at the casualness of her statement. The same woman who blushed when she'd seen me naked for the first time.

"Yeah, really," she teasingly taunted. She tried to move up the bed but my weight kept her pinned right where she was.

"Am I crushing you?"

"No, but I'm starting to freak out about . . . you know."

"My dick?"

A raised brow from me had her smiling again.

"Yeah."

"Don't worry. We'll take it slow." The last thing I wanted was for her to be so tense she didn't enjoy herself. But the reality was that my size was sometimes more of a hindrance than a blessing. I know, poor me, but that was the truth of it.

"Okay," she said, her muscles already tensing.

"Try to relax," I coaxed, kissing her sweetly to let her know everything would be great. We were meant to fit together; it just might take a bit more work on my end to ensure she felt nothing but pleasure.

Rising up on my forearm to balance myself, I reached for the condom I'd pulled out earlier and quickly sheathed myself. Lining myself up at her entrance, I teased her with my finger one last time to make sure she was completely ready.

"Tripp?"

Looking down into her trusting eyes, I knew I was never gonna be the same man ever again. "Yeah?"

"What's your real name?"

Without hesitation that time, I said, "James."

CHAPTER TWENTY-EIGHT

Reece

FINALLY. HE'D TOLD ME HIS real name. Then again, he couldn't use the excuse that he didn't know me well enough, seeing as he was poised to have sex with me.

Every time I thought about the size of his cock, what it would feel like stretching me open, I tensed. I tried to listen to him and relax, but he wasn't the one who was gonna get a huge dick shoved inside him. Most women would be ecstatic to find out the guy they were gonna sleep with was well-endowed, but this was going overboard just a bit.

"Are you ready?" he asked, concern mixed with lust dancing behind his beautiful green eyes.

"I think so."

He lowered his mouth to mine, his tongue sliding over my bottom lip and deliciously teasing me. The thrust of his tongue soon mirrored the thrust of his body. Gentle and patient. If his restraint teetered on the edge, he didn't show it. Placing his hand under my knee, he widened my legs, pushing my thigh up toward me to open me up a little more.

"You're beyond tight, baby," he groaned, nipping my lip before kissing along my jaw, eventually burying his head in the crook of my neck and panting heavily. "Are you okay? How do you feel?"

"It hurts a little, but it feels good at the same time." And it did hurt, even with how wet he'd made me. But it wasn't as painful as I thought it would be.

"I have an idea," he said before pulling out of me. "Come here." He grabbed my hips and pulled me down the bed. He rested back on his haunches and spread my legs as far apart as possible. His hands braced underneath my knees, pressing my thighs back toward me like he'd just done with my leg moments earlier. "Wrap your hand around me and put me inside you." When I looked hesitant, he said, "Trust me. Do it."

With my hand fully wrapped around his cock, I lined him up at my entrance. He swiveled his hips before pushing back inside me, that time going in with much more ease, although he still took his time. An ache that'd bloomed inside me intensified, my body hungry for every inch of him. After slowly working himself in, we were fully sheathed. I felt so incredibly full. Tripp remained still until he took a few deep breaths and pulled back an inch.

"I'm gonna start to move now." His expression looked pained and I wondered if I was somehow inadvertently hurting him.

"Are you okay?"

He clenched his jaw. "I'm more than okay. I'm just tryin' to hold back so I don't hurt you. But it's so hard." The sexiest moan flowed from his incredible lips, seducing me even more than he already had.

"Yes it is," I said, laughing after I realized how cheesy my reply was. He chuckled, and whatever tension had existed between us instantly evaporated.

Every corded muscle of his chest constricted as he rocked in and out of me, the vision in front of me purely animalistic. His lips parted, his eyes hooded as he lost himself to the feel of my body. The sight of Tripp lost in his own bliss was intoxicating, and if I were a woman who could come from an image alone, it would have happened right then.

Several minutes later Tripp found a steady rhythm, thrusting inside me, gently at first and then a bit more aggressive the more my body opened for him. All traces of pain disappeared. Every time he swiveled his hips, he hit my sweet spot, the strangled "yes" which flew from my lips affirmation enough.

"Right there?" he asked, hitting the sensitive place inside me over and over. He knew damn well that was the spot.

"Yes. Oh . . . yes. Right there." I tried to move with him, but the position he had me in made it near impossible to do so. "Tripp, let go of my legs. I want to feel you against me. Please," I begged. It didn't take but a second for him to comply.

Resting on top of me, some of his body weight held up by his forearms, his mouth found mine again as he fucked me senseless. "I can't believe you're takin' all of me, baby. So fuckin' good," he panted. "You feel incredible. So warm. Tight. Do you love my cock?" The only response I could muster was a moan. "Tell me you love my big cock," he demanded, plunging his tongue into my mouth. I should have known Tripp would talk dirty, his past sexual innuendoes surely laying the groundwork.

As we continued to taste each other, I felt my body crest on the wave of pleasure, climbing higher and higher until the sensation was so overwhelming there was nothing to do except count the seconds until my body detonated into the abyss of my impending orgasm.

I couldn't believe the words that were about to come out of my mouth, but before I could stop myself, I shouted, "Fuck me harder. I'm right there. Oh my God. Yes . . . I'm right there." My fingers clenched his tight ass as he picked up his pace, reaching underneath me to pull me closer while he pounded into me, although I suspected he still restrained himself. A twinge of pain erupted but was quickly absorbed by my orgasm. Every nerve inside me fired into the heavens, the feeling so strong and powerful I almost lost my breath. Tripp latched on to my mouth and swallowed my screams, his own moans mixing with mine as he lost himself to his own high.

When we'd finally come back down, our breath regulated and reality came back into focus. Tripp remained on top of me, his weight starting to crush me the longer he laid there. I tapped his ass. When he still didn't budge, I slapped his rear.

"Ow," he grumbled.

"You . . . have to . . . move." My strangled words were enough for him to roll off me.

"Sorry." He laughed. "I forget my size sometimes."

"You could've killed me," I teased, turning on my side to face him.

"It'd be a hell of a way to go out, though, don't ya think?"

I never answered, the curve of my lips enough to tell him I agreed. To look at him right then was the best sight I'd ever laid eyes on. A thin sheen of sweat covered his large, muscled body, the tips of his hair sticking to his forehead from all of his exertion. I never thought a sweaty man could be alluring, but Tripp had proved me wrong. His semi-erect arousal lay across his belly, the condom he'd worn disposed of in a nearby wastebasket.

Lost to the image of the man lying next to me, he startled me when he reached out to pull me close. He smiled and kissed my temple, wrapping his arm around me as I snuggled into his side. Without thinking, the pads of my fingers danced over his skin. When I came to a scar, I stopped, but only briefly before continuing on.

"Does it still hurt?"

"Sometimes when it rains, but other than that, not really."

I decided to continue to be inquisitive, hoping in his contented state that he wouldn't hold anything back. "I thought all big bad biker boys were inked up. So where's yours?" I continued to trace his skin, the circling rhythm comforting me enough I felt my eyelids grow heavy.

"First off," he said, grabbing my hand and placing it over his manhood, "I ain't no boy." He thrust his hips for effect and laughed when I playfully pulled back and smacked his arm. "Second, people usually get inked to tell a story. My wounds are my story." His words were poetic yet haunting. I couldn't even imagine what he'd experienced, the horrific ordeal he had to live through. But live he did, which proved Tripp was a fighter. If I hadn't realized it before, I did in that moment.

To lighten the mood, I decided on a lighter topic. "Where did you get your nickname from?"

"Well, if you must know," he says, licking his lips, "girls were always tripping over themselves to get my attention. Hence the name Tripp." He stopped talking and just stared at me, and it wasn't until he grinned that I realized he was just messing with me. Although I had no doubt that women did trip over themselves to gain his interest.

"Nice one." I laughed.

"Seriously, though, I was quite the clumsy fucker when I was younger. I was always trippin' over my own damn feet. Always fallin' and breakin' somethin'. My dad was the one who gave me the nickname." His eyes darkened for a brief moment, no doubt at the recollection of his father. Before I could inquire, however, his mood switched back to one of lightheartedness.

"Ready for round two?" He turned his head toward me and captured my lips. I was sore but definitely up for some more of what he was offering.

"I guess so," I answered, rolling my eyes on purpose as if his request was an inconvenience. He flipped me on my stomach and slapped my ass, but as soon as his hands parted my legs, his cell rang.

"Dammit!"

"Do you have to get it?"

"Yeah. Shit's not good right now, and it could be important."

Hopping off the bed, he snatched his phone from the end table and strode toward the hall, returning a minute later. He looked pissed while he quickly dressed, sitting on the edge of the bed to pull on his boots. "Look, I have to get goin', but I promise I'll be back as soon as possible."

"Can I ask what it is you have to do?"

"You can, but that doesn't mean I can tell you."

I shrank back on the bed, annoyed by his statement. I'd dealt with secretiveness before and it only led to bad things.

Seeing the look on my face, Tripp laced his fingers with mine and tried to make me feel better. "Listen, Reece, when it comes to the club I won't be able to tell you about a lot of stuff that goes on. I hope you can understand."

"I do," I lied. What else was I gonna say? Demand he tell me everything? We'd only slept together one time, and while I wanted nothing more than to claim Tripp as my man, the truth was we still didn't know each other all that well.

"You okay?" he asked, leaning over to give me a parting kiss.

"Yeah."

"You sure?" His questioning gaze comforted me.

I nodded that time, pressing my lips to his before he rose from the bed.

"I'll set the alarm before I go."

"Hurry back." I pouted, disappointed he had to leave so soon after we'd been together. He shot me his sexy grin and winked before disappearing from the room, the close of the front door signifying when he'd left the house.

Lying back against the headboard, I couldn't stop my heart from racing to keep up with the adrenaline and giddiness I felt. I knew we'd only just met, but whatever was happening between us was exciting. The sexual chemistry was off the charts, but more than my attraction toward him, I felt safe, which was something completely new for me.

For the next twenty minutes I lost myself to thoughts of the man who'd just left my bed, and what'd we'd be doing as soon as he returned. Then a sudden noise from downstairs drew my attention. At first I thought I heard something hit against the front door, but then I couldn't be sure. Sitting up in bed, I strained to listen for any signs that Tripp had returned. When all was silent, I laid back on the bed only to jump to my feet when the alarm shrieked through the air. Wrapping the sheet around me, I raced toward the top of the steps, the front door wide open below.

I didn't hear anything over the piercing sound. I should've locked myself in the bedroom, but instead I slowly descended the stairs and cautiously peered around the room. After shutting the door, I punched in the code and the alarm finally silenced. I checked out all of the rooms. No one else was in the house, but that realization didn't stop my heart from pounding against my chest so rapidly I feared having a heart attack right where I stood.

CHAPTER TWENTY-NINE

Tripp

WHEN I'D WALKED INTO THE clubhouse, Trigger, Ryder and Jagger were crowded around the door to Chambers, talking quietly while they glanced over at Marek every now and again, who was subsequently slumped over the bar. I knew exactly what'd they'd been discussing. The possible relation between Marek and Sully seemed like the only topic we talked about when together.

When Stone ripped out a chunk of Psych's hair and swiped his blood on a piece of cloth, he did so when Marek was in the middle of his break with reality. It wasn't until the next day that he revealed to his best friend and leader just what he had planned. At first Marek refused, but after a little coaxing he relented, realizing it was better to know either way than to continue to torture himself. He'd given Stone some of his hair as the final step.

"What the hell are we gonna do with him?" Jagger asked, pacing in front of us like he was the only one put out by the new state of our president. "He can't go on like this."

"We know," Ryder barked, glaring at the rest of us as if we were the cause of the new shit storm.

"Calm down. We don't need to deal with your pissy mood on top of everything else." Trigger gave Ryder a look before turning his attention to me. "Where are we with the results for that fuckin' test?"

"I don't know. Stone gave the stuff to Adelaide and asked her to put a rush on it. That was a week ago."

The tension brewing between the four of us was enough to push any one of us over the edge with anxiety, as if the energy we shared was tangible, feeding on our state of mind.

"What the fu . . . fuck are ya yellin' 'bout?" Marek slurred, slapping the top of the bar for emphasis, although with the way he wobbled on top of his seat, I was surprised he had enough energy to even raise his hand. I'd seen Marek fucked up before—actually quite a bit over the years—but never like this, and not for this long. While I completely understood his turmoil, I also knew it was in his and his wife's best interest to do something about it, and quick. Otherwise, I feared shit was gonna hit the fan, and irreversible damage was gonna be the result.

No one answered his outburst. In fact, we tried to give him his space, although what he'd been doing with that space had been destructive. From what Stone had told me, Marek and Sully had been fighting—or to be more accurate, Marek had been blowing up at his wife for no reason. None that Sully could understand, at least. He'd barely spent time at his house, only stopping in for a few minutes at a clip before coming back to the clubhouse, where he proceeded to get shit-faced.

"Trigger!" Marek yelled over his shoulder, almost falling on his ass from the simple movement. Once he righted himself, he shouted, "I need another fuckin' drink."

"Goddammit," Trigger growled. "I can't take much more of this." He continued to grumble to himself as he walked across the room and then behind the bar.

"And don't water it down," our prez ordered.

"I *should* water that shit down. Maybe then you'd sober up and take your ass home." Bold move on Trigger's part, but someone had to say something.

"Fuck you!" Marek shouted in response, rising off his stool and stumbling toward the back, no doubt heading to the bathroom to either piss or vomit.

As soon as he disappeared, the door opened and in strolled Stone.

At first I was happy to see the guy. Then Adelaide and Sully appeared right behind him.

"What the hell?" Ryder quickly walked over to him and pulled him aside. They huddled in the corner, our VP glancing over at his woman and Sully every few seconds. I knew their presence wasn't gonna go over well as soon as Marek came back from the bathroom, and I only prayed he'd passed out back there.

Approaching the two women, I gave them both a tight smile. "What are you doing here?" I knew Stone never told Adelaide exactly whose DNA was being tested, but she wasn't stupid. And while I believed she'd never guess what was really going on, she had to know something was off. Stone's moody ass had only intensified.

In truth, all of us had been on edge since that fateful day when Psych spewed his final admission. Or lie. The truth was yet to be determined.

Jerking her head to the side, Adelaide had me follow her until we stood away from Sully. Once her friend was out of earshot, Adelaide started talking. "Sully called me this morning crying because she's worried about Marek. He won't talk to her, snaps at her for the smallest things, and he hasn't spent the night at home in a week." She looked at me expectantly, as if I was gonna tell her something her own man wouldn't. "I don't know what the hell is going on, Tripp, but this is bullshit. She's been through enough. She doesn't deserve this, and if you know what's goin' on you need to tell her."

"You know I can't do that." My shoulders slumped forward. I wished I could put their minds at ease, but it simply wasn't my place. Marek had to handle this on his own, and although I didn't agree with the course he'd taken, it was essentially his call.

"Why?" Her voice rose. "Is it some kind of man code? Is he cheating on her?" she finally asked, lowering her voice to ensure Sully didn't hear. The whole time we'd been standing off to the side talking, Jagger had been keeping Sully occupied, giving her a quick hug when she started to cry.

"No, it's nothin' like that. That much I can tell you," I told her honestly.

"Then what is it?"

I opened my mouth to tell her she wasn't gonna get anything out of me when I heard a crash come from down the hallway. The noise grabbed everyone's attention, and I held my breath for what was to come. I knew damn well Marek wouldn't be happy when he saw Sully, which was awful. If anything he should've been seeking comfort in her arms, but he turned the other way, hurting her in the process.

The whole situation was beyond fucked-up, and the longer he had to wait to find out if his wife was actually his fuckin' sister, the more he unraveled.

The second Marek appeared all conversations ceased. Everyone turned toward him and waited to see his reaction. At first he didn't see his wife; it was apparent in the way he ambled back toward the bar, stumbling over his feet and almost falling on his face. Twice. He was a sad sight and when I glanced over at Sully, the tears flowed more freely than before.

Adelaide had left my side to console her friend, and it was when a sob erupted from Sully that Marek finally turned around, noticing her for the first time. A mix of anger and torture distorted his expression at the very sight of her. As if his heart was being ripped out all over again. I walked the few feet and stood next to the women and Jagger, Ryder, and Stone approaching our group as soon as they saw Marek's reaction.

None of us knew what he was capable of at that point. Would he ignore his wife or rant and rave until he forced her to leave? He'd never lay his hands on her, that much we knew, but what words would come out of his drunken mouth was anyone's guess.

It seemed as if time stood still as Marek and Sully locked eyes with one another, the tension in the air building until Marek finally spoke.

CHAPTER THIRTY

Tripp

"WHAT THE FU . . . fuck is sh . . . she doin' here?" he slurred, walking as swiftly toward us as he could in his inebriated state. His eyes were bloodshot and his hair disheveled. He reeked of alcohol and his clothes were a little worse for wear. All in all, he looked like shit.

The closer he came the more we huddled around Sully, preparing to deter him from whatever he planned on doing.

When he stood a few feet from his wife, he wobbled and tried to reach for her, but Jagger stepped directly in front of her. His move of protectiveness only served to infuriate Marek, the look of astonishment on his face quickly giving way to boiling anger.

"Move!" Marek shouted, continuing to sway on his feet.

"Not gonna happen, Prez," Jagger said, crossing his arms over his chest but looking a little apprehensive. "Why don't you go sleep it off?"

Stone stepped in and stood directly in front of his friend. "Yeah," he agreed. "Why don't you go sleep it off? You can talk to her later."

"I don't wanna talk to her," he growled, clenching his fists until his knuckles turned white.

"Why?" Sully suddenly shouted, shoving past Jagger so she could look at her husband. "What did I do? Why won't you tell me?" Her voice trembled, tears cascading down her cheeks while she waited for him to answer. "I love you, Cole. Why are you treating me like this?" She stepped closer—too close, in my opinion. Emotions ran high and I feared the worst.

Before anyone could stop him, Marek grabbed Sully's arms and drew her in, their noses almost touching they were so close. "I. Don't. Want you here," he enunciated. "Go home." He shoved her back, but not hard enough to cause her to stumble. He took a step back, glaring at her the entire time.

I understood why Marek didn't want to fill Sully in on exactly what was goin' on, not until he absolutely had to, but there was no reason for him to be treating her like this. It was uncalled for, and certainly unnecessary. Then again, he wasn't in his right mind. Hadn't been for a while now.

As if shit weren't already spinning out of control, Adelaide stalked toward Marek, Stone trying to pull her back before she reached him. "I don't know what's going on, but you're a real shit for treating your wife like this. A real shit," she repeated, hitting his chest for emphasis. "You better get your act together, and soon, before you lose the only good thing that's ever happened to you." They stood toe-to-toe, Adelaide throwing Marek icy daggers and Marek swaying from side to side, trying to keep his balance.

"Stone, get your fuckin' woman outta my face or else," Marek threatened, continuing to clench his hands at his sides. The sight disturbed me. The guy I knew would never raise a hand to a woman, yet there he was essentially threatening Adelaide. Would he really do something? I had no idea, and that realization rattled me.

The icy expression that crossed Stone's face alarmed everyone present. "Don't you fuckin' talk to her like that. You hear me?" he asked, stepping in his best friend's face. His drunken, out-of-his-mind, heartbroken, and confused best friend. I would've bet Marek's mental state, drunk or not, was the only reason Stone didn't physically attack him.

As the two men squared off, we all backed up to give them some room to sort out their issue, if that was at all possible right then. After an intense stare-down, Marek still wobbly on his feet, Stone leaned in and whispered something in his ear. Resting his hand on Marek's shoulder, Stone continued to speak, but only on a level our prez could hear. A minute later I saw some of the tension evaporate from Marek, although he still appeared to teeter on the edge. Shaking his head, he stumbled back before turning around and heading toward the hallway to no doubt escape everything and everyone.

Sully continued to cry, resting her head against Jagger's chest while she expelled everything she'd been feeling.

"Stay with her," Stone told Jagger, grabbing Adelaide's hand and tugging her behind him into Chambers. He motioned for the rest of us to follow with a jerk of his head. Normally, women weren't allowed inside Chambers but this was one of the rare exceptions, the last time being when Sully had forced her way inside to demand that Marek trade her for Adelaide and Kena after her father had orchestrated their kidnapping.

I had an idea what Stone wanted to ask his woman, and the seclusion of the room would certainly provide the privacy we needed. The tension coming off the VP built and built until he looked like he was gonna explode. Pacing in front of all of us, he ran his hand through his hair before clenching his fists at his sides, much like Marek had done moments before.

"Why haven't we heard anything back about those results?" he asked to no one in particular, although there was only one person present who could give an honest answer.

Ryder and Trigger mirrored Stone, pacing and glancing over at Adelaide every few seconds. I'd chosen to lean against the wall, content to just listen to whatever was about to unfold. Someone had to be the semi-calm one.

"Like I told you yesterday when I called them, the lab is backed up. There's nothing I can do about that," she said. "Why is that DNA so important, anyway?" There was a small part of me that thought maybe Stone had told Adelaide everything, but thankfully I'd just been proven wrong.

Stone ignored her question, instead edging closer until he towered over her. "You didn't call today?"

"Not yet, no."

"Are you fuckin' kiddin' me right now, Addy? I told you how important those results are. That I needed them back right away," he bellowed, the veins in his neck bulging the more he continued to speak. Or rather yell. Stone started pacing again, mumbling incoherently to himself.

"What the hell is wrong with you?" She looked to each of us standing in the room, her nervousness displayed on her face. "Whose DNA is it?"

"None of your business," Stone yelled over his shoulder. I'd seen those two shout at each other before but this was on another level, and Adelaide knew it. Before she could respond, however, Stone gripped the back of his neck in frustration and headed toward his woman again, backing her against the door before she could react. He loomed over her once more, intimidating her with his size and aggression. "Get your fuckin' ass on that phone and get the goddamn results, Addy. Now!" He slapped the doorframe above her head for added effect.

My eyes popped wide as I looked around at everyone in the room. To say we were surprised Stone had yelled at his woman like that was an understatement. Sure, our VP was hotheaded and went overboard sometimes, but I'd never heard him speak to Adelaide in such a way.

Sure enough, in true Adelaide fashion, she didn't let him get away with it. I saw what was gonna happen before Stone did, her hand cracking across his face before he took his next breath. The sound shook the room and everyone gasped, me included—an odd reaction coming from three grown men, but it was the truth. We'd all been through the mental wringer for what seemed like forever with no end in sight, and right then was the culmination to the ever-growing tension.

Stone backed away, the look on his face softening as if she had indeed just slapped some sense back into him. "Baby, I'm sorry," he apologized, reaching out to touch her, but she shrugged away from him.

"Don't even think about touching me," she fumed. Stone had a condition where he was immune to physical pain, but right then I could see that he was hurtin'. Not from the slap, of course, but because he knew he'd crossed the line, and it'd take quite a while for him to grovel enough for Adelaide to forgive him. She never put up with his shit, pushing back as often as Stone tested her.

Shoving him, the adrenaline pulsing through her surely enough for her to move him, or he allowed her to do so, she continued to speak. "There's obviously something detrimental going on here to have Marek treating Sully like shit, and for you to have lost your damn mind and yelled at me like that." Adelaide was the one to advance on Stone that time, looking up at him and throwing him a stern glare. "You better get your head out of your ass, Stone, and until that happens you can stay here. I don't want you at home."

Again Stone tried to draw her into him but she dodged his touch. Looking every bit the apologetic man, he raised his hands in submission. "I'm sorry. I was outta line. It's just . . . there's so much goin' on and—"

"I don't care what's goin' on here. That's no excuse for you to talk to me like that." Anger and hurt shrouded her expression.

"I know. I'm sorry, baby," he repeated.

Adelaide continued to glare at him, even when he attempted to grab her hand, which he failed at yet again.

"Don't," was all she said before she threw the door open and hurried from the room, Stone hot on her heels. I could hear him apologizing over and over, but it was no use. Adelaide was as stubborn as Stone, and I knew—we all did—that his sullen ass would be staying here at the clubhouse for at least the next few days.

As if whatever had just transpired in the past hour hadn't been enough, I noticed two missed calls from the alarm company when I pulled my phone from my pocket.

CHAPTER THIRTY-ONE

Tripp

RUSHING INSIDE THE HOUSE, I shoved past the officer standing in front of Reece and pulled her close. "Are you okay? What happened?" I looked between the both of them, impatiently waiting for one of them to answer me.

"I'm fine." She tried to pull away but I wouldn't let her.

"Do you live here?" the officer asked, flashing me a stern look before glancing back toward Reece. The guy was young, a rookie maybe?

"Yeah," I lied, deeming him unworthy of a full explanation. "What happened?" I repeated.

"Apparently the front door was opened, setting off the alarm." Nothing further from him before he jotted something down in a notepad.

"How the hell did that happen?" I finally let go of Reece and neared the doorframe, searching for any sign of foul play but not readily finding any. "Did you check the house?" I wasn't sure who I directed that specific question to.

"Yes," they both answered, Reece dipping her head for a moment before looking back at me. I had a suspicion she was hiding something from me.

"And?"

Reece spoke first that time. "I checked the house after the alarm went off, and thankfully didn't find anyone. Officer Bauer did another check when he arrived. Just in case." She gave the cop a thankful smile, and I didn't like it. I saw the way he kept checking her out, right in fuckin' front of me. Brazen little shit.

Needing him to leave, I threw my arm around her shoulder and leaned down to kiss her. "Well, it looks like maybe a faulty door. I'll have it checked out. No need for you to stay here." My tone left no room for misunderstanding. Or argument.

He gave me a final once-over before smiling at Reece. "Miss." He nodded before leaving, still writing something down on that damn notebook of his.

After I'd shut the door, I asked, "Are you sure you're okay?"

"Yeah. Just a bit frightened. But that alarm probably scared me more than anything." Putting her finger in her ear and wriggling, she said, "It's really loud."

"That's the point. A deterrent." I took some time before blurting out my next statement, figuring it was as good a time as any to let her in on my plans. Plans that had formed on my way over. "You're gonna stay with me at my place."

I expected some sort of argument, some sort of refusal, but she had none. A simple nod from her and I'd been put right back on edge when I should have been relieved.

She was definitely hiding something from me.

CHAPTER THIRTY-TWO

Reece

DESPITE THE FRIGHT I'D ENDURED two days back, I never imagined my life could turn out normal. Well, as normal as it was working in a strip club and being involved with a biker. I was smart enough not to put too many hopes and dreams on a new relationship, if that was even what this was, but I couldn't help but picture myself with Tripp for the long haul.

His incessant need to make sure I was safe was sweet. Something I certainly wasn't used to. He'd increased security even more at the club after the mysterious issue with the front door. Not sure why, seeing as how it had happened at the house and not at Indulge, but I couldn't help but feel a sense of relief either way.

What I failed to tell Trip was that I'd been a little more than freaked out, and while I tried not to show my vast relief at his suggestion to stay with him at his house, a calm had descended over me when he uttered the words.

"You wanna go dancing after work?" Carla asked, giving me a quick smile while she poured a beer for a customer. "I know a place that's open late."

She busied herself wiping off the counter and taking orders while I contemplated her offer. After the hang-up I'd been worried. Then when the door at the house had been mysteriously opened, thankfully setting off the alarm, I'd been rattled to my core. For as much as I wanted to relieve some of my anxiety about both incidents, I knew I shouldn't go anywhere Tripp wasn't able to accompany me, and I highly doubted he was the dancing kind.

"I don't think I should," I finally answered.

"Oh come on," she prodded.

I gave her my most apologetic smile. "Maybe another time."

"Does this have anything to do with Tripp? Is he keeping you under lock and key?" Her question wasn't meant to be a serious one, but when she saw the fleeting widening of my eyes, she changed her tune. "Are you serious, Reece? Did he tell you that you can't go anywhere without him? I've noticed how the two of you have been attached at the hip recently. The man is relentless, and while I think Tripp is a good guy, don't let him push you around. You do what you want, when you want. Do you hear me?" Her hands found their way to her hips, her brow arched in wait.

"It's not like that." She looked at me skeptically. "Honestly. He just wants to keep me safe." Carla had no idea what I'd been through in the past. If she did then she'd fully understand my need to relent to Tripp's slightly overbearing tendencies.

"Fine, but if I think he's being too possessive over you, I'm gonna say something to him."

I had no doubt she would. Carla had come to be a good friend over the short time I'd known her, so I didn't take any offense to her threatening to stick her nose further into my business. Besides, I thought it just might be worth watching that interaction between the two of them. For amusement purposes.

The next few hours passed relatively quickly. The crowd grew in size, and thankfully everyone seemed to be on their best behavior. Surely the overly large bouncers spread throughout the club didn't have anything to do with it. Coming back from the ladies' room, Carla caught me before I walked back behind the bar.

"Hey, there's a guy over there asking for you."

Craning my neck around her and the few men blocking the view to the other end of the bar, I didn't see anyone I knew.

"Is he a customer?"

"I don't think so."

Again I tried to see anyone who might look familiar, my heart racing inside my chest all of a sudden. "What does he look like?"

"Cute. Tall. Slim build. Blond hair. Oh, and he has a small scar on his chin." Carla nodded toward one of the dancers needing her assistance before leaving me to stand there all alone, my fear taking hold and wrapping its horrid arms around me so tightly I suddenly found it hard to breathe. My eyes bounced all over the club and still I didn't see him.

Not until one of the drunken patrons hopped off his stool and staggered toward the stage.

A terror I was unfortunately all too familiar with ripped me apart from the inside, threatening to destroy my very existence. My sudden panic stole my remaining breath as soon as my eyes connected with his. A wry, lecherous smile spread across his face before he shoved away from the bar. Each step he took toward me warned me to run, but I couldn't. My body froze, locking me in place. My heart rammed against my ribs as fearful tears stung my eyes.

A cold sweat broke out over my skin when he'd finally reached me, his fingers curling around my small wrist and tightening. He saw fear in my eyes, a reaction he'd come to love from me.

"What's wrong, sweetheart?" I didn't answer. I couldn't. My brain fired off a plethora of words, but my lips refused to give them sound. "You didn't honestly think I'd let you leave me? That I wouldn't find you?" He sucked on his teeth while he shook his head, an indication that harm was about to find me. But surely he wouldn't do anything in public. Right?

Breaking eye contact, I glanced around the club in a panic, desperate to find one of the security men Tripp had hired. I saw a couple of them, but they were busy keeping the customers in line. I screamed in my head for one of them to look over at me but it was useless. They obviously couldn't hear me as they weren't mind readers. Next I searched for Carla, but she was busy serving drinks.

When my eyes found his again I flinched. His cold stare froze me.

The way he looked me up and down, wearing a disgusted expression as he did so, told me his rage was building.

"What the fuck are you doin' here, anyway? And dressed like some kind of street whore?" His hold on my wrist intensified, making me wince from the pain.

"Please let me go," I pleaded. "Please."

All of a sudden we were nose to nose. "Don't you think you deserve to be punished for running away?" My only reaction was to shake my head. He disagreed with my silent response. "I think you do." His eyes darkened as his other hand seized my upper arm, turning me around and shoving me in front of him toward the hallway. I tried to look over my shoulder to see if anyone had noticed the man gripping me up, but the club was packed. As he pushed his way through the crowd, I knew there was no hope of being rescued.

CHAPTER THIRTY-THREE

Reece

DREAD FILLED MY VEINS AS he shoved me into one of the empty private rooms. In that moment I would have preferred that bastard who'd attacked me the night Tripp saved me over the soulless man standing in front of me right then.

The way his cold stare devoured me made me feel weak and pathetic. Gone was any ounce of strength I'd gained since fleeing from him all those weeks prior, only to be reduced to the sniveling, pleading shell of a woman pushing short pants of air from my lungs.

"Rick . . . please don't do this," I begged, raising my hands in front of me as if my feeble attempt to ward him off wasn't laughable.

"Don't do what?" He cocked his head. "Make you see the error of your ways for taking off? For forcing me to hire someone to track you clear across the fucking country?"

I'd been so careful, disposing of the single credit card I had and only paying with cash. I thought I'd fled far enough, leaving him back in Maine, but his daunting presence just reiterated how much of a fool I'd been to think I could ever escape him.

With each word he spoke his voice became louder, raising the hairs at the nape of my neck. I knew what would happen once he ran out of rhetorical questions.

Threats.

Pain.

Bruises.

"Fuckin' answer me," he roared, spittle hitting my face as he backed me against the wall. "Did you really think I'd let you go?" Running his fingertip down my arm, he sneered at me before puncturing my skin with his nails. Blood trickled down my arm and I flinched in pain, praying this was the worst he'd subject me to. But I should have known better. "I swear to Christ if you don't answer me, you're gonna regret it." The lower half of his body pinned me to the wall behind me.

"No," I meekly whispered.

Placing his fingers at his ear he said, "Sorry. What was that?"

"No," I repeated, choking on my fear.

"Then why did you leave?" His voice was low and deep. Menacing. I wasn't sure which I preferred, him shouting or the calm tone he chose to use right then. Both warned me of what was to come.

He slammed his palm against the wall by the side of my head, his breaths coming out harsh and quick. "Why do you make me do this, baby? Why do you keep testin' me? You know once I'm angry I can't control myself." I saw the devil in his eyes when his fingers wrapped around my throat. Images of Tripp flashed before me, and my heart ached at the thought that I'd never see him again. That pain was worse than anything Rick could ever inflict on me.

The tighter he squeezed the closer the darkness crept, bursts of light behind my lids warning me I was going to dive into unconsciousness very shortly. Just as my vision tunneled, someone banged on the door.

We hadn't been in the room but for five minutes, although it felt like a lifetime. More banging, followed by a man yelling. "Reece," he shouted. "Open the door." More pounding against the locked door. Surprisingly Rick released me, and as soon as I drew in air I started coughing, rubbing at the tender affected area around my throat. Rick reached for the handle, flipping the lock before swinging open the door. I was too busy trying to breathe to bother to see who had thankfully interrupted us.

"What the fuck do you want?" Rick growled, shrouding the doorway so I couldn't see who it was. Not until Mike, one of the bouncers I'd tried to signal earlier with my silent plea, shoved past him and approached me.

"Reece, are you okay?" He reached out to touch me but I shrank toward the wall, confused as to what was happening. My wits hadn't fully returned yet, my body still in preservation mode, trying to take in as much air as my lungs would allow.

"She's fine. Now get the fuck outta here," Rick yelled, stepping in front of Mike, his back facing me.

Before Mike could forcefully remove Rick, Tripp appeared in the doorway, his eyes instantly finding me. He seemed frozen in place, taking in the entire scene in front of him, but it only lasted for a few seconds before he rushed inside and shoved both Rick and Mike away from me.

"What the hell is goin' on here?" he asked, never taking his eyes off me. The vein in his neck bulged and I knew he was doing his best to control himself, his gaze pleading with me to fill him in on why I was in one of the private rooms with a man he didn't know and one of the club's security men.

Tripp's eyes trailed over my face before falling to my throat. I hadn't even realized my fingers were still rubbing at the area. When he gently removed my hand I swore I saw his eyes turn red with rage. "Who did this to you?"

"Don't touch her!" Rick shouted, sidestepping Mike and shoving at Tripp's shoulder. Rick was a tall guy, lean but certainly strong, although he was no match for the likes of Tripp—and he was about to find that out very soon.

Spinning around, Tripp lunged toward Rick and pounced on him, both men falling to the ground with a heavy thud. "You dare put your hands on her?" Tripp roared, his fist connecting with the side of Rick's face. I didn't feel sorry for the beating Rick was about to endure, but the last thing I wanted was for Tripp to be dragged into my mess.

"Tripp!" I shouted. "Stop. Please." I took a step forward, but Mike moved in front of me.

"Not a good idea," he warned, flicking his eyes back to the two men on the ground. Tripp was on top of Rick, expelling his rage onto the man who'd terrorized me for years.

A garbled sound erupted from the bastard's mouth but was quickly silenced by another hit from Tripp. In a blur of movement to my left, Hawke and Ryder rushed into the room and ran toward Tripp, attempting to pull him off Rick. After the third try they were finally successful.

Tripp stumbled backward until he righted himself, but as soon as Rick tried to speak Tripp attempted to go after him again.

"What the fuck?" his brother shouted.

Leaving the scuffle, Ryder asked me, "Are you okay?"

"Yeah, I'm fine," I lied. I was anything but fine, but the last thing Tripp needed to see was just how scared and upset I was. It would only add to his fury.

Once Rick had finally risen to his feet, he stupidly tried to approach me. His eye was already starting to swell, his nose and mouth all bloody, but that didn't stop him from boldly trying to shove past the man who'd just beaten him and try to get at me. It showed how crazy he was when it came to me.

"Don't you fuckin' touch her," Tripp growled, his voice dipping low with unbridled rage.

"Don't *you* fuckin' touch her," Rick retorted, wiping the blood from his face and then running his palms down the front of his jeans.

"Are you insane?"

Little did Tripp know the answer to that question was a resounding yes.

With a crazy look in his eyes, Rick stood rigid, glared at Tripp, and then uttered the words I'd feared as soon as I saw Tripp enter the room. "Get away from my wife."

CHAPTER THIRTY-FOUR

Tripp

I MUST HAVE HEARD HIM *wrong.*
Did he just say that Reece was his wife?
She's married?

Whipping my head in her direction, my feet quickly followed until I loomed over her. Her head was lowered, her eyes either closed or staring at the goddamn ground. I couldn't tell, but either way she was gonna look at me and tell me what the hell was goin' on. No way she was married, and to that fuckwit to boot. My brain refused to believe it. Plain and simple.

"Reece," I bit out, anger, adrenaline and confusion battling for first place. "Tell me what's goin' on," I demanded, the bite in my tone obvious. Still no movement from her, except for the shudder of her shoulders. Trying a softer approach, I lifted her chin with my finger until she finally looked me in the eyes. Hers were filled with unshed tears, but as soon as she saw the look on my face, an expression I wasn't sure was clear as I battled with pinging emotions, they fell down her cheeks.

"I'm so sorry," she said, grabbing my arm.

"Tell me it's not true," I pleaded, brushing off her hold before finally backing up. She cried harder before looking toward the ground again. "Tell me, Reece. Tell me right now that it's not true," I repeated. "Tell me you're not really married."

"She is," the bastard behind me yelled.

Desperately needing privacy, I instructed Hawke and Ryder to take him to another room and wait for me. I refused to acknowledge that he was her husband, even though I knew in my heart it was true. And even though I was sure she had a good explanation, it didn't change the sting of betrayal that sliced me in half.

Reece and I didn't know each other that well, this was true, but the connection I'd found with her was unlike any other I'd ever experienced. I knew the feeling was reciprocated. I saw it in her eyes when she looked at me, felt it in her kiss when she demanded more from me. But to think that she was hiding such a huge secret made me question everything I'd been feeling for her.

Once we were alone, I paced in front of her, silence compounding the tension which now existed between us. Finally, after what felt like forever, a soft sound drifted through the air and caught my attention.

"Tripp, I'm so sorry," she whispered, the lilt of her voice softening my anger toward her and the entire situation. "I wanted to tell you . . . but I didn't know how. I just wanted to forget."

"Forget you were married?" I crushed the small distance between us and crowded her personal space once more, giving her no other option than to look me in the eye while she tried to explain. Trust me, the last thing I wanted to do right then was deal with this shit, but I knew it would only fester and drive me insane, making me even angrier if we didn't have the damn discussion.

"Yes." Because of her anguish, her eyes took on a deeper hue of blue than gray. "I've left Rick a few times, but he always finds me." I hated the sound of his name on her lips, but I did my best to rein in my simmering fury. She slowly raised her hand and traced the scar on the bridge of her nose. "He threatened to kill me if I ever left him again. He probably would've had Mike not interrupted him.

"Was he the one who broke your nose?" I already knew the answer, but I needed to hear it from her.

"Yes." She blew out a pent-up breath before quickly revealing what'd happened. "He'd come home drunk, like he often did, and accused me of cheating on him. Even though I wasn't, and never had. It was the first time he'd punched me." A few tears escaped and trailed down her cheeks. "Before, he would only grab me and slam me against the wall, or slap me across the face. But he never balled up his fist, not until that time."

The silence was deafening as I continued to try and process everything Reece had just told me. My emotions had me feeling like I was on a damn roller coaster, jolting me back and forth between sadness, anger, betrayal and, oddly enough, possessiveness.

"I knew I should've never let you leave my house," I mumbled more to myself than her. But she'd heard me loud and clear.

"There's no way you could've known. I didn't lie to you, per se, but I did omit certain things about my life."

"Which is the same as lyin', by the way. Just so you know." I couldn't help the anger in my tone, pushing to the forefront of my tangled emotions. "You definitely should have told me before we fucked."

My crassness startled her, and the look of regret on her face tore at me. A deep sadness shrouded her eyes. It'd been there the first time I saw her, but I'd dismissed it to the lifestyle she'd chosen. Apparently it hadn't been from her choice of profession but from years of being beaten down so much she never thought she was worth anything. While I was still very upset with her for not confiding in me, I knew I had to protect her from her husband.

Fuck! I hated even thinking that word, but there it was.

Reece was married.

But that wouldn't stop me from claiming her.

CHAPTER THIRTY-FIVE

Tripp

AS IF I DIDN'T HAVE enough shit to deal with, now I had to take care of the issue with the shitbag who'd made Reece's life a living hell. Even though she'd only divulged a small amount of their life together, I knew there was much more to that damn story.

The last thing I wanted to do was leave her alone, so I instructed Mike to stay with Reece until I returned, knowing damn well she was still scared after what happened.

Striding toward the room where Rick was being held, I took a deep breath before turning the handle, knowing I had to control myself so as not to kill him right then and there. Don't get me wrong; I had no problem snatching his life, but taking such a rash step wasn't smart. If it came down to whether or not he had to die, I wanted to make sure everything was set in place before he drew his last miserable breath. Killing was never something I aspired to do, but I knew it was necessary sometimes.

Rick was slumped over on the small couch set against the far wall. Drawing my brows close together, I stared at Ryder with a questioning look, since he was the one closest to him.

"What?" Ryder asked, shrugging. "I saw Reece's neck. Just thought I'd make him see the error of his ways." The slow smirk on his face would have been comical had I not been so torn up inside over the whole situation.

Nodding, I approached. I slapped the side of Rick's head, a groan escaping him before lifting his head up. His eyes rose to mine briefly before closing. He was coherent enough to hear what I had to say. "You are never to come near Reece again. Do you hear me?" No response from him except an incoherent grunt. "I know you understand what I'm telling you, but let me break it down for you, just in case. If I so much as see you anywhere in the same vicinity as her, I'll kill you. Slowly. If you don't believe me then just test me, although it'll be the last thing you ever do." I stood to my full height. "Reece is mine now. Forget you ever knew her."

Jerking my head toward Ryder and Hawke, I instructed, "Break his legs."

"Both?" Ryder asked.

"I said *legs*, didn't I?"

"Okay, just making sure." I would have done it myself but I needed to get back to Reece. Ryder grinned while stepping toward Rick. My brother closed in on his other side and the two of them dragged the no-good piece of shit from the room and out the back door of the club.

Even if he tried to come after Reece again, it wouldn't be for quite some time.

CHAPTER THIRTY-SIX

Reece

I COULDN'T EXPLAIN MY EMOTIONAL roller coaster where Tripp was concerned. I'd been through the entire gamut since I'd met him, starting with fascination when I first saw him standing at the edge of the stage during one of my routines, to undying thankfulness when he'd rescued me from that bastard in the back room, to anger when he'd fired me, to sexual unease—of the good kind—when he looked at me like he wanted to devour me, to guilt for not telling him I was married. Then back to untold gratitude when he saved me yet again.

I'd never felt so alive before, yet I feared whatever was developing between us would fizzle out and die. Nothing good ever lasted in my life, and while I'd come to accept that, I could honestly say I was teetering on the edge, waiting for the other shoe to drop, so to speak. And it almost did when Tripp found out I was married. I really thought my betrayal would have driven him away, but he'd proven again that he was a good man.

We talked for hours and, justifiably, he went back and forth. One second he understood my need to withhold the truth about Rick, and the next he'd tell me it was wrong of me not to share that kind of information. We eventually agreed to move on and put the incident behind us. Easier said than done, of course, but at least we both made the attempt.

Before I could dismiss the topic of Rick altogether, though, I needed to know what had happened to him. Tripp didn't want to tell me at first, but thankfully he realized I had a right to know. Initially, all he would reveal was that Rick had been taken care of, and my heart skipped a beat. At first I assumed he meant that Rick had been killed, a thought which made me both uneasy yet relieved. I pressed further, practically begging him to tell me exactly what happened. I'd held my breath in case he told me that my first assumption had been correct. It turned out that Tripp had spared Rick's life, although he'd had him incapacitated by breaking both his legs. He also told me that he warned Rick that if he ever came near me again he'd kill him. I believed that he'd actually follow through if given another opportunity.

While there were so many things I had yet to learn about Tripp, what I did know told me he was a good man, present debacle included. Not the 'put your best foot forward until you finally show your true colors' type of man, but a genuinely good-hearted, 'do right by you' type of man.

While I hated that my brain conjured up images of Tripp and Rick together, I couldn't help but compare the two. Tripp had a good heart while Rick did not. Of course, Rick had been nice in the beginning, and me being so young I simply didn't have the experience to spot a wolf in sheep's clothing.

He'd come into the restaurant I worked at after school and sat at the counter, making small talk for two hours. I thought he was handsome with his shoulder-length sandy blond hair and green eyes, eyes which were deceptively perilous, although I didn't know it at the time. A handsome stranger paid attention to me, and I ate it up.

Rick showed up every time I worked, and once when I joked that he'd been stalking me, he simply shrugged and gave me a mischievous yet what I thought was an endearing smile. Looking back I should have seen the signs, but like I said, I was young and inexperienced.

When Rick found his opportunity he pounced. And I say pounced because he was most certainly a predator. We soon began dating and when the accident happened, the only person I had to turn to was Rick. He had become my only family, readily taking me in and letting me live with him. He dug his clutches in deeper after we'd been together about six months. I'd finally decided I was ready to have sex, and soon afterward the sides he'd kept hidden started to emerge. Becoming enraged when I talked to another guy, even when they were customers at the restaurant, he'd accuse me of cheating. I'd vehemently deny it, of course, because it wasn't true.

After I graduated from high school we were married. I'd convinced myself that once I became his wife he'd no longer have a need to be jealous. How wrong I'd been.

I had big plans of going to college, but Rick only became more suffocating, refusing to allow me to go anywhere without him. I had to quit my job, solely relying on him for everything. About a year into the marriage, he started drinking more, and that's when the real abuse started. At first he shook me when he yelled at me. Then he graduated to slapping me across the face until he eventually elevated to punching and kicking me. Since I didn't have a job, or go to school, or socialize with friends, and had no family to speak of, I had plenty of time to heal after one of his beatings. No one to witness the abuse.

The first time I tried to leave him was when one of his beatings had caused me to miscarry our child. I was twelve weeks along and although I was only twenty, I desperately wanted the baby. In some warped way I thought if we had a child that he would change, but in fact my pregnancy only heightened his paranoia and abuse, claiming he wasn't the father and that I'd been messing around on him. Looking back, having miscarried my child had been a blessing in disguise. I had no right bringing another person into that kind of world.

Over the course of our relationship, I left him a total of four times, this last time being the fourth. He'd made good on his promises and had found me each and every time. Only this time, I hoped and prayed Rick would heed Tripp's warnings and stay away from me for good.

Against Tripp's advice, I returned to work the following night, reminding him that there was no way Rick would be bothering me anytime soon—his words. I repeated them to him to drive home that I was safe. True, there was a part of me that believed Rick would saunter right back inside Indulge and hurt me, even kill me, but then I remembered that he couldn't walk.

"MOVE," ARIANNA DEMANDED, SHOVING PAST me without giving me the opportunity to shuffle to the side to allow her to pass. Her mood toward me had shifted from mere annoyance to downright hatred, or something very close to it. I knew the reason why, but I never played into her sourness by engaging her.

Coming back from the restroom she bumped into me again, that time pushing me against the wall. "What the hell is wrong with you?!" I shouted, pissed off that she wouldn't give me a break. Whatever her issue was with me was all on her. I did nothing wrong and I wasn't going to let her give me shit any longer. I had enough on my plate at the moment as it was.

She stopped and spun around, advancing on me until she stood so close I could smell cheap men's cologne all over her. "My problem," she sneered, "is that you waltz in here and think you're the best thing that's ever graced that stage."

"I don't work the stage anymore, or did you forget?" Not working the pole any longer was just one of the things she hated about me, Tripp's interest in me being the main reason, of course. At every available opportunity Arianna would sneak up next to him and press her fake tits against him, pawing at him and offering herself. She wasn't subtle about it, making sure to remind me that they'd been together every chance she had. He assured me that he wasn't interested in her, and that the times they did hook up he was drunk, and that he never wished to repeat that mistake ever again. Even with his admissions, though, I couldn't help the jealousy that captured me whenever she touched him.

"You're stupid if you think he'll keep you around for much longer. Tripp loves variety, always coming back to me in between his new interests." She'd completely switched topics, focusing on the one that was the real reason why she'd decided to harass me that evening.

"What does that say about you, then?" I asked, scoffing when she looked confused. "If that was true, which it's not and we both know it, he'd just be using you until he found someone better. You're the idiot for waiting around for whatever scraps he'll throw your way."

If looks could kill I would have been dead already. I could tell by her expression that she didn't know what to say, but she was trying to think of something anyway. Several awkward seconds passed with us simply glaring at each other, until finally she mumbled, "Fuck you," and walked back toward the front of the club.

Rolling my eyes, I took a moment to compose myself before returning to the bar. Even though I tried not to let Arianna see me flustered, my insides were twisting and turning from the implication that Tripp would eventually go back to her.

As soon as I stepped behind the bar I saw Tripp, and low and behold Arianna was standing next to him, jabbering on about nonsense, I was sure. A fire lit my temper and, with barely controlled fury, I stalked to where they stood. He saw me approach, his eyes never leaving mine as I wrapped my arms around his neck and pulled him down for a sensual kiss. As soon as my tongue found his, he growled into my mouth and pulled me close, shoving Arianna away from him at the same time. I heard her gasp but I wasn't about to break our kiss to look at her. After I regrettably pulled back, Tripp had the biggest grin on his face.

"I think I know what that was for, but I don't care. You can stake your claim on me anytime your little heart desires." He gave me a quick peck on the lips before taking a seat.

"Since you've given me permission, you should be prepared for me to stake my claim over and over again." I'd meant to keep the tone light but I couldn't help it, even though I'd silently warned myself earlier not to go there. "You need to stop letting her hang all over you like that."

"I will. I promise." *Well, that was easy enough.* "You're the only woman I want hangin' on me. Pinned underneath me. Sittin' on top of me." He cocked his head to the side and appeared as if he were deep in thought. "What else?" he asked, tapping his chin with his index finger.

"Bending over in front of you," I offered, letting out a startled shriek when he grabbed me and pulled me on his lap.

"That's my girl." He laughed, nuzzling my neck before sucking on my earlobe.

I heard Carla laugh, not even realizing she was paying attention to us. I should have known better, though, as she had become protective over me, warning Tripp that if he ever hurt me he'd have to deal with her.

I'd decided to tell her everything pertaining to Rick, from my history with him up until what had just happened at the club. She was my one true friend, even though there were times when she was more like a mother figure.

CHAPTER THIRTY-SEVEN

Tripp

LOST TO MY OWN THOUGHTS about Reece and everything that'd just happened with that shitbag husband of hers, I nearly ran right into Stone when I walked into the common room at the clubhouse.

"We finally got 'em," he hurriedly announced, completely disregarding the fact that I'd almost knocked him over.

"The results?"

He nodded.

The last thing I wanted to deal with was this shit, but I knew it was of the utmost importance, the future of our club, and our president, basically hanging in the balance.

"Where's Marek?" I glanced around the room, trying to locate our downtrodden leader.

"He just went to piss."

"Is he drunk?"

"What do you think?"

Ryder waltzed out of the kitchen with a half-eaten sandwich in hand, stopping and looking at us standing together. "What?" he mumbled as he shoved the rest of the food in his mouth. Once he swallowed, he asked, "What's goin' on?"

"We got the results back," Stone offered, glancing down at his watch.

"Fuck," Ryder grumbled, looking between the two of us. "Wait, is that good news or bad?"

"Let's wait for everyone to get here first, and then we'll tell him together."

As soon as Stone stopped talking he looked uncomfortable, which immediately made me uneasy. I'd known Marek for years, and without sounding too much like a pussy, the first time I'd seen him really come alive was when he met Sully. Well, more like 'took.' Or 'saved' was more the honest truth. Over the time they'd been together, married for all of it because he'd initially forced her into it, I'd seen his eyes light up with life. Again, not wanting to sound all pussified and shit, but he'd changed.

While he'd become more on edge where his wife was concerned, constantly fretting about her safety knowing her father had still been out there, he smiled more. Okay, so I wouldn't go so far as to say he smiled, per se, but the corners of his mouth curved up more than ever before. And the way he looked at Sully, watched her when she wasn't looking, told me he'd fallen head over heels in love with her. Their beginning had certainly been the furthest from ideal, but they were meant to be together.

For all the happiness Sully brought into our president's life, she also brought him a ton of worry. Waiting for the other shoe to drop where her father was concerned, the constant fear she'd be taken from him, it all weighed heavy on him, showing in the deepened lines around his eyes. Then when he found out about what Rico Yanez had done to her, which unfortunately was the same thing Vex, her ex-man of sorts, and her father had done, he started to slowly unravel.

We'd all witnessed his slow descent into hell, his main focus not on club business but instead on making Vex, Yanez and Psych pay for what they'd made Sully endure, even though all that shit happened before Marek had even met her. It didn't matter, though, and I now understood his need for justice where she was concerned. I knew without a doubt that I'd snatch Rick's life if he ever came near Reece again.

To add something like this to the mix after everything Marek had been through, I feared he'd dive off the cliff of sanity and never resurface. I only prayed the results would be the ones he needed. The ones we all needed them to be if we wished to keep our president. Our leader. Our friend.

Ten minutes later the rumble of bikes sliced through the growing tension, my unease heightening with the thought that we were about to possibly deliver the worst news of Marek's life.

The door to the clubhouse swung open and in walked Trigger and Jagger. Thankfully no one else was with them. Marek had made us swear not to tell anyone else what was going on until he figured out what to do, which he never did. Instead, he chose to shut out his wife and drink himself half to death. The other guys had questioned the change in Marek, and we all chalked it up to his dealings with Psych. And by dealings, I meant Psych's torture and death. Cutter wasn't buying it, though, insisting Marek would have taken great pleasure in exacting revenge on the Savage Reapers' leader and not shut down afterward. Even though he was suspicious, he stopped trying to get any of us to talk after the third time we didn't give him anything.

"Hey," Jagger called out, coming to stand by my side, looking as reserved as the rest of us. Trigger mirrored our expression but remained silent, feeding off the palpable strain surrounding all of us.

We chatted amongst ourselves about the upcoming meeting when the man of the hour stumbled down the hallway and into the common room.

"What the fuck?" he growled, heading straight for us, albeit slowly so as not to fall on his face. "Is this a fu . . . fucking irrevention?" He looked haggard, but that was nothing new.

"No," Stone answered, striding the few feet until he stood directly in front of his best friend. "This ain't no intervention. We got the results." It took but a few seconds before understanding crossed Marek's face, and just when I thought he'd be relieved to finally find out whether or not Sully was actually his half-sister, he almost crumbled. Holding on to Stone's shoulder for support, Marek's eyes became glassy, unshed anguish pooling behind his blue orbs.

"I don't think I can do this," he garbled.

"You can, and you will," our VP gritted out. "Enough is enough. This shit's gotta stop. Today." Placing his hand on Marek's shoulder in return, he leaned in and whispered something in his ear, our president's face falling even more before he reluctantly nodded.

"Let's do this in Chambers," Trigger suggested. "Just in case some of the other guys show up."

All of us agreeing, we entered our sacred meeting place, shut the door and took our seats.

CHAPTER THIRTY-EIGHT

Tripp

"I SWEAR TO CHRIST, IF someone doesn't say somethin' soon I'm gonna lose it," Jagger blurted, pounding the table in frustration.

"Calm down," Trigger berated him, quickly glaring at him before turning his attention back to Marek, who was leaning back in his chair with his head tilted and looking up at the ceiling.

All concern was focused toward our leader, preparing for the results to be bad but hoping for the best. The envelope in Stone's hand was still sealed, indicating he himself didn't even know yet. We were all in limbo.

The tearing of the envelope made me shudder, but my reaction was nothing compared to Marek's. Forcing himself to his feet, he kicked his chair behind him with as much force as he could muster.

"I c-can't fuckin' do th-this," he stammered, the reality of his predicament sobering him slightly. "I can't," he mumbled before heading toward the door. Stone jumped up from the table and rushed forward, stopping Marek before he turned the handle.

Flinging the results toward me, our VP shouted, "Just open it."

My fingers trembled slightly as I pulled out the folded piece of paper. I scanned the document but had no idea what the hell I was looking at. There were multiple columns with a bunch of numbers.

"Well?" Stone shouted over his shoulder, pinning Marek against the wall to ensure he finally faced what he'd been running from ever since Psych fucked with his head.

Stone had given Adelaide Psych's DNA as well as Marek's, both in their own baggie. He feared if he labeled one 'Father' and the other 'Child,' she might've been a bit more suspicious, and that would've opened up a whole other can of worms. Instead, he just asked that they be tested to see if the two samples were related.

"I don't know what the hell I'm lookin' at," I grumbled, trying to read over the piece of paper once more. "Give me a sec." Starting from the top, I searched for anything that made a lick of sense to me. It wasn't until I reached the bottom, after all the bullshit columns, letters and numbers that I came to the fields I needed.

Probability of relation . . . 0%

I read it again just to be sure. Releasing a breath, one I hadn't even realized I held trapped in my lungs, I looked over to Stone and slowly shook my head, making sure to accompany the gesture with a grin.

"Oh, thank God," I heard Ryder say under his breath, understanding quickly spreading to Jagger and Trigger as well.

The rustle of Stone's cut bristled in the silence. I saw his grip on Marek's shoulders tighten. "She's not your sister, man." Marek raised his head. "Psych wasn't your ol' man, which means Sully is not related to you."

I thought Marek would've been elated, but instead he crumpled to the floor and the eeriest sob escaped. "Motherfucker. I can't . . . can't believe I push . . . pushed her away," he cried out, knocking his head against the wall a couple times. Stone sank to the floor beside him and threw his arm around his shoulder before looking to us and jerking his head toward the door. We understood right away, all of us disappearing from the room so they could have some privacy.

If anyone had any chance of consoling Marek, it was his best friend.

CHAPTER THIRTY-NINE

Reece

THE NEXT SEVERAL WEEKS PASSED way too quickly for my taste, but at least Tripp had remained in my life. Even after everything with Rick happened he stayed true to his word and stuck around, insisting I stay at his place with him.

"I want to talk to you about something," I said, tugging on the hem of my nightshirt as I walked toward the bed.

He swung his legs over the side and reached for his phone. Quickly checking a text, an annoyed expression passed over his face before he placed the device on the nightstand. "If this is about you paying for shit, I told you I don't want your money." He leaned back on his elbows, his nakedness completely distracting me. The way his muscles flexed with any simple movement entranced me. The man had the most amazing body, and I knew he was using it to sidetrack me. "My eyes are up here," he joked when he saw I'd been staring at . . . well, all of him.

"Very funny, but I'm serious."

"Then if you're so serious stop gawking at me like I'm a piece of meat." With one sudden movement, he hopped off the bed and picked me up off my feet, hooking my legs around his waist before I even realized what he was doing. "Or maybe some meat is exactly what you need right now."

"I told you we can't do that. Not for the next couple days." A mischievous grin appeared on his gorgeous face. "What?"

"There's always the back door." I gave him a blank stare. "You know . . . anal," he clarified, just in case I'd been confused on what 'back door' had meant, which I wasn't.

"Are you serious?"

His only response was to wriggle his brows.

I gripped the back of his hair and tugged. "If you think for one second I'm gonna let you stick that anaconda in my ass, you're crazy."

"Anaconda?" He laughed at my word choice, but that was exactly what his dick was.

No way. Not gonna happen.

"Fine. For now. We'll work up to it."

I attempted to object but he silenced me with his mouth, his tongue teasing my bottom lip before deepening the kiss. One hand gripped my backside, anchoring me to him, while the other held the back of my head, his fingers seizing my hair and positioning me exactly how he wanted. Tripp took control every time we'd been intimate, and this time was no different.

"Wanna wash up?" Already en route to the bathroom, his strong legs carried us toward the shower. Placing me on top of the vanity, he spun around and turned on the faucet, testing the water until it heated to the temperature he wanted.

While his back was to me, I removed my nightshirt. The only piece of clothing remaining was my black panties. When Tripp caught sight of me topless he groaned, reaching for his cock which already seemed painfully hard.

"What are you doing to me, woman?"

"What? We're gonna take a shower, aren't we? Well, I have to get naked before I get in, don't I?"

"Yeah, I guess." His eyes roamed my entire body, and when I hopped down from the counter and lowered my panties, he growled—literally growled, like some kind of hedonistic animal. It was extremely hot.

"Give me a minute and maybe I'll think about giving you some. As long as we're in the shower," I made sure to add. I acted like I was doing him some kind of favor, but in reality it was me who was going crazy over not being able to have sex with him. Tripp had become like some sort of drug. The way his touch ignited my skin. The way he looked at me, which made my body hum. The way his kiss made me wet. The way he moved his body when deep inside me like the most blissful, erotic escapade.

"Hurry up." He disappeared, but not before giving me one of his famous smirks.

I called for him to come back inside once I'd finished taking care of necessary business, stepping under the water while I waited for him to appear. A gust of air cooled my skin when Tripp opened the shower door. I soaked in the sight of him, taking my time raking my gaze over every inch of his body. When my eyes landed on his, he smiled. No smirk, no mischievous grin, just an honest-to-goodness happy, peaceful, enthralled smile.

Clicking the door shut, he backed me against the far wall, slowly reached for my hands and pulled them above my head. "Tell me you want me," he instructed, dipping his head and kissing my neck, licking and sucking until his lips nipped my earlobe. "Tell me how much you want me to fuck you." His warm breath triggered goose bumps across my skin.

"Yes," I panted, licking my lips and praying he'd kiss me again soon.

"Nope. Not what I wanna hear." His teeth snagged my lower lip, the quick shot of pain exciting me more than I thought possible. "I want you to tell me how badly you want my cock. Don't be shy either." His hold on my arms tightened while his lower half held me in place, the cool tiles warring with the heat of the spray.

I wasn't particularly skilled in the art of dirty talk, but if Tripp wanted to hear some filthy things then I'd try. But first I was gonna have some fun.

"I love your big penis," I moaned, holding back the smile threatening to give me away.

He pulled back, and the faux irritated look on his face was already making the corners of my lips twitch. "What the hell, Reece? 'Penis' is such an unsexy word. In fact, I can feel my *penis* deflating as we speak." He was lying, of course; his arousal was hard and thick, pressing against my belly. "Try again," he urged.

I kissed him quickly before pursing my lips as if in deep thought about what I should say. "I'd love for your cock. . . ." I paused for effect, to which his eyes lit up. " . . . to fill my vagina—" Tripp cut me off before I could continue with my 'sexy talk.'

"No *vagina* either."

I couldn't help it, the laugh I'd been holding bursting forth.

"I knew you were fuckin' with me." He chuckled, reaching down and lifting me up the wall. "Stop messin' around and tell me what I wanna hear or else."

I wrapped my legs around his waist and anchored myself to him. "Or else what?"

"Or else I'll spank that plump ass of yours," he threatened, the tilt of his mouth telling me he might just like to do that.

"You keep threatening to spank me. What if I want you to?" I teased, biting my lip while waiting for his reaction, which was immediate.

"Then I'd say that in a couple days when we can really play, I'll redden your ass, all while making you beg for me to fuck you hard."

I swore my temperature rose ten degrees, and it had nothing to do with the hot water raining down on me. "Well, until then. . . ." I took a deep breath, and leaned in to lick the shell of his earlobe before spouting, "I want your big, thick cock deep inside me." His muscles tensed. "I want you to fuck me like you've always wanted. Don't hold back."

"Fuck me," he growled before releasing my hands and unhooking my legs from around his waist. He didn't say another word, instead surprising me by spinning me around as soon as my feet hit the floor of the shower and pushing between my shoulder blades to bend me over.

"What are you doing?" I stupidly asked, knowing damn well what he had planned.

"I'm gonna take you from behind," he answered, his authoritative tone screaming for me to obey without reserve. "Brace yourself against the wall."

As my hands connected with the tile, he palmed my breasts,

teasing one and then the other until my nipples were painfully erect. "Spread your legs for me, baby. Good." The sounds of the water and our heady breathing were quite intoxicating. Anticipation licked at my insides, warmth flooding me with eagerness and hunger. As I opened my mouth to plead with him to give me what I needed, he aligned himself at my entrance and slowly pushed inside.

"Yes," was all I could manage to say as he worked himself in inch by inch. At that angle I took him deeper, his thickness hitting against the sensitive spot inside me. He grabbed my hips and dug his fingers into my skin, pushing in and then pulling back, his cock electrifying all my nerve endings as he thrust in and out of me.

"You feel amazing," he panted, his grip bordering on painful. "I can't get enough. I don't ever wanna stop," he confessed, driving me higher and higher toward a place I'd quickly become addicted to. His touch had awoken me, promising me a life I'd never dreamed possible before I'd met him.

I moaned his name over and over as the first wave of my orgasm crested, pushing back against him every time he drove himself deep. Tripp was still holding back. I could feel it in the way his fingers bruised me, his muscles tensing when he thought he pushed too hard.

"Let go, Tripp. Take me how you want," I begged, my muscles beginning to clench in pleasure.

"I'll hurt you," he said, continuing to drive me insane with his body. "I . . . I can't," he mumbled, the spray of the shower muffling his refusal.

"Oh God!" I cried out. "I'm gonna come." My lungs seized my breaths as I rushed toward ecstasy at top speed. "Oh . . . Tripp . . . please. Please let go and fuck me." I steadied myself when a string of expletives flew from his mouth. Within seconds his grip punished me while his body destroyed mine. His harsh thrusts swirled pain and pleasure into the most beautiful, mind-numbing feeling.

"Goddammit!" he roared, pulling me back until I was flush against his chest. He rocked into my body over and over until he pushed me over the edge, free-falling so deliciously I couldn't think straight.

Euphoria.

It was the only word I could think of to describe the way he made me feel. He fell right after me, the warmth of his seed filling me, making me even slicker.

Our bodies continued to glide together, slowing with the passing moments. Still pressed against one another, he turned my face toward his, his lips drifting over mine before he demanded more from me. The man certainly knew how to kiss, that was for damn sure. Our tongues battled, his taste slowly imprinting on me for life.

All too soon, he slipped from my body and turned me to face him. "Did I hurt you?" He genuinely seemed concerned, and it was sweet.

"Nothing that won't pass in a few minutes," I assured. I knew my answer was sort of cryptic but I didn't want to tell him that he had hurt me a little, especially after I begged him to let go and fuck me with wild abandon. Truth was Tripp was overly large, so sex with him so far had been slightly painful, but the pleasure he evoked definitely outweighed the twinge of discomfort.

Tripp frowned at my response but when I rose up on my tippy toes and linked my fingers behind his neck, he relaxed. Pressing my lips to his, all of the worry quickly evaporated. His posture relaxed and we melded together.

"I'm clean," he blurted.

"Oh, you wanna get out of the shower now?" I asked, confused by his sudden statement.

"No. What I meant was that I'm clean. You know, no rashes or shit down below," he joked, chuckling when I realized what he'd meant.

"Oh. Good. Yeah, I guess we should have discussed that before going bareback, huh?"

How could I have been so careless? I seemed to lose all reason as soon as Tripp looked at me, let alone touched me. "I got tested at my annual exam, and since Rick and I hadn't had sex for a few months prior. . . ."

I stopped talking when Tripp's jaw muscles clenched and his nose flared in anger. He pushed away from me and flexed his hands at his sides.

"The last fucking thing I wanna picture is you with that prick." I'd seen Tripp angry before, usually when he was defending me, but his reaction right then was different. It was like he was upset with me, a feeling I certainly didn't like.

I lowered my head and apologized. "Sorry, I just wanted to let you know that you're safe." I stared at his feet, fearing that if I looked back up at him I'd start to ramble and reveal something else he didn't want to hear.

"Shit," he mumbled. Hooking his finger under my chin, he raised my head until our eyes met. "Listen, Reece. I'm sorry. I didn't mean to snap at you like that. I just don't ever want to hear that bastard's name. I can't fathom the thought of him touching you. And what he did to you . . . I should have done more than had his legs broken."

"No, you shouldn't have. I don't want you any more involved than you already are." It was the truth. While Rick deserved worse than having his legs broken, I didn't want his evilness to infect Tripp, making him feel as if he had to deal with Rick on my behalf. Silence wrapped around us both, and before things became tense between us, I decided to change the topic.

"Are you ever going to invite me to your club?" I would've been lying if I'd said I wasn't curious about where Tripp spent a lot of his time. I didn't even know if women were allowed there, but it couldn't hurt to ask.

"Funny you should ask," he answered.

CHAPTER FORTY

Tripp

"I'M NERVOUS," SHE WHISPERED, FIDGETING in the passenger seat of my new truck. Reece continued to be adamant about not riding on the back of my bike, something which I was definitely gonna remedy someday soon, so I went out and purchased something she felt safe riding in for the time being.

"Don't be. They're gonna love you." Reece had been a bundle of nerves ever since I asked her to come with me to Riley's baptism. She smiled but I knew she was on edge, and no matter how much I tried to calm her, my efforts were useless.

Stone and Addy had finally set a date to have Riley's ceremony at the clubhouse, and the day had arrived. That precious little girl was the apple of not only her parents' eyes but the rest of us as well. I tried not to fawn all over her whenever they brought her around, but she stole my heart. So innocent. When she looked up at me, I saw the trust in her eyes. Her tiny smile always made me happy, even when I'd had the shittiest day. It wasn't until I met Reece that I had even entertained the idea of having one of my own, although it was way too soon in our relationship to even discuss something like that. But nonetheless, the thoughts were forming.

"Do I look okay?" she asked, fiddling with the hem of her light blue dress.

"You're gorgeous," I confirmed. When she'd strolled into the living room earlier that day and twirled around, I caught sight of the back of her dress. The majority of her skin was exposed. She'd worried it wasn't appropriate, but with the hemline hitting just above her knee and the dress covering everything in front, it was more than suitable. Before we left the house, however, I showed her just how sexy I thought she looked, my desire for her uncontrollable as I backed her against the nearest wall, lifted her dress, moved her flimsy panties to the side and devoured her. Her taste was still on my tongue.

Pulling off the main highway, I drove another half mile until I reached the compound. The gate was open and manned by a few of the newest prospects. If these guys turned out to be half the man Jagger was, our club would be stronger than ever.

Once inside I easily found a space, most of the lot still empty. Once I'd killed the engine I glanced over at Reece, the anxious flush of her cheeks making my dick twitch. She reached for the door handle but I stopped her. "Here, let me get that for you. One second." I jumped out and hurriedly walked around the back, coming to stand by her side in a few seconds flat. I extended my hand as soon as I opened the door, the heat from her palm promising the warmth her body would provide mine once this shindig was over.

Leaning down I placed a chaste kiss on her mouth, knowing she was anxious and doing my best to try and calm her. "You'll be fine. Trust me. After about ten minutes, it'll be like you've known them forever. The women are super cool, so you'll have no problem there. The guys are as well, although if I notice any of them being *too* nice, don't get freaked out if I let them know about it." I winked, but she knew from the tone of my voice that I was deadly serious on that last point.

"Oh stop," she chided, slapping my arm in mock annoyance, doing anything she could to help ease her worries.

I walked beside her, my hand resting on the middle of her back. My fingers brushed back and forth over her bare skin. "I hate that you're showing so much skin," I rumbled.

She stopped walking and turned toward me. "You don't like my dress? Why didn't you say something back at the house? I know my back is exposed, but I thought you said it was appropriate for today. Besides, I'm not showing any cleavage or anything." She would have continued to ramble had I not interrupted her.

"Calm down, baby. I just meant that I hate that you're showing *any* skin. Not because the dress isn't nice, because it is, but every fucker here is gonna notice." I tried to smile but my expression was strained. "You look gorgeous. Stop freakin' out." I snatched her hand and led her the rest of the way through the large open lot.

Stone and Adelaide had picked a perfect day. The sun was shining and the light breeze helped to soothe the midday heat. A large tent with numerous tables and chairs littered the grounds, providing shade and seating for everyone attending.

"Nomad!" Breck shouted as he walked toward us, beer in hand and already half empty. I liked Breck just fine, until he consumed a few drinks; then he became sort of obnoxious. Usually, I'd just shout for Cutter, his father, to reel him back in or I'd be forced to deal with him. Most times, Cutter would intervene if he was there. If not, and I had to take care of business myself . . . let's just say that Breck had been knocked out once or twice. He wasn't my favorite, but I didn't dislike him either. He was loyal as fuck to the club, and that went a long way in my book.

"Get ready for this one," I warned Reece, the flare of her eyes almost making me laugh.

"Breck," I greeted, tightening my hold on Reece's hand unknowingly.

"Ow," she whined. "My hand."

"Sorry." Turning my full attention back to Breck, who was now staring at my woman, I took a step closer and crowded his personal space. "Don't even think about it, man. She's mine." The gravel in my voice was unmistakable.

"What?" He played dumb. "I didn't say anything." He grinned.

"You didn't have to. I know you." We stepped around him to join the others, but not before I warned him. "And don't get shit-faced,

Breck. We're not at a fuckin' ruckus."

He mumbled something before walking in the opposite direction.

"What's a ruckus?" Reece asked, walking quickly just to keep up with my long strides. I slowed down when I noticed.

"It's a party the club throws every so often when we're celebratin' something or need to blow off some steam. But there's no wives or girlfriends allowed, just wannabes and the guys." I had no idea all of that shit was gonna come flyin' out of my mouth until it was too late.

Why the hell did I just tell her all that? Damnit!

She stopped walking and yanked her hand from mine. I closed my eyes in regret and tried to think of something to say that would undo some of the damage I'd undoubtedly just caused.

"What's a wannabe?"

"Women looking to attach themselves to one of the members. But it never happens. They're pretty much there to entertain the guys."

Oh my God! Seriously . . . shut up, Tripp.

"What?" Her question was accompanied by an indiscernible look on her face. Was that confusion? Jealousy? Anger?

"I have no idea why I just told you all that, Reece."

"Does your club throw these types of parties all the time?" She'd ignored my last statement.

"They used to. But not so much anymore." I was being honest, so I prayed it would gain me some brownie points. "We actually haven't had one in quite some time."

"If another came up, would you go?" She crossed her arms in front of her and kept her gaze on me the entire time. The heat of her stare fueled me. She was tryin' to lay claim on me and I found it exciting. I wanted to test her, to see how far she'd go, either with her words, her expression or her body language.

"Yeah, I'd go." I ran my hand through my hair, gripping the back of my neck as if I weren't giving much thought to her line of questions about my club. I'd told her the truth. I would attend the next ruckus the club had. I just wouldn't participate in the free pussy that was offered.

"Why?" Reece attempted to mask her anger.

"Because it's a club party. Why not?"

"Would you sleep with one of the women who came?"

"Do you care if I sleep with one of them?" I knew how irritating it was to answer a question with one, but I wanted to see what she'd say.

"Yes, I would care. A lot."

It was all I needed to affirm that she felt something deeper for me than just the byproduct of our rushed circumstances. I'd come to develop strong feelings for Reece, no matter how annoying I felt they were. After all, feelings equated to possible hurt and agony in the future.

"Then you have my word that I won't sleep with anyone else. But you have to promise the same. I meant what I told Breck. You're mine."

A look of what I could only describe as happiness fluttered across her gorgeous face when I verbally staked my claim on her. "So does that mean that we're . . . ?" Her eyes darted from me to the ground then back again.

"Together?" She nodded. "Yes. That's what it means."

She smiled, which made me smile, the thud of my heart relaxing into a steady rhythm, a calm spreading through me I'd never experienced before. In truth, it terrified me.

We stood there staring at each other, allowing the brief silence stretching between us to comfort us. There were so many things I wanted to say, but if I rambled on right then I'd come across as some crazy man. And after everything she'd been through, not only with Rick but since I'd met her, the last thing I needed to add to her list was an all-consuming man who wanted to possess her. My emotions were a lot for me to handle, and I could only imagine how she'd feel if I tried to express them.

CHAPTER FORTY-ONE

Reece

"RELAX," TRIPP SOOTHED, KISSING MY temple in an attempt to calm me. His touch soothed me, but not enough to stop the fluttering anxiousness in my belly as we approached some of the people already gathered.

"I'm trying," I answered, grasping his hand tighter. There were a group of women huddled together at one of the tables, laughing and having a great time together. It was then that I longed for someone, other than Carla, who I could let loose with and confide in. Don't get me wrong; I was beyond grateful that Carla was in my life, but sometimes I wish I just had a couple more girlfriends. Rick had kept me so secluded that the few friends I had back home had eventually stopped trying to reach out to me.

"You'll have fun. I promise," Tripp said, raising his free hand to someone who'd acknowledged his arrival. Our arrival.

"Well, look who decided to show up," a dark-haired man called out, quickly walking toward Tripp to greet him. He was handsome. Very handsome, in fact.

"Prez. How are ya?" They shook hands and did that half-hug thingy guys do. Since I had nowhere else to look, I studied both men, hoping to God I wasn't being obvious. The interaction between them was intriguing. They passed a silent message back and forth with the flick of their eyes and a subtle nod. Their body language was even heightened, elongating their coded communication.

"I'm good. Better."

"How's Sully?" Tripp's question caused his friend to tense, but only for a second. Had I not been paying such close attention I would've missed it for sure.

"She's good. We're gettin' there." Finally looking away from Tripp, the handsome stranger looked in my direction. "Who did ya bring with you?"

"This is Reece." Tripp looked at me for the other part of his introduction. "Reece, this is Marek, our club's president." It was then that my eye caught the 'President' patch on the front of his leather vest.

"Nice to meet you," I greeted, flashing a small smile before looking toward the ground. Bad habit after years of being with Rick. If I looked at another man for two seconds too long he became angry.

"Glad you could come today. Someone's gotta keep this guy in line."

I looked back up at the both of them and found two pairs of eyes on me. Marek's comment was one made in jest, but his expression remained stoic. Something told me the guy was more on the serious side, which I guess made sense seeing as how he was in charge of the entire club. But there was something hidden beneath the blue of his eyes that indicated there was more to him than what he revealed to others. Mainly strangers.

Tripp leaned away from me and spoke in a low voice, Marek acknowledging what he'd said with a jerk of his chin and a slight twitch of his lips. After they parted, Marek stood straight, glancing back at me one more time before turning around and walking toward a building to the left of where we were standing.

We continued to walk forward, and it was only then, as I scoured the expansive area, that I came to realize there was no baby present. I wasn't Catholic, but I knew enough that the child was usually clothed in a white gown of sorts for the ceremony, which would have made her easily detectable. Then again, maybe these people did their own thing, had their own traditions.

"I wonder where Stone and Adelaide are," he mused, as if he'd read my mind.

"I was just thinking the same thing."

He opened his mouth to speak but quickly snapped it shut, his recent smile morphing into a vicious scowl. The faltering of his steps put me on alert. Tripp cursed under his breath, and as I perused the crowd I knew exactly why.

"What the hell is *she* doing here?" I asked.

"I have no goddamn idea, but I'm about to find out." We stalked toward the person in question—or I should say that Tripp stalked forward, dragging me behind me. His steps were rushed and I had to break out into a slight jog just to keep up with him.

"Arianna," Tripp barked, startling not only her but the couple people standing close by. Lowering his voice so as not to call anyone else's attention, he said, "What are you doing here?"

I'd told Tripp about the way Arianna had treated me at work, telling me that I wasn't gonna hold his interest and that he would eventually choose her over me. I'd also revealed how she taunted me with their past escapades. I'd tried to play off her antics as juvenile and those of a jealous woman, but she'd managed to affect me. Tripp and I were still so new it was only logical I'd have my doubts.

Tripp shut down every insecurity I had where she was concerned, assuring me that he'd never touch her again, even if I weren't in the picture.

"I was invited, of course," she said sweetly, false bravado spewing forth as she put on airs she couldn't quite pull off. Her outfit was inappropriate for such an event. If I'd thought my dress was borderline questionable because of the open back, my reservations halted at the sight of her short, red, skintight excuse for a dress. Sure, some of the others' dresses were form-fitting, but they weren't slutty. There was a time and a place for such clothing, and a baby's baptism celebration wasn't one. Her face was overdone with way too much makeup, and her hair was high and ratty. Tame everything down and she'd pass for attractive, but not like this.

"By who?" he asked. Her eyes flicked to mine, narrowing slightly before focusing back on the man standing next to me.

"Breck."

"Of course," Tripp mumbled before shouting for Breck, who was fast approaching with a beer in hand. He stopped next to Arianna and snaked his arm around her waist.

"What?"

"Why did you invite her here?"

"Because I could. What's it to you?" Breck's eyes shot to mine before a lascivious grin flashed across his face. "Oh I get it. You fucked her so now you don't want anyone else to have her. Well, too bad." Breck pulled Arianna close and she laughed, but her eyes never left Tripp.

"I don't give a shit who you fuck." I believed he was speaking to the both of them, but couldn't be sure. "Just make sure you stay away from us, or else." Tripp stopped speaking, turned around and guided me back toward the parking lot. I heard Breck and Arianna mumble something behind me, but again we were walking so fast I couldn't make out any of it.

"Tripp, please slow down. I'm gonna break my neck in these heels." I yanked on his arm for emphasis.

"Sorry." He slowed but not by much. Once we were far enough away, he dropped my hand and leaned against the building Marek had entered not ten minutes prior. "I'm sorry you had to hear that, Reece. If I could change parts of my past I would."

"Ditto," I responded, leaning in to him so I could feel the heat of his body. Was I upset at the reminder that Tripp had been with Arianna? Of course. Did I believe he wanted nothing more to do with her? Wholeheartedly.

Tripp's arms encased me, drawing me in so I could rest my head against his chest. The hasty thrum of his heartbeat told me he was upset. Over the next several minutes we remained silent, existing in the comfort the other provided. His fingers danced over my exposed skin, heat blossoming between my legs at his subtle touch.

"Reece," he whispered, his fingers pressing harder on my back before lowering to cup my ass cheeks. Pulling back to look into his face, I saw a plethora of emotions cross his features. His green eyes darkened with remorse and apology, but a deepening lust existed just under the surface, overpowering his regret at the situation that had just occurred. "Can we escape inside so I can show you how sorry I am that you had to endure that?"

I knew it wasn't his fault. He had no idea she was gonna be there, and I wanted more than anything to give him a reprieve from his guilt, if that was even the correct word to describe what he'd probably been feeling since the encounter. However, I knew it wasn't the right time or place. The last thing I wanted was to be caught by his friends, especially since they didn't know me. It was important these people viewed me as someone other than just the stripper Tripp hooked up with from the club.

Rising up on my toes, I pressed my lips to his. When he groaned into my mouth, I thought for sure I would've thrown all caution to the wind and taken him up on his delicious offer, but I restrained myself. Barely.

"This isn't the place. But I promise that as soon as we get home I'll let you apologize over and over again."

He ignored me, instead pressing his lower half into mine. "Please. Don't make me beg, baby," he pleaded. "I'm so fuckin' hard right now." His warm breath fanned my face before his mouth descended over mine, the flick of his tongue enough to tempt me once again.

The roar of motorcycles interrupted our heated moment. Three bikes followed by an SUV soon entered the lot, gravel kicking up around their tires before they backed into the available parking spaces.

The engines kicked off and the men rested their feet on the ground on either side of their impressive machines as they removed their helmets.

"Yo," one of the men yelled, laughing at something one of the others had said while approaching us. "I thought for sure you'd be the last to arrive." He stopped a couple feet away, his smile wide and inviting. He appeared younger than the rest of them, probably somewhere in his early twenties. The way the sunlight hit his dark golden hair, it appeared as if he had natural highlights—an attribute any woman would kill for, me included. His amber eyes flicked from me to Tripp a few times before any introduction was made.

"I'm not the one who's always late. That's Ryder."

"Stop callin' me out," a dark-haired man yelled from across the lot, continuing to talk to the others as if he hadn't just had an outburst.

"You're a close second," the guy jested, his hand extended to me in the absence of introduction. "I'm Jagger," he said, snagging my hand as soon as I raised my arm. He seemed pleasant.

"Reece. Nice to meet you," I replied, relaxing in the acceptance of his friend.

"Why are your women already here?" Tripp asked his friend. "Some business I should know about?"

"Nope. Nothing that exciting. They didn't wanna ride with us 'cause they didn't wanna ruin their outfits." He shook his head as if the women were being ridiculous, but I completely sided with them. "Hey, before I forget. Can you come to my next bout? Ryder was supposed to but he said he's got somethin' going on."

"Yeah. No problem." Tripp had told me that they had an undefeated, underground MMA fighter in the club. I guessed this was him.

"Great. Okay, I better go find Kena before Breck makes another attempt."

"Fuckin' Breck," Tripp grumbled. "He brought Arianna with him."

Jagger's eyes flicked to mine. "Asshole."

"Yeah."

And that was it for their exchange. Jagger rushed across the lot, and I found his eagerness sweet. Or maybe it was to protect his woman from the likes of Breck. Either way, I liked him.

The next to approach was Hawke. Him I knew, having talked to him on occasion at Indulge when Tripp had sent him in to watch over me. He'd told me he was just there to make sure there were no issues, but I knew his presence had been geared toward me. I couldn't say I minded, though; after everything that'd happened, I welcomed the extra sense of security.

"Hey, Reece. How are ya?" Surprisingly, he leaned in to kiss my cheek, a gesture which earned him a growl from his older brother.

"All right," Tripp admonished. "That's enough."

"What? I'm just sayin' hello." Hawke chuckled, seeming to love riling up his brother.

"Uh-huh." Tripp looked around the lot before asking, "Where's Edana? I didn't see her with the others."

Hawke's expression darkened. "She didn't feel good," was the only explanation he gave. Tripp had told me that his brother had had a rough go of it lately due to his girlfriend being attacked. But he said he was getting better each day, although still much more reserved than he used to be.

"Maybe next time," Tripp said, gripping his brother's shoulder in a show of support.

"Yeah. Maybe." Hawke flashed us a tight smile before disappearing.

Before anyone else could advance our way, the driver's door to the black SUV opened and out stepped a tall, blond man in a dark blue suit. His hair was shorter on the sides than on top, pulled back in some sort of faux Mohawk. He looked nervous.

The other men standing around hooted and hollered at the sight of him, and I guessed he was another member of the club, although I wasn't sure because he didn't match their attire of leather vests and jeans.

"What the fuck?" Tripp whispered next to me.

"Who is that?"

"Stone. He's the VP. And Riley's dad." We watched him open the back door and fiddle around for few seconds before exiting with a little girl in a long white dressing gown. I guessed they were sticking to tradition after all. The sight of him holding who I naturally assumed to be Riley was beautiful. In that short amount of time, I could tell how much he loved his daughter. The way he ignored his friends and focused on the little girl, as if he was lost in her, instantly told me he was a good man.

He walked around the vehicle and opened the passenger door, and soon a woman came into view.

"Is that Adelaide?" The woman was stunning. Her dress was sleeveless and the most beautiful shade of pale yellow I'd ever seen. The material hit just below her knee, and even though it flared out at the cinched waist, there was no hiding her gorgeous form. Her beautiful blonde hair was pulled back in a stylish half updo.

"Yup. Sure is." Tripp smiled wide at the sight of her, and as soon as she caught his attention she returned the expression, striding over to us within seconds. Once she was near, she wrapped her arms around his neck and gave him a big hug.

"Not today, Addy," Stone shouted across the lot. The look on his face was part serious, part joking. The little I did know about the woman was that she had tended to Tripp after he'd been left for dead just outside the club's gates. She nursed him back to health and still checked in on him from time to time.

"Oh shush," she shouted over her shoulder, turning her attention to me when she looked back. "And you must be Reece," she said, pulling me in for an impromptu hug. She was certainly friendly, I'd give her that.

"Yes, I am." I smiled, and for once it hadn't been forced. My nerves had loosened their hold and I reveled in the feeling. "So nice to meet you. Tripp has told me a lot about you."

"Well, this guy," she laughed, gripping his upper arm, "and I have a special bond. I hope you don't mind that, because I know Stone certainly does."

"No issues whatsoever." I'd spoken the truth. My newfound jealousies didn't extend to Adelaide. "I'll be forever thankful that you saved him."

"Okay, okay. All this mushy talk is gettin' to me." Tripp leaned in and kissed Adelaide's cheek before walking away. He'd snatched Riley from Stone's hands, turning his back on his friend so he could fuss over the precious little one.

"He loves that little girl. They all do," Adelaide revealed. "I just hope she doesn't mind so much as she gets older."

CHAPTER FORTY-TWO

Tripp

"I NEVER THOUGHT I'D SEE the day." I held Riley close while her father fixed his tie.

"What are you talkin' about?"

"I'm talkin' about you in a monkey suit. What the hell's gotten into you?" Riley grabbed my finger and tried to suck on it, but I pulled it away at the last second. "Where's her sucky thing?"

"Her binky?"

"I don't know what the hell it's called."

"It's in the truck." He opened the back door and rooted around for what felt like forever.

"If you don't hurry up, I'm gonna let her suck on my finger, and you probably know where that's been." I laughed at the words that came out of his mouth. I would've never done such a thing, but the fact that Stone thought I would, and how distressed he became, made me laugh harder.

Gently placing the binky in Riley's mouth, he said, "I know where those hands have been. Keep them away from my daughter."

"Oh relax." Looking closely at him, I saw he was nervous. "What's wrong with you? Seriously? Why so uptight?"

"No reason." He shifted his attention away from me and onto his woman, who was chatting with Reece. "How's that goin'?" He jerked his head toward the women. "Heard you had some issue with her husband. Not cool fuckin' around with a married woman, by the way." His dark eyes chastised me. He obviously didn't know the full story.

"I'm not fuckin' around with a married chick. Well, she's technically married, but she doesn't wanna be." Stone stood there staring at me, waiting for the rest of the story. I didn't want to bring it up, but I didn't want him thinking badly of Reece either. "He beat and terrorized her for years. She finally got away, but he tracked her across the country. He found her at the club, and thank God we got to him before he dragged her out of there. He probably would've killed her this time." I hadn't realized how much the entire situation had affected me until I clutched my chest after speaking. The thought that Reece could've been ripped from my life gutted me.

"Fuck," Stone replied. "Sorry, man. I didn't know that." He looked back toward Reece and Adelaide. "Is she okay now? And where is her hus . . . that bastard?"

"Ryder and Hawke broke his legs in warning never to come near her again. I would've done it, but I probably wouldn't have been able to stop at just his legs."

"Speak of the devil," Stone interrupted as Ryder drew closer.

"I'm the devil? I think someone sold their soul for an Armani suit." Ryder chuckled. "Why you all dressed up?"

"Will everyone get off my back already," Stone sneered, shoving his hands in his pockets in another bout of nervousness. It was extremely odd to see our VP acting in such a way. It almost made me think something else was up with him. But he wouldn't tell me even if I asked, so I let it go.

Cutter and Trigger joined us, coming out of the clubhouse and smelling like booze. Nothing too crazy, though.

A black sedan pulled up in front of the gates, the prospects inspecting the vehicle before allowing it to pass. As soon as the car came to stop, a priest stepped out and smiled at Stone. Adelaide appeared suddenly, stealing her daughter from my arms.

"Time to get things started," I heard Stone shout as we all walked toward the back of the compound.

THE CEREMONY WAS QUICK. MAREK and Sully had been chosen as Riley's godparents, and I had to admit that Stone and Addy had definitely chosen wisely. I saw the longing in Sully's eyes when she held the little girl, and I only hoped they could have one of their own someday. Marek stood rigid beside her, although he relaxed some when she reached for his hand. I could sense they were still dealing with the strain of what'd happened, but there was a light back in Marek's eyes that had been missing over more time than I cared to acknowledge.

We were an hour into the party when Stone stood, clearing his throat to gain everyone's attention. Once all eyes were on him, including Adelaide's, he finally spoke.

"Addy and I want to thank everyone for coming today to help us celebrate. And if Riley could talk, she'd say thank you too." Everyone smiled, glancing at the baby girl before turning their gazes back to Stone. "You're all aware of the difficulty Addy and I went through while she was pregnant with Riley, and it was by the grace of God that she was able to give me a healthy child. Now I'm not a religious guy at all." He looked over at the priest. "Sorry, Father Houston, but it's true." The collared man simply nodded. "But I'd never prayed as much as I did during those months."

A solemn look briefly passed over everyone present. We'd all been praying for not only Adelaide's life but for the life of their daughter. She'd been dealt a tough hand, having been told she had ovarian cancer *and* that she was pregnant. Thankfully everything turned out great, and Adelaide was in remission.

"After everything we've been through, baby, I don't want another day to go by without the world knowing how much I love you." Stone moved toward Adelaide, gently taking Riley from her arms and passing their daughter to Sully. Then he helped his woman to her feet and did something I never thought I'd see—he lowered himself to one knee and took her hand in his. Wide-eyed and astonished, Adelaide's lower lip started to tremble. "I even asked your dad for permission, so that tells you how serious I am." She laughed and looked across the table at an older man sitting next to Trigger. He looked back at her with such love there was no mistaking that he was her father.

"Baby . . . ever since I met you I've become a better man. I'll admit there've been hurdles along the way, and I'm not sayin' I won't trip and fall on my face from time to time, but knowing you're there to help me up and make me see the error of my ways means more to me than I can ever say." We all laughed because we knew Stone had a temper which landed him in hot water with Adelaide sometimes. But he always came around, and my God did he love that woman.

He licked his lips and blew out a nervous breath. It was then that I understood his previous anxiety and the reason why he'd decided to don a suit. He wanted to put forth the effort Adelaide deserved. "Adelaide Reins . . . will you marry me?"

"Of course I will," Adelaide proclaimed, tears streaming down her beautiful cheeks. She pulled him to his feet and threw her arms around his neck. Everyone clapped in celebration. Stone kept it clean, even though I knew damn well all he wanted to do was make a spectacle and kiss the hell out of her. But her father was present, and I knew even though his relationship with him had been rocky, he respected him enough not to openly defile the man's daughter in front of him.

CHAPTER FORTY-THREE

Tripp

I STAYED AS CLOSE TO Reece as I could, with the exception of when I had to piss or grab another drink. I knew she was still a bit nervous, although she'd relaxed some over the past couple hours. Adelaide and Sully had engaged her in conversation, doing their best to make her feel welcome. Kena and Braylen had even sat down next to her in an attempt to get to know her.

While Arianna made sure to stay away from Reece, I saw her staring at me from time to time. I never acknowledged her presence, which I knew irritated the fuck out of her, but I didn't give a shit. Reece had caught one of Arianna's glances and stiffened beside me. I relieved her tension with a soul-scorching kiss, almost forgetting we weren't in private. It wasn't until Hawke yelled for me to let her breathe that I pulled away from her delectable lips.

"Wanna join us?" Sully asked Reece, shuffling past us in a hurry.

"Where you goin'?" I asked before Reece could.

"Bathroom. If that's okay with you," Adelaide snickered, half sloshed herself, no doubt celebrating her engagement. Good thing Stone was driving them home.

"Want me to join you?" I asked my woman, laughing at her reaction.

"You can't go in the bathroom with us."

"Who says?"

"We say," Adelaide and Sully replied in unison. They pulled Reece away from me, and I hated to admit that I already missed her.

Fuck! I have it bad.

I couldn't draw my eyes away from her, staring after her like a lovesick puppy. Thoughts of her beneath me consumed me, and I counted the seconds until I could make the images in my head a reality.

I knew someone had sat down next to me, but I took a sip of my drink and ignored whoever it was, having a feeling I knew exactly who dared to approach me.

"You know she can't satisfy you the way I can."

Anger instantly boiled in my veins at the sound of her voice. I didn't respond, not until she shifted closer and put her hand on my thigh, too close to my dick. I seized her wrist and tossed her hand away as if she'd burned me.

"Don't fuckin' touch me, Arianna. I mean it. Do it again and I'll have you thrown out of here." I was doing my best not to cause a scene, but she tested my patience for sure. "Where's Breck?"

"I don't know. I think he's passed out somewhere. Besides, he can't keep up with me. He's not like you, baby," she slurred, daring to touch me again. I jumped up from the table and backed away, glaring at her before turning toward the clubhouse. No way was that bitch staying here without Breck present. I strolled inside and walked across the common room, finding the guy in question passed out cold on the couch.

"Goddammit!" I swore, punching the back of the couch. He didn't even move. As luck would have it, one of the prospects came out of the kitchen carrying two trays of food. "Hey, prospect. Call a cab."

"For who?" He was young and new. Too new to realize he didn't ask the questions, only did what we told him to.

"Just. Do. It." I turned on my heel but not before Arianna stumbled into the common room, no doubt having followed me inside. This was all I needed. Reece would be walking through there any second and I didn't want her to have to deal with my past mistake yet again.

"There you are," Arianna cooed, batting her heavily coated, fake lashes at me. "Wanna take me in one of the back rooms? Or we can do it right here if you want." She didn't bother waiting for my refusal before she hiked up her skirt and leaned against the bar. She wasn't wearing anything underneath.

"Pull your skirt down," I barked. "No one wants to see that shit." I was pissed, even more so when Arianna pushed off the bar and stalked toward me, her skirt still hiked up to her waist and exposing herself.

"You still want me. You know you do. Stop wasting your time with that skank." I found it funny that she referred to Reece as a skank when it was she who fucked anyone willing, often for money. Thank God the few times I'd been with her I'd been smart enough to use a condom.

I'd been so enraged that she'd put me into this position, I hadn't noticed Reece had walked into the room, halting her steps once she saw the scene in front of her.

Arianna hanging on my arm with her skirt around her waist.

CHAPTER FORTY-FOUR

Reece

TO SAY I WAS LIVID would have been an understatement. The sight of that bitch hanging all over Tripp, and with her skirt bunched up showing everyone her goodies, made my blood boil. Heat shot through me and my skin flushed red. My fists clenched at my sides and while tears formed, they were from anger. Not sadness or hurt. Okay, part of me was hurt, but mostly it was from anger.

Although rage best described what I felt right then.

I didn't misconstrue the scene in front of me. I knew damn well Tripp didn't want to have anything to do with Arianna. I saw it in his rigid posture, in the way his eyes flared with his own fury that she dared to come near him after he'd warned her earlier. It was then I saw Breck passed out on the couch, explaining why that bitch made her bold move on my man.

I'd finally found my sliver of happiness and there was no way in hell I was gonna let some low-class whore snatch that away from me. I was done brushing off her attacks, done second-guessing my relationship, done giving in to the small bouts of paranoia that maybe what Arianna spewed was true. That Tripp would eventually tire of me and go back to her.

It was time I stepped up and claimed what was mine. Oh yeah, my possessive side came bursting out, and I embraced the hell out of it.

Slowly walking toward the two of them, Tripp shoved her aside as I approached. "Get the hell away from him," I seethed, trying to convince myself not to tackle her and beat the hell out of her once and for all. For as much as I wanted to teach her drunk ass a lesson, this wasn't the time or place. I didn't want to make a scene, nor did I want the women behind me to think badly of me.

"Or what?" She tried to put her hands back on Tripp, even though he took a few more steps away from her. Before I could answer or even reach her, a blur of blonde hair pushed past me and headed straight for Arianna. Grabbing her by the back of her hair, Adelaide pulled her toward the door, Arianna stumbling behind her the entire way, trying to catch her footing.

"Get off me, you crazy bitch!" she yelled, trying to dislodge herself from Adelaide's hold. But it was useless; she was simply no match.

Adelaide was stronger than she looked. I laughed out loud as she finally tossed Arianna out on her ass, screaming, "Don't ever show your ugly face around here again or you'll regret it!" before she slammed the door on her. Turning toward us, she threw up her hands and said, "Anyone else need disposing of?"

We all burst out laughing at what she'd done. She saw the look on my face and decided to step in on my behalf, and I'd be forever grateful to her for doing so. She winked at me and said, "I got your back, sweetheart."

When Tripp drew me into his side, he kissed me before saying, "I told you they were cool chicks."

"They certainly are," I agreed.

All of a sudden a serious look shrouded his face. "Do you want me to fire her? I know you said you didn't want to see anyone lose their job, but I think she's only gonna get worse. Especially after tonight."

That time I didn't have to think too long before answering. "I think it's time. After the shit she pulled tonight, she's gone too far."

"Okay, consider it done. Now how about we get outta here so I can ravage you properly." The seductive tremor in his voice instantly made me wet, the ache that had been present the entire day kicking into overdrive.

"How can I say no to that?"

"You can't." He reached for my hand and pulled me toward the exit. Once outside, we walked right into another commotion. At first I thought Arianna still hadn't left, causing one last scene before she was finally booted off the property.

But as we approached, I saw a few of the men crowding the gates, a car on the other side with a woman blaring on the horn. It was obvious she wanted to come inside, but for who I had no idea.

Not until she laid eyes on Tripp.

I would have liked to say that the rest of the evening passed without incident, but I would've been lying.

CHAPTER FORTY-FIVE

Tripp

MINDLESSLY WALKING TOWARD THE GATES, I tried to dispel the image in front of me, but no amount of blinking or wishing would make her disappear.

"Tripp," Rachel shouted. "Tripp, tell them to let me in."

My only response was to shake my head, releasing Reece's hand as I prepared myself for one helluva scene. I had to make sure she was real. That she was really there. Only then would I summon up the anger necessary to tell her to go to hell.

"How the fuck did you find me?" Out of all the questions rattling around inside my confused brain, that was the one that chose to escape. Peering at her through the bars, gripping the metal tightly while I pushed angered breaths from my mouth, I shouted again, "How did you find me?"

"I . . . I remember you telling me about this place." Even in the dim light of the lot I could see her pupils were dilated. She had an issue with drugs back when we were together, but I always chose to look the other way because it hadn't affected me. Well, not until I found her fucking some guy, her lapse in judgement surely a side effect of the drugs. Or maybe it was simply because she'd been a selfish bitch. *Yeah, let's go with that second one.*

Other than her eyes, she appeared okay, even though I knew she wasn't. "What are you doin' here?"

"I need to talk to you."

Looking at Rachel now, I realized I'd never loved her. She was simply someone I'd fucked and had a good laugh with on occasion.

"What could you possibly have to talk to me about? I haven't seen you in over a year. What could be so damn important that you just show up here out of the blue?" I backed up and turned away from her, fully intending on hightailing it back inside the security of the clubhouse to bark orders at someone to make sure she left without further incident. But I didn't make it that far. The next words out of her mouth froze me to my spot, disabling any thoughts from forming, let alone allowing my body to flee as I'd initially intended.

"Your son."

I whipped around so fast I was surprised I didn't fall over. The weight of her words crushed me. No way. It wasn't true. She wasn't pregnant when I left her. Or was she? I had no idea, but then again why would I have even bothered to ask? She'd cheated, and the guy I'd found her with probably wasn't the first. If she'd popped out a kid, what were the chances that he was mine? Slim. The chances just had to be slim. Otherwise, I had no idea what I was gonna do.

Instead of confronting Rachel with her ridiculous allegation, I sought out Reece. I didn't have to look too far, seeing as how she was standing next to Sully, the look on her face utter disbelief. We'd just started our relationship; how would she handle me having a son all of a sudden? That was a lot to ask of someone. I clearly had deep feelings for her if I was more concerned about what she thought than what I was goin' through.

Striding toward the woman who'd taken over my entire world, I reached for her but she simply shook her head and stepped back. I could hear Rachel shouting something behind me, but all of my focus was on Reece. The look in her eyes told me she was confused and . . . was that embarrassment?

"Reece." Her name was the only word I could form. I had no idea what to say, but I knew damn well I needed her to talk to me, to tell me what was goin' through that head of hers. I could only imagine, but I refused to give in to my own paranoia. Maybe it wasn't that bad . . . or maybe it was worse.

As I opened my mouth to say God knew what, she turned on her heel and fled toward the clubhouse, rushing inside and disappearing as my world fell down around me. For the first time in my life I was happy, genuinely happy. It figured my contentment with life wouldn't fuckin' last.

All because that bitch at the gate decided she wanted to swoop in and ruin everything. Anger tore through me as I finally lost my temper and hauled ass toward Rachel.

"Open the fuckin' gates!" I roared, shoving past whoever stood in my way. "Now!" The creak of the steel fueled my rage, the match to ignite the inferno swirling around inside me. Once I stepped foot on the other side I came face-to-face with her.

"Tripp!" I heard Stone shout, but my name was muffled. My only focus right then was ripping the truth from her filthy, lying mouth if it was the last thing I did.

"You better tell me right now that you're lying," I seethed as I towered over her. Rachel was selfish, proving it when she fucked around on me. She didn't care about me then and she sure as hell didn't care about me now. Rachel was only there because she didn't have anywhere else to go, no one else she could think of who'd help her. If the kid turned out to be mine then I'd have no choice but to step up, but if I found out this was just a ploy of hers to wriggle back into my life, she was gonna regret it for sure.

Her shoulders shook. Her body trembled. Her eyes filled with tears, though I highly doubted they were genuine. Rachel had always been good at playing upset to get my attention. I'd fallen for it in the past, but not anymore.

"I'm not lyin'," she muttered. "He's your son."

My eyes scoured the length of her. She didn't look like she'd had a baby, but then again she had always been conscious of everything that passed her lips—with the exception of dick, of course. My fury heightened and it wasn't from the memory of her fuckin' someone else. I didn't care about that. I didn't care about her. I cared that she was messin' with my relationship with Reece by just being there.

"Where is he?"

She remained silent and pointed toward the back door. The muscles of my jaw ached from clenching so hard, but my expression was enough to make her move out of my way as I reached for the handle.

As soon as I ripped the door open, I saw a tiny baby sitting in a car seat, his eyes wide and staring right back at me. His lower lip quivered, so before he started wailing, I looked behind me to search for someone I could trust to help. I didn't want to touch the little guy for fear my anger would transfer to him and scare him more than I was sure he already was. But I needed to see him up close, and I sure as shit didn't want Rachel handing him to me.

I caught Sully's attention and motioned for her to come over with a simple jerk of my head. Marek released her hand but he didn't look happy about it. Rachel never objected as Sully brushed past her. She knew I'd shut her down or make her leave before I'd even seen my so-called son.

Sully silently reached inside the car and pulled the baby from his seat. The infant wasn't even strapped in, nor was the car seat securely in place. *Careless bitch.*

Cradling the baby in her arms, Sully held him out to me. Still Rachel said nothing. All she could do was fidget next to me.

"I can't." I just wanted to look at him up close, but under the illumination of the security light I couldn't determine if he truly belonged to me or not. All goddamn babies looked the same at that age.

Speaking of which, I asked, "How old is he?"

"Three months."

"Three months? How in the world can you possibly say he's mine? You got knocked up months after I left you." I took a step to the side and stood so close I pinned her against the car. "Did you think I couldn't add? That I was so fuckin' stupid I'd think this kid was mine when there is no humanly way possible he could be? Unless you saved my cum and had someone inject it inside you months after I took off. Is that what you did?" Before she opened her mouth to lie, I yelled over to Adelaide, interrupting her conversation with Stone. "Addy, how long is cum good for?"

"What?" she shouted back, confusion written all over her face. She started toward me, Stone hot on her heels.

When she was near, I repeated, "How long is cum good for?"

"If you're asking how long semen is viable, the answer depends on what's being done with it."

"Stop it," Rachel shouted, slapping my chest with both her hands. I didn't move. She'd always hated when I intimidated her by standing so close, but I'd only acted that way whenever we really went at it. I'd never laid my hands on her, my presence enough to shatter whatever shit she'd tried to lay at my feet. Whether it was coming home drunk dressed like some kind of whore, smelling like men's cologne, or high as a kite, stumbling into our place in a daze I thought she'd never come down from. I excused her behavior and I think deep down I knew not to trust her. When I caught her cheating, it was more of a shot to my ego than anything else, but I took the opportunity for what it was and finally walked away. And what happened afterward set the direction of my future. I couldn't blame Rachel solely for me getting piss drunk, jumped by the Reapers, and shot to all hell, but I held her partly responsible.

"Stop what?" I shouted right back.

"I have nowhere to go," she cried, a few dramatic tears escaping and falling down her cheeks. "I can't take care of him by myself. It's too much."

"It's only too much because you're still addicted to that shit." It was an open-ended statement. 'That shit' could be anything. She'd tried it all, her dilated pupils and sunken skin proving she'd engaged the devil just hours prior. Cocaine was her favorite, though. No doubt if I searched her purse there'd be a vial in there.

"I'm tryin'," she lied.

"You're not," I countered. "And now I want you to take your kid and get the hell out of here." Lowering my face to hers, I said, "And if you ever come back, you *will* regret it."

"Please," she begged. "Please just take him." Whatever light had been hidden somewhere inside her had been completely blown out. Her blank stare worried me, not so much for her safety but that of her kid.

"I'm not takin' care of your son, and I sure as hell ain't raisin' some other fucker's kid." I turned my back on her, the sight of her sniveling pissing me off. She had no right to just show up out of the blue, claim the kid was mine, when he clearly wasn't, disrupt my night, let alone my relationship with Reece, and then beg me to take her baby off her hands.

What the hell is wrong with her?
Selfishness.
Drugs.
That's what's wrong with her.

The baby started crying, all of the commotion happening around him finally tipping him over the edge. Sully held him close, whispering something to him while rocking him back and forth. He seemed to have calmed in her arms, and while I didn't want to take him from her, he had to go back to his mother. I used that term loosely because I could already predict what kind of life this poor kid would have—a mother chasing whatever high she craved, caring only for herself and putting her kid second.

When I turned around to reach for the baby, Rachel made her move. She jumped back into her car and kicked over the engine.

"Don't you fuckin' dare," I shouted, racing toward the car as she hauled ass in reverse. "Rachel!" I yelled. "Get back here!" The bald tires squealed as she whipped the car around and took off, kicking up rocks and dust in her haste to escape.

What the fuck just happened?

CHAPTER FORTY-SIX

Reece

STARING INTO THE MIRROR, I tried to get a handle on everything that'd just happened outside. Some woman showing up claiming Tripp was the father of her baby. What the hell? I knew the other shoe was gonna drop, so why was I surprised? Because for once in my dreaded life I thought I'd finally get my happily ever after.

Did he know she was pregnant when he left her? He told me briefly about their relationship and how she'd cheated on him. Tripp never seemed torn up about it, though, telling me he never really loved her, although he may have thought so at the time.

What if the baby if his? What will I do? Continue our relationship, or allow him to try and work it out with her in an effort to give his sudden family a chance? I guess I won't find out until I leave the bathroom I've been holed up in for the past ten minutes.

Slowly turning the handle, I reentered the common space inside the club. Kena and Braylen, who I'd met earlier that day, were standing close together in the far corner. Kena's hands were going a mile a minute, her sister trying her best to interrupt her at every turn. Tripp had told me about Kena's condition soon after I'd met her, explaining that she wasn't deaf but that she simply couldn't speak.

I needed to see Tripp, to talk to him and try to figure out where we stood. Before I reached the door, it flung open and a crowd of people barreled inside. As soon as Tripp saw me he rushed forward and pulled me into a hug. His embrace was strong, borderline suffocating, but I relished the feel of his arms around me.

"I'm so sorry, Reece. I had no idea. I never expected to see her ever again." He stroked my back in reassurance, but all I wanted was answers. I pulled away from him so I could look into his eyes when I asked my question.

"Is it true, then?" I held my breath until he answered, which thankfully didn't take but a millisecond.

"No. The kid is too young to be mine. I have no idea what the hell she was thinking." He vigorously shook his head. "That's a lie. Yes I do. She's so far gone she actually thought I'd buy into her bullshit. Hell, she was high when she came here."

Looking around the room I saw the baby, but no Rachel. "Where is she?"

"She took off." He raked his fingers through his dark hair. "She fuckin' took off and left her kid here. And now I gotta deal with it."

I parted my lips to tell him I would help him when he squeezed my hand before walking toward Sully, who'd been coddling the infant.

I walked behind him and stood next to Adelaide, who was on the other side of Sully. I felt so out of place, but I didn't want to add to Tripp's stress by letting him know as much.

"He's adorable," I said, reaching over to touch his tiny hand. He had the bluest eyes I'd ever seen on a baby, although to be honest I hadn't seen many infants up close.

"He sure is," Sully whispered, nuzzling him close when he started to fuss.

"What the hell am I gonna do with a baby?" Tripp asked no one in particular. I gave him his space, continuing to stand next to Adelaide and Sully while he tried to work it out. I searched the rest of the room and saw Kena next to Jagger. They looked content, although she still looked frustrated, something definitely weighing heavy on her mind. She smiled at her man, but worry halted the expression from reaching her eyes. Next I saw Braylen standing next to Ryder, his arm slung over her shoulder while she rested her head on his chest. They were silent, watching everything unfold in front of them.

"Can you take him? Until I find Rachel?"

"Who the hell are you talkin' to?" Stone asked, looking over his shoulder as if there were someone standing behind him Tripp had been speaking to.

"Come on, brother. You already have one. How hard is it to take care of another one?"

"Are you kiddin' me right now? You have no idea how hard it is to raise a kid. I love my daughter more than life itself, but she requires constant attention. We hardly get any sleep, and forget about sex. No, we can't do it. You're gonna have to take him until you find that bitch. We just can't take care of two kids," Stone argued.

"Well, you better get used to it, sweetheart," Adelaide yelled over her shoulder, turning her attention back to Sully and the infant. "And that bullshit about no sex is a lie. How else did I get pregnant again?" She smiled, waiting for realization to dawn on her soon-to-be husband.

CHAPTER FORTY-SEVEN

Tripp

"COME ON, ADDY. I DON'T wanna hear that shit," Trigger yelled from across the room. He was behind the bar serving some of the guys a drink. That was gonna be my next stop for sure. I could definitely use a stiff one.

Stone mumbled something before crushing the small distance between him and his woman, reaching her in only a few strides. "What did you say?" The look on his face was priceless, and I had to stop myself from busting out laughing at his astonishment.

"You heard me." Adelaide kissed him before placing his hand on her belly. "Riley is gonna be a big sister." The light in her eyes filled me with warmth. I knew how much shit she'd gone through not that long ago, and to be able to have another kid was definitely a blessing for them both. Stone nodded before finally smiling. He pulled her close and kissed her, all the while remaining silent. He was obviously shocked. Shit, we all were.

"We can take him," Sully blurted, diverting the conversation and suddenly looking desperate to keep the baby in her arms. "I can watch over him while you try and find her." She looked over at her husband who was sitting at the bar, the pleading look in her eyes pulling at my heartstrings.

"I don't think that's a good idea, baby," Marek answered, sorrow laced deep in the lines of his face. He tipped his shot glass and swallowed the contents before rising to his feet.

"Please. I know it's not permanent. I promise I won't get attached to him." Sully looked down into the infant's face and smiled, the baby's tiny hand wrapping around her finger.

"You're already attached," Marek said, coming to stand next to her.

Deciding to add in my two cents, I said, "Come on, Prez. I promise I'll find her as soon as possible. I could really use your help." I rested my hand on his shoulder for emphasis.

Several tense seconds passed, keeping us all on edge as to what he would decide. Finally he huffed out a frustrated breath and relented.

"Fine. But you better find that bitch soon, Tripp. I mean it," he admonished. Even though he appeared put out by the request, his eyes filled with something akin to pride when he gazed at his wife holding the little one.

"I will. First thing tomorrow, I'm on it." Giving him a quick nod, I turned my attention to Reece. "Any time you wanna leave, just say the word. I know it's been one helluva day, and I don't blame you at all if you just wanna get outta here."

Whatever tension she'd been holding onto dissipated as soon as I wrapped my arms around her.

"I'm okay to stay a little while longer."

"Are you sure?"

"Yeah." Pulling back, she rested her hands on my chest and looked up at me, the thrum of my heart picking up speed from her simple touch. "Go talk to your friends. I'll be on the couch with my new favorite badass." Looking over her shoulder, I saw Sully and Adelaide had moved to the sofa, huddled together and fawning over the baby.

"I think I can take her," I teased, winking at Adelaide when she briefly looked over at me.

"I don't think so." Reece laughed. "You're no match for that woman."

"You might be right about that." Leaning down, I pressed my mouth to hers, the softness of her lips conjuring up all sorts of sordid images. Before I became a slave to what my body wanted, however, I ended our kiss. "I won't be long." I lightly smacked her ass before sauntering toward the bar to join some of the men. Marek occupied the corner seat, nursing his drink, while Stone was surprisingly engaged in conversation with Trigger. As I neared I could hear them discussing the VP's future child. Words such as 'karma' and 'hope you have another daughter' flew from Trigger's mouth, a smirk lifting the corners of his lips as Stone's face turned ashen.

Slapping Marek on the back, I swung my leg over the stool and sat down next to him. "How ya doin'?" It was meant to be a rhetorical question at first, but after the words left my mouth I really wanted to know how he'd been faring, especially after everything he'd been through. Him and Sully both. I'd asked him a similar question earlier and he gave me a coded look accompanied by a generic sort of answer, which was to be expected seeing as how Reece had been present.

I was the guy who witnessed the first slice into Marek's soul when Psych spewed the lies about the two of them being related. I saw all hope fade from his eyes, only to be replaced by fear and uncertainty. I saw it only fitting that I was the one who delivered the good news by reading the DNA results, almost coming full circle from desperation to elation.

"I'm good," he answered, continuing to nurse the amber liquid in his glass, the ice cubes clinking together and drawing out the staleness of his response as he lowered his drink. Marek glanced over at me when I simply bumped his shoulder. "What?"

"You know damn well that answer ain't gonna fly. Not now. Not after everything we've been through." Sure, Marek had been the one to bear the brunt of Psych's lies, but I'd been affected by his reaction to the entire situation.

"What do you want me to tell ya? That I withdrew so far into my own pain and misery that I practically pushed Sully away, treating her like shit and not givin' a fuck about how she was feelin'? That I thought about eatin' a bullet if it turned out that she was indeed my half-sister because my heart would've been shredded and there wouldn't've been any reason to live in a fuckin' world where she wasn't mine?" He ran a hand through his hair, the blue hue of his irises darkening with his still-present pain. "It took everything in me not to grab her and hold her close, fearing the outcome every second of every goddamn day. But Sully didn't deserve to be put through that shit, to drive herself crazy waiting for the final results."

"And you did?"

"It was my cross to bear," he answered quickly, and I truly believed he thought he spoke the truth. "Anyway, we got through it."

"Barely," I uttered, flashing him a smirk when he turned to look at me once more.

"Yeah. Barely."

The chatter in the clubhouse swirled together, all bodies present involved in their own conversations, allowing me time to delve deeper into what happened when he finally told his wife the reason he'd withdrawn from her.

"How did Sully take the news? You know, when you eventually fessed up as to why you were actin' like such a prick?"

A gruff laugh escaped my fearless leader.

"She was beyond livid." Marek leaned over the bar and grabbed a bottle of whatever he could reach. Normally Trigger would be on point in serving the drinks, but he was still too busy razzing Stone. "Actually, I'd never seen her so furious. She called me every name in the book. Not that I didn't deserve it."

"I can only imagine."

"No, you can't. I'm tellin' ya, I saw a side to my wife I never even knew existed. She was pissed that I chose to hide what her father said from her, sure, but she was more hurt than anything. She thought I didn't love her anymore and that eventually I'd leave her altogether. She told me she kept thinkin' she'd done something to deserve the way I treated her, that she was just waiting for the emptiness to creep back into her life when I finally decided to walk out the door for good." Marek hung his head, breathing quickly to regain his fleeting composure. "All of her hurt and fear manifested into rage. She almost scared me, and I'm man enough to admit that."

A slow smile spread across his face as if he was proud of his wife's reaction, that she was able to let go and not bottle everything up inside. Then again, it proved what I'd always thought about Sully, that she was a fierce woman underneath all the calm. His smile disappeared as quickly as it had appeared, however. "I'll always regret putting her through what I did, treating her as if it was her fault that I couldn't even bear to look at her, let alone touch her."

Clasping his shoulder, I said, "You two will get through this. I can already see that she's forgiven you. No one can mistake the way that woman feels about you, man."

"Forgiven, maybe, but it'll be a long time before I can prove that I'll never hurt her like that again."

I didn't know what else to say in support so I chose to remain silent. That was until he started his own sort of interrogation on me.

"What the fuck happened with that crazy bitch showin' up here like that?" He abruptly changed the topic and I couldn't say that I blamed him. Marek wasn't a touchy-feely kind of guy, and the fact that he told me as much as he had was a rarity in and of itself.

"I have no goddamn idea. I'm still tryin' to wrap my head around it. I haven't thought about Rachel since the night I left her, and for her to show up out of the blue, and claiming she has my son of all things, is mind-blowing. Then she fuckin' takes off and leaves her kid behind." A heavy exhale passed my lips. "Everything happened so fast. One minute she was here and the next she was gone."

"Crazy shit," Marek mumbled before pouring himself another drink.

"You can say that again."

A half hour later, we were all still trying to relax and find our footing after the evening's events. Riley and the baby boy, whose name we didn't know, were resting in one of the back bedrooms. It seemed like the night was gonna end on sort of a good note when all of a sudden one of the prospects—I believed his name was Cod—rushed inside.

"You guys better get out here," he shouted, the panic on his face unmistakable.

CHAPTER FORTY-EIGHT

Tripp

"FUCK!" MAREK YELLED. "WHAT THE hell is goin' on now?" All the members hurried outside, the women following close behind. But as soon as we saw who was waiting for us, I turned toward the females and shouted for them to go back.

"I got 'em," Trigger offered, thankfully following the confused women back inside the clubhouse.

As we approached the gates, badges were flashed and a few more SUVs appeared.

"Open the gates, Marek," Sam Koritz shouted. The crooked DEA agent who'd raided our club, and who was still in bed with the Savage Reapers, I was sure, had the audacity to show up out of the blue, without cause, and put the cherry on top of one of the shittiest days I'd had in a long time. Granted, I hadn't been there when he and his goons had stormed in, but I heard all about it.

The man was around ten years older than me, yet he looked at least twice that. A huge potbelly hung over the top of his cheap khaki pants, a laughable comb-over doing shit to hide his receding hairline.

"Why?" Marek's stance was unyielding. He didn't want to deal with Koritz any more than the rest of us did, but being in our position it was part of the deal, I supposed.

"Do it or we're gonna ram 'em."

"Why don't you go set up someone else?" Hawke shouted from behind me. I twisted around and shot him a warning look. We didn't need any reason for Koritz to put a target on our backs again. Granted, the club was legit now, no longer dealing with Los Zappas Cartel, but we did have a few decomposing bodies under our belt. Recent ones, at that.

Koritz signaled for the men still occupying two of the SUVs to back up, no doubt waiting for his go-ahead to lurch forward and slam into our gates.

Before they could make another move, Marek threw up his hand and rotated his finger in the air, signaling for the prospects to open the gates. The defiant part of me wanted to stand in front of the gates and tell them to fuck right off. In order to get rid of them, however, we had to comply.

The groan of the metal infuriated me. None of us understood the reason for Koritz's visit, but I was sure he was gonna fill us in real soon.

All five SUVs entered the compound, our men stopping them from going much farther than the entrance. No way in hell they were gonna make themselves at home and traipse all over our lot. My heart picked up pace the longer we stood in silence, waiting and wondering just what the hell brought them all out that evening.

Koritz finally stepped closer, a few of his men behind him with their hands on their weapons. None of us were armed. Well, let me clarify. As soon as Cod ran into the clubhouse shouting for us to come outside, all of us strapped up, the cold of the metal tucked safely in our waistbands. But Koritz didn't know that, and we sure as hell weren't gonna let him in on our little secret. For all he knew we were unarmed. Element of surprise and all that shit, in case it all went south.

"What the hell are you doin' here?" Marek spit out, taking a single step closer to the bastard stupid enough to think he could just show up out of the blue and there wouldn't be any consequences.

"We're looking for Psych Brooks," he cockily responded, arching a brow as if that reaction alone was enough to make us think he knew what we'd done to the Savage Reapers' president.

"What makes you think we know where that piece of shit is?" I took my place by my prez, offering a united front of sorts, denying any involvement in Psych's disappearance. A lie, but they'd never know that little tidbit of information. Henry 'Psych' Brooks was exactly where he should be—rotting in the ground. Marek had done the world a service when he'd extinguished that bastard's existence. Granted, his demise had been more brutal than what we were used to, but the ends justified the means.

"I have it on good authority that you were the last ones to see him alive."

"Oh yeah? Who told ya that?" Marek questioned. I personally couldn't wait for the day when we could teach Koritz a lesson, snatching his life once and for all.

Did I mention that the Knights were riding the legal side of the fence these days? Because that theory gets tested every once in a while.

A man who was a couple inches taller than Koritz sidestepped one of the DEA men and came into full view. It was dark and I couldn't make out much except that he was bald and stalky. When he moved under one of the lamps, however, I saw he wore a cut, but I couldn't make out the patch.

"You know where he is, and if you don't tell me I swear to Christ I'll rain holy hell down on your club." It was then I recognized his voice, had heard it a few times before. Unfortunately.

All of a sudden, an eruption the likes of which I'd never experienced before exploded around me, men screaming and barreling toward the intruder.

Rabid.

VP of the Savage Reapers.

Psych's right-hand man.

He dared to set foot on Knights soil?

Inside our compound?

The closest any fuckin' Reaper got to our clubhouse was outside the gates when they'd left me for dead, shot to all hell.

Koritz, along with his men, drew their weapons, and it was then we decided to show our cards as well. The smirk on the DEA agent's face would have been alarming if I'd thought enough to give a fuck.

"Well, it looks like you boys are in a bit of trouble." He puffed out his chest as best he could given his girth. "I'm sure those guns aren't registered." He made a move but stopped when Marek started shouting.

"Take one more step and I'll blow your head off, Koritz. Agent or not." The malice in Marek's voice left no room to wonder if he'd actually follow through or not. A glint of reservation flashed in Koritz's eyes, his men looking to one another for guidance. But they wouldn't find it. They dared to disrupt us, to show up on our doorstep asking about a worthless piece of shit. Adding to their stupidity, they brought Rabid with them. We should've killed them all just for that shit, but we didn't just have ourselves to worry about right then. The women in our lives took precedent over our need to show those fuckers who was boss. That didn't stop Hawke, Jagger, Stone, Ryder, and Cutter from spouting off at the mouth, though.

"Just get rid of 'em," someone shouted behind me, everyone's voices blending together and making it difficult to distinguish who was saying what.

"Fuck them for bringing that Savage piece of shit here," another yelled. If Marek didn't do something soon, all hell was gonna break loose, that much I knew for sure. Thankfully, Trigger had been able to keep the women away from this shit; otherwise, I had no doubt we'd be engaged in a whole other kind of standoff. And fuck Breck for passing out earlier. We needed all hands on deck in case shit went down, and based on all the hardware pointed at everyone's heads anything could happen.

Tense moments passed and still we all stood there, threatening the others in complete silence. Until our prez finally spoke up. I released the breath that was stuck in my lungs. I had no idea what Marek was gonna say, but at least it was somethin'.

"We don't know where Psych is, and we don't care. We're done with the war, have been for some time now," Marek spewed, his conviction a practiced one. If I hadn't known better I would've believed he spoke the truth. "Now unless you have a warrant, get the fuck outta here."

I got the feeling Marek wanted to say something else, but he surprisingly held his tongue. Probably for the best. We didn't need to invite any more trouble into our lives than was already present, although I was sure Koritz wasn't gonna stop until he'd buried us somehow. Literally or figuratively. Either way would be bad.

And Rabid . . . fuck! I thought for sure we were done with the Reapers, what with extinguishing their leader and all. But it looked like he was itchin' to start up a whole new war with our club.

Koritz eventually lowered his weapon, his men following suit. "I'll be in touch. You can count on that." The only thing we could do was watch in silence as they filed back into their vehicles and slowly backed out of our lot.

There was no resolution that evening, and there wouldn't be one for a very long time. I was sure of it.

Rabid knew our club was the last to see Psych alive, Marek, Stone and Jagger agreeing to meet him at the warehouse to exchange Sully for Adelaide and Kena. The rest of the men who'd accompanied Psych that day had all been extinguished, and looking back we should have chased down Rabid and taken him out as well, tied up all loose ends. But the VP of the Reapers had always been a follower, and we honestly thought once his prez was no longer in the picture, along with their supply being cut off from the cartel, that their club would've imploded from the inside.

Our arrogance had just come back to bite us in the ass.

EPILOGUE

Tripp

THE PAST TWO MONTHS HAD flown by in a blur. No matter how hard I tried, I couldn't find Rachel. It was as if she'd disappeared off the face of the earth, abandoning her kid like she didn't give a shit about the little boy. Then again, actions spoke louder than words, and while I'd initially been outraged at what she'd done, I came to believe that she knew she wasn't a fit mother, her selfishness for drugs clouding any maternal instinct she could have possibly had toward her own baby.

Even though only a short time had passed, the infant was growing quickly. Whenever Sully brought him by the clubhouse, there was a look of love and adoration in her eyes for the baby she cradled in her arms. I saw a peace come over not only her but Marek as well. The tension between husband and wife seemed to have evaporated, replaced by exhaustion, mostly due to late nights with the little boy would be my guess. If I asked my prez I was sure he'd tell me he'd prefer sleepless nights caused by a baby over all the other shit that had kept him up until the early morning hours.

All had been quiet where Reece's ex-husband had been concerned. She'd filed for divorce but her lawyer couldn't locate Rick, which wasn't a surprise to me, although I never let Reece in on that little tidbit of information. Not until now. I couldn't hide my secret any longer. Sure,

I'd been a vault in the past, most of the club's dealings requiring the utmost discretion, and even though that would always remain, the situation with Reece was different. Outside the scope of what I was used to dealing with, so to speak.

"Reece?" I whispered. "Are you awake, baby?" She groaned, snuggling closer and slinging her arm over my chest, her head buried in the crook of my neck. The heat from her naked body made my dick twitch, as if I hadn't just exhausted him over the past couple hours.

"Reece?" I repeated, trying my best not to move because the feel of her next to me was too good.

"Uh-huh," she grunted, sleep still struggling to steal her from me.

"It's about Rick," I confessed. I hated bringing up his name while lying in bed with Reece but I had to tell her what happened. What I'd done. I knew I was risking her, risking *us*, but I didn't want that kind of secret between us.

Her eyes fluttered on my chest, her lashes causing an odd tickling sensation. The strands of her long hair cascaded over my arm as I continued to hold her tightly.

"I don't wanna talk about him." She was more awake than before but still groggy. "He's dead to me."

"Well, speaking of. . . ." I waited for the dawn of recognition to blossom in her brain. It didn't take long. She pushed herself up and bent her legs behind her, waiting for me to elaborate.

"What?" she prompted, rubbing her eyes with her palms to drive away the sleep once and for all. "Why did you say it like that?"

Not sure how to start off this particular conversation, I reached for her hand, wound my fingers with hers, opened my mouth and let the words flow. "He tried to come after you again." She gasped and I shook my head to stop her from responding. "Hawke was the one who actually spotted him. That guy was brazen."

I couldn't stop her from interrupting that time. "Was?" She tried to pull her hand from mine but I only held on tighter. "What are you telling me?" Her voice shook and her eyes widened. I feared she wouldn't understand what I'd done, even though she'd lived with the fear he'd find her and most likely would've ended up killing her.

"When Hawke saw him waiting in his car across the street from Indulge, he called me right away. My blood boiled at the thought that he was never gonna leave you alone. Never," I reiterated, trying like hell to drive home that she would've been in constant danger as long as he still breathed air into his lungs. "When we approached him, he tried to leave, but I ripped open his door and flung him onto the pavement before he could. Hawke did a quick search of his car and found a loaded gun in the console, along with a half empty bottle of whiskey."

"What did you do?" she whimpered, finally withdrawing her hand from mine. She moved back on the bed, the small distance between us like a knife to the chest.

"I had to, Reece. I had to get rid of him. Right before I shot him, he drunkenly confessed that he was gonna punish you for leaving him. That he was gonna kill you and then kill himself."

"He said he was gonna kill me?"

I wasn't sure why she was shocked by that.

"Yes."

"So you shot him?"

"Yes." My expression was blank. I wanted to smile, knowing Rick would no longer ever be a threat to Reece, but I knew it wasn't appropriate.

"Dead?" She looked to be in a state of shock.

"Yes." I kept repeating the same one-word answer, but it said everything. The truth. I'd snatched lives in the past, but this one felt more justified than most.

Because I loved her.

"Oh my God." Her eyes never left my face. Her expression mirrored my own, which was not good. It meant I couldn't get a read on what she was thinking or feeling.

So what did I do? I revealed feelings I'd been harboring for a little while now, blurting them out at the most inopportune time.

I reached across the bed and drew her close. Thankfully she didn't struggle, her surprise at what I'd told her incapacitating her refusal. Placing my hand on the back of her head, I pulled her so close the tips of our noses touched.

"I love you."

Her warm breath hit my lips, the need to kiss her more powerful than ever before. Her mouth parted but she didn't speak, not for an excruciatingly long minute.

"You do?"

Not the response I was hoping for, but at least she didn't pull away in revulsion.

"Yes." Again with the one-word answer.

She continued to speak, glossing over the fact that I'd just told her that I loved her. Maybe she was in shock. Maybe she didn't feel the same. It didn't matter. I wasn't gonna lie; I would've loved to hear her say those three words back to me, but as long as she didn't run from me after hearing what I'd done, everything would be fine.

"I can't believe I made you kill him. I'm so sorry, Tripp. I never meant to drag you into my mess."

Wait . . .

What?

I pulled back so I could see her whole face. I needed her to really hear me, to understand that she wasn't responsible for any of what I'd chosen to do.

"You didn't make me do anything. I made that decision. More so for me than for you." Her frown showcased her confusion. "When I realized he'd never leave you in peace, it gutted me. To know that you could be snatched away from me at any given moment terrified me. And the only way to extinguish that worry was to snuff out the threat. So when I got the call from my brother, I seized the opportunity and ended it. Ended him."

Silence stretched between us, the slightly uncomfortable kind that was mixed with realization of our new reality.

I'd killed someone who had meant something to her at some point in her life, even though he turned out to be her worst mistake—her words, not mine.

When I couldn't take the quiet any longer, I asked, "What are you thinking?"

Reece moved the few feet toward the edge of the bed and swung her legs over, sitting upright next to me. She hung her head, her hair covering the side of her face. Gripping the edge of the mattress, she crossed her legs at the ankles. Her nakedness distracted me for a split second, memories of burying myself inside her enough to make my dick start to harden. Then she finally spoke, pulling all my attention back to the topic at hand.

"I'm not sure," she confessed. "On one hand I'm relieved that Rick will no longer come after me." She raised her head and looked at me. "I'll never be able to repay you for making me feel safe, Tripp. For the first time in my life . . . I feel free."

"But. . . ." I knew there was a 'but' in there somewhere.

Tears pooled behind her eyes. "But you killed him."

"Yeah, I did." A pain rippled through my chest, my breathing strangled and debilitating me while she continued to lock me in her gaze. I silently pleaded with her not to leave me because of a decision I felt I needed to execute—every fuckin' pun intended.

"I'm glad he's dead," she whispered, averting her eyes while lowering her head. "Does that make me a bad person?"

I gripped her thigh, my desire to touch her mixed with the need to gain her approval for what I'd done. "Does it make me a bad person that I killed him?"

"Yes." My heart sank. "No." A faint tremor of hope appeared. "I . . . I don't know."

This shit was all new to her, but unfortunately for me, it wasn't. Reece wrapped the sheet around her and stood, walking across the room and only coming to a stop when she'd reached the bedroom door. "I need some time to think," she said, clutching the sheet tighter before walking away from me.

Reece

FOR AN ENTIRE WEEK, I'D successfully avoided Tripp. He'd given me the time and space I wanted without complaint. He refused to budge when I'd suggested staying somewhere else. Instead, he said he'd stay at the clubhouse until I decided to talk to him again. He understood why I needed to think about what'd happened, but the truth was that him killing Rick was only part of the reason why I needed to be alone.

The other reason was so I could wrap my head around the fact that his child was growing inside me, and I had no idea how he'd feel about that. His reaction to Rachel showing up and claiming he was the father of his child had set him off. Understandably, he was upset because he knew she was lying. Add in the mix that she'd cheated on him and it was a recipe for disaster when they saw each other again. But how much of his anger was because he thought for a brief moment that the baby was actually his? Did he even want kids? Would he react in a similar manner when I told him my news?

I could move past him killing Rick. I really could, even though it scared me that he'd taken a life. And while such a thing should terrify me, I hadn't been completely shocked. I may have been somewhat sheltered, all due to Rick's overbearing and suffocating ways, but I wasn't stupid.

Tripp was part of the Knights Corruption. They hadn't always been choir boys. Okay . . . 'choir boys' was a bit of a stretch, but my point was made. The men were intense, Tripp being no exception, but their love for their families overshadowed any wrongdoings that had been committed. Naïve? Maybe, but I'd had the opportunity to really get to know Tripp, and what I knew was that . . .

I loved him.

Unequivocally.

Even before he'd expressed his feelings for me, I knew I'd fallen for him. The way he'd treated me, the way he'd made it his mission to keep me safe, the way he'd smile at me, touch me, kiss me—it all proved he loved me well before he'd uttered the words.

After another restless night's sleep, I'd finally decided to talk to Tripp and tell him everything.

———◆———

I PACED AROUND THE KITCHEN, glancing up at the clock for the millionth time that evening. How was I gonna broach the topic? Would I just blurt out, "I'm pregnant?" or would I beat around the bush, never quite finding the right words? What would happen if he didn't want the baby? If he no longer wanted me? I tried to put myself in his shoes, but I couldn't see past my own fears and paranoia. Our relationship was still new, and although we were learning more about each other every day, to introduce a baby now could destroy what we'd been trying to nurture.

My hand rested on my belly. I wasn't showing yet. I'd suspected I was pregnant the night Tripp told me everything, but I needed to see a doctor to confirm what the three store-bought tests revealed. The doctor said I was around eight weeks, and when I'd done my calculations, I figured it had happened when we had sex in the shower, the only time we hadn't used protection. We'd had discussions about birth control, both of us wanting to stop using condoms, but my body had always had a negative reaction to the pill. Funny thing was I'd made an appointment with a gynecologist to discuss other options. That appointment was set for the following week. I guessed there was no need to keep it anymore.

The roar of a motorcycle cut through my thoughts, increasing my anxiety over how our conversation would go. If Tripp decided that he wanted no part of the baby, or me going forward, then I'd walk away and raise him or her on my own. I knew it would be hard, and my heart would be broken, but my love for my unborn child was already growing deeper with each day that passed.

Taking a few deep breaths, I turned the handle of the front door, opening it up as Tripp walked up the front steps. I stepped back to allow him to enter, and as soon as he walked past me I knew I'd be more than heartbroken if he decided he didn't want to be a father. I'd be devastated. Seeing him again only drove home how much I loved him.

He headed toward the living room, choosing to stand near the couch instead of taking a seat. "Why did you want to see me?" His question was straightforward, a small bout of hesitation wafting off him. He was nervous. *Join the club.*

My eyes raked over him as he stood in front of me. His dark hair was disheveled, and three-day-old stubble prickled his jawline. He looked tired, but he had also never looked more beautiful. Odd word to describe a man like Tripp, but it was the God's honest truth. He was beautiful, inside and out. The rustle of his leather cut was a most welcome sound, and I had to remind myself to stop ogling him and get straight to it.

"Maybe you better sit," I instructed, pointing toward the sofa directly behind him. Without a word, he plopped down on the cushions, glancing up at me and waiting for me to tell him the reason I'd asked to see him.

"Okay, you're startin' to freak me out," he said, trying to grin but his expression fell flat. "Why don't you come sit next to me?"

"I need the space."

"Don't you think I've given you enough space? I mean, I know it's only been a week but I haven't called you, or shown up at the club to bother you. For fuck's sake, Reece, I told you I loved you and all you said was that you needed some time to think. I know you're unsure of me because of what I did, but don't tell me that you don't sleep better at night knowing that sick fucker can no longer hurt you." He took a deep breath, and I knew he would have continued had I not blurted out the real reason why I'd asked him to come over.

"I'm pregnant." My eyes widened at my bluntness. I'd planned on a different delivery, but I wanted him to stop rambling and saying things that only made me feel badly about the way I'd chosen to handle things between us.

He rose to his feet, his presence overwhelming me more than normal. He took a single step closer. "What did you say?"

Was he angry? Disappointed? Happy? I couldn't tell. His face was void of any expression.

"I'm . . . I'm pregnant."

He reached for me but I retreated. I had no idea why. Was I preparing myself for the hurt I'd start to feel as soon as he uttered the words I feared? Was I still in a state of shock myself over the news that I was gonna be a mother? That my life was forever changed?

"Reece." My name flowed from his lips, his tone soft yet commandeering. "Come here." He reached out his hand and left it in midair, waiting for me to accept. He didn't have to wait long. As soon as our palms touched, I felt his love. His acceptance. He drew me closer, the small quirk of his lips telling me everything. He wasn't upset at all. The longer we looked at each other, the more apparent it became that Tripp was happy about my news.

"So you're not upset?" His delicious smell intoxicated me, almost to the point that I'd forgotten what we were talkin' about. Almost.

"Why would I be upset? Sure, it's a shocker, one I'm not quite sure how to process right now seeing as how we always used a condom, but I could never be upset about you telling me you're gonna have my kid."

"It happened when we had sex that one time in the shower . . . when I had my period," I blurted.

"That can happen?"

"Apparently," I responded.

"Good to know for next time." He chuckled, his attitude and demeanor toward the news making me love him that much more.

"There's something else I have to tell you." I snaked my hands around his neck and pulled him down so I could kiss him. He was so damn tall that sometimes I forgot how much shorter I was than him.

His breath tickled my lips. "If you tell me it's twins, I think I'm gonna have to sit back down for a minute." Although he was joking, I saw the flash of nervousness in his eyes.

"If I were having twins, I'd be joining you on that couch."

"So what is it?" His arms held me close, his fingers interlocking behind my back.

"I love you." No use in waiting a second longer to tell him how I felt. I should have said it the night he told me.

"That's the hormones talkin'." He tried to joke, but I knew he wanted to hear me say it again, possibly believing I hadn't meant those three precious words.

"No it's not." I smiled before pressing my lips to his once more. I needed to taste him, to breathe his air into my lungs and steal a small piece of his soul for my own. "I love you. More than I ever thought

I could love someone. Ever since the first day we met you made me feel safe and protected. You gave me back a piece of myself that'd been missing for as long as I could remember." Tears welled up in my eyes, and although I told myself not to cry they came rushing forth anyway. "I can never repay you for that."

"You just did," he said, smiling before resting his hand on my belly.

COMING SOON

Ryder
Knights Corruption MC Series, book 5
April 2017

ACKNOWLEDGEMENTS

TO MY HUBBY- THANK YOU for your continued support while I lose myself for hours on end in my office. Thanks for holding down the fort and entertaining our furry children while I'm lost inside my head. Love you, baby!

A huge thank you to my family and friends for your continued love, encouragement and support. What a wild ride this journey has been, and hopefully will continue to be for many years to come.

To the ladies at Hot Tree Editing, both editors and beta readers, I can't say enough great things about you. You continue to amaze me and I can't wait until our next project together. You have been beyond fantastic!

To Clarise from CT Cover Creations, what can I say other than you're freaking amazing, woman! Your work speaks for itself. I'm absolutely thrilled with each and every cover you've magically created for me. They just keep getting better and better, Tripp being number 10! Can you believe it? Rest assured, there are countless books in our future. ☺

To Kiki, Ruth and all of the other amazing ladies at The Next Step PR- You work tirelessly to promote my work, and "thank you" just doesn't seem adequate enough. For all of your love and support, and for helping to guide me through this wonderful book world we all love so much, I'm eternally grateful. And for the times I'm stressed beyond belief, you're words of encouragement mean the world to me.

To Elmarie, thank you so much for taking the time to beta read Tripp. Your feedback enabled me to polish parts of the story that were missing that certain something. I'm beyond thrilled we've met and become friends, and I have no doubt you'll be reading the next book very soon. ☺

To Beth -Your love and support is truly priceless. I'm beyond thrilled we've become such dear friends. I don't know what I would do without you! You cheer me on when I'm nervous, and celebrate when I succeed. Love you! Here's to many more wonderful years to come.

To all of the bloggers who have shared my work, I'm forever indebted to you. You ladies are simply wonderful!

To all of you who have reached out to me to let me know how much you loved my stories, I am beyond humbled. Thank you so much, and I'll continue to do my best to bring you stories you can lose yourself in, even if it's only for a few hours.

And last but not least, I would like to thank you, the reader. If this is the first book you've read from me, I hope you enjoy it. If this is yet another story from me you've taken a chance on . . . THANK YOU from the bottom of my heart!

ABOUT THE AUTHOR

S. NELSON GREW UP WITH a love of reading and a very active imagination, never putting pen to paper, or fingers to keyboard until 2013.

Her passion to create was overwhelming, and within a few months she'd written her first novel, Stolen Fate. When she isn't engrossed in creating one of the many stories rattling around inside her head, she loves to read and travel as much as she can.

She lives in the Northeast with her husband and two dogs, enjoying the ever changing seasons.

If you would like to follow or contact her please do so at the following:

Website:
www.snelsonauthor.com

Email Address:
snelsonauthor8@gmail.com

Also on Facebook, Goodreads, Amazon, Instagram and Twitter

OTHER BOOKS BY S. NELSON

Stolen Fate
Redemption
Addicted (Addicted Trilogy, Book 1)
Shattered (Addicted Trilogy, Book 2)
Wanted (Addicted Trilogy, Book 3)
Torn
Marek (Knights Corruption MC Series, book 1)
Stone (Knights Corruption MC Series, book 2)
Jagger (Knights Corruption MC Series, book 3

Printed in Poland
by Amazon Fulfillment
Poland Sp. z o.o., Wrocław